TONY PANG

Shadows Of The Asasiyyin

The Asasiyyin Chronicles Book 1

First published by MESAI Global LLC 2023

Copyright © 2023 by Tony Pang

All rights reserved. No part of this publication may be reproduced, stored or transmitted in any form or by any means, electronic, mechanical, photocopying, recording, scanning, or otherwise without written permission from the publisher. It is illegal to copy this book, post it to a website, or distribute it by any other means without permission.

This novel is entirely a work of fiction. The names, characters and incidents portrayed in it are the work of the author's imagination. Any resemblance to actual persons, living or dead, events or localities is entirely coincidental.

Tony Pang asserts the moral right to be identified as the author of this work.

Tony Pang has no responsibility for the persistence or accuracy of URLs for external or third-party Internet Websites referred to in this publication and does not guarantee that any content on such Websites is, or will remain, accurate or appropriate.

Designations used by companies to distinguish their products are often claimed as trademarks. All brand names and product names used in this book and on its cover are trade names, service marks, trademarks and registered trademarks of their respective owners. The publishers and the book are not associated with any product or vendor mentioned in this book. None of the companies referenced within the book have endorsed the book.

First edition

This book was professionally typeset on Reedsy.
Find out more at reedsy.com

Contents

DEDICATION

Dedicated to the best creative writing instructor Canada ever had. Ed Griffin, may you Rest In Peace.

Acknowledgement

I'd like to start by thanking Allah (SWT), for giving me everything

I'd like to thank my mom, who was the main inspiration behind this story. *"You are the wind beneath my wings"*

Thank you Kareemah for checking my grammar and giving the encouragement and support to keep me going.

Thank you, my lovely readers, you followed me and stayed with me.

Finally, I can't leave without expressing my gratitude to everyone over at JustWrite who made this book what it is today. I do not know what I would do without you guys!

If you enjoyed this story, then please be sure to show your appreciation by leaving a review on either Amazon or Goodreads. It would mean more than I can express!

Unearthed Secrets

Anastasia Asma'u stood at the corner of Russell and Wilkins, her gaze sweeping across the bustling Eastern Market district of Detroit. The air was thick with the scent of spices and fresh produce, a cacophony of voices rising above the din as vendors hawked their wares. Her dark, expressive eyes seemed to pierce through the chaos, searching for answers hidden amongst the vibrant tapestry of people and cultures that surrounded her.

"Agent Asma'u, the captain wants an update on our progress," her partner called out to her. His words were almost drowned out by the roar of a motorcycle revving nearby.

"Tell him we're still gathering information, Jackson," she replied, her voice calm yet authoritative. She turned her attention back to the market, her eyes flitting from the colorful displays of fruits and vegetables to the lively conversations between patrons.

As a devout Muslim, Anastasia took a moment to say a silent prayer under her breath, asking Allah for guidance in her work as an FBI special agent. It was a simple ritual that grounded her amidst the chaos of her job, reminding her of her purpose and dedication to justice.

"Hey, Anastasia, I heard there's a stall selling halal food down the street. Maybe we can grab lunch there later?" Jackson suggested, glancing over at her.

"Sounds good," she agreed, nodding towards him. "But first, we need to find our witness."

Their search led them deeper into the heart of Eastern Market, passing stalls selling everything from artisanal cheeses and cured meats to vibrant textiles and intricate jewelry. The diverse mix of people and cultures seemed to meld together into a harmonious cacophony, much like the city of Detroit itself.

"Excuse me, ma'am," Anastasia addressed a vendor selling fragrant bouquets of flowers. "Have you seen this man around here today?" She held up a photograph of their key witness, a middle-aged man with a distinctive scar running down his left cheek.

"Ah, yes," the woman replied, her accent thick but her words clear. "I saw him earlier, near the fish market. He seemed…nervous."

"Thank you," Anastasia said, offering a polite smile before heading in the direction the woman had indicated.

As they walked, she couldn't help but feel a sense of pride in the work she did. Serving her community and upholding the law was a sacred duty to her, one that she never took lightly. It was this dedication and determination that had earned her a reputation as one of the top agents in the Detroit field office.

"Hey, look, there's the fish market," Jackson pointed out as they approached their destination. "Let's ask around and see if anyone else spotted our guy."

"Good idea," Anastasia agreed, steeling herself for another round of interviews amidst the sensory overload of Eastern Market. But no matter the challenges that lay ahead, she knew she would face them head-on, guided by her unwavering faith and commitment to justice.

The sun dipped below the horizon, casting long shadows across the Eastern Market district as Anastasia Asma'u and her partner, Jackson, approached the scene of the crime. The murder of a prominent businessman had sent shockwaves through the city, and the pressure on Anastasia to solve the case was immense.

"Alright, we're here," Jackson said, glancing at Anastasia. "Remember, this one's high profile. We can't afford any mistakes."

"Understood." Anastasia nodded, her resolve steeling her as they ducked beneath the yellow police tape and stepped into the dimly lit alleyway where the victim had been found.

As they surveyed the scene, Anastasia couldn't shake the feeling that there was something different about this case. A chill crept down her spine as fleeting visions of her ancestral homeland in Nigeria flickered at the edges of her consciousness. She could almost hear the whisper of her grandmother's voice telling stories of magic and mystery from their lineage.

"Hey, you okay?" Jackson asked, noticing Anastasia's momentary distraction.

"Uh, yeah. Just thinking." She shook her head, pushing the strange sensations aside for now. There would be time later to ponder the mysteries of her heritage; right now, she had a job to do.

"Alright, let's see what we've got," she said, crouching down beside the body. The man lay sprawled on his back, his eyes wide with fear, as if he'd seen something truly horrifying before his death. Anastasia examined the scene meticulously, noting every detail, from the peculiar angle of the broken glass shards to the faint, otherworldly scent that lingered in the air.

"His wallet and phone are missing," Jackson reported, rifling through the victim's pockets. "Could be a robbery gone wrong."

"Or it could be something else entirely," Anastasia murmured, her instincts telling her that there was more to this case than met the eye. She couldn't ignore the gnawing feeling that something otherworldly was at play. The visions of Nigeria, the strange scent—she couldn't help but wonder if they were somehow connected.

"Hey," Jackson said, snapping her out of her thoughts, "I found this." He held up a small, intricately carved stone covered in symbols that Anastasia recognized as West African. It seemed to pulse with an energy that sent shivers down her spine.

"Interesting," she mused, taking the stone and examining it closely. "This could be significant."

"Let's hope so," Jackson replied, his voice tight with the weight of their responsibility. "We need a break in this case."

As they continued to work, Anastasia couldn't shake the feeling that she was being watched. Glancing around, she caught a glimpse of movement in the shadows, like a figure vanishing into the night. A chill settled in her bones as she wondered if the line between reality and the supernatural was blurring before her very eyes.

"Let's wrap this up and get back to the station," she said, her voice steady despite the unease that gripped her. "We've got a lot of work ahead of us."

And as they walked away from the crime scene, Anastasia Asma'u couldn't help but feel that they had only scratched the surface of a mystery that would test the limits of her faith and her understanding of the world.

Anastasia Asma'u stood at the edge of the crime scene, her dark eyes scanning the area with a mixture of curiosity and apprehension. The alleyway was dimly lit, its shadows casting eerie patterns on the crumbling brick walls. The pungent smell of rotting garbage mixed with the metallic tang of blood, making her stomach churn.

"Another odd detail," Special Agent Jackson murmured from behind her, pointing to a patch of strange symbols etched into the ground near the victim's body. "I've never seen anything like this before."

"Neither have I," Anastasia admitted, crouching down to examine the markings more closely. They seemed familiar, yet foreign – reminiscent of the fleeting visions she'd been experiencing lately. Her heart raced in her chest as she tried to make sense of the connection. "Jackson, have you ever had the feeling that something you're investigating might be… beyond the realm of what we normally deal with?"

"Like supernatural?" Jackson raised an eyebrow, his voice tinged with skepticism. "Isn't that a bit far-fetched, even for us?"

"Perhaps," Anastasia conceded, trying to dismiss her growing unease. "But there's just something about this case that feels different. I can't quite put my finger on it."

As they continued examining the crime scene, Anastasia's attention was drawn to the victim's body, which lay sprawled on the cold, damp pavement. His face was twisted in a horrifying expression of pain and terror, as if he'd seen something truly monstrous before his death. What could have caused such fear?

"Look at these scratch marks," she said, gesturing to the deep gashes that marred the man's clothing and skin. "They don't match any known animal or weapon. And the way his body is positioned – it's almost as if he was thrown against the wall with incredible force."

"Strange," Jackson agreed, his brow furrowing in concentration. "But it doesn't necessarily have to be supernatural. Maybe we're dealing with something new and dangerous – some kind of experimental weapon or technology."

"Maybe," Anastasia murmured, though she couldn't shake the feeling that there was more to this case than met the eye. The strange symbols, the eerie visions, the unexplainable evidence… they all seemed to hint at a hidden world that defied logic and reason.

"Are you alright?" Jackson asked, noticing her furrowed brow and troubled expression. "You seem… distracted."

"I'm fine," she lied, forcing a smile onto her face. "Just trying to make sense of all this."

"Let's keep digging, then," he said, clapping her on the shoulder. "We'll figure it out eventually. We always do."

As they resumed their investigation, Anastasia couldn't help but feel torn between her duty as an agent and her faith as a Muslim. She had always believed that there were limits to human understanding – mysteries that could never be fully unraveled. But now, as she peered into the darkness that shrouded the crime scene, she wondered if those limits were beginning to crumble.

"God, guide me," she whispered under her breath, her hands shaking as she collected another piece of evidence. "Help me find the truth – whatever it may be."

The sun dipped below the horizon, painting the sky in shades of pink and orange as Anastasia Asma'u stood at the edge of the bustling Eastern Market. The cacophony of voices and the scent of spices filled the air, but her focus remained on the crime scene before her.

"Agent Asma'u, meet Detective Torres," said a tall, broad-shouldered man with salt-and-pepper hair as he approached. "She's been working this case from the local angle."

Anastasia extended her hand, shaking Detective Torres' firmly. The detective was shorter than Anastasia, but her piercing gaze exuded confidence. "Pleasure to meet you, Agent Asma'u," she said. "I've heard good things about you."

"Thank you, Detective," Anastasia replied, appreciative of the compliment. "What can you tell me about the victim?"

"His name was Henry Blackwood," Torres began, flipping through her notepad. "Prominent businessman, well-respected in the community. No known enemies. It doesn't make sense why someone would target him like this."

"Perhaps it wasn't personal," Anastasia suggested, her mind racing as she considered all possible angles. She felt the weight of the case pressing down on her, but her determination only grew stronger.

"Maybe," Torres conceded. "But there's something else – we found strange symbols carved into the walls and floor near the body. No one on our team can make heads or tails of them."

"Symbols?" Anastasia asked, her interest piqued. She had seen similar marks at the crime scene earlier, heightening her suspicions that something supernatural was at play.

"Right here," Torres said, gesturing to several photographs in her notepad. Anastasia took a closer look, her brow furrowing as she tried to decipher the intricate patterns. They seemed familiar to her, as if they were a part of her ancestral memory, yet remained just out of reach.

"Have you tried consulting experts on the occult or ancient languages?" Anastasia asked, hoping to gain more information.

"Already in progress," Torres replied. "But so far, nothing."

"Detective, may I keep these photos for my investigation?" Anastasia inquired politely, her mind already formulating theories based on the limited evidence available.

"Of course, Agent Asma'u," Torres agreed, handing them over.

"Thank you. We'll be in touch if we find anything," Anastasia assured her, tucking the photos into her pocket. As she turned back to the crime scene, she couldn't help but feel a chill run down her spine, as though she were being watched by unseen forces.

"God, grant me wisdom and protection in this investigation," she murmured under her breath, her faith anchoring her amidst the storm of uncertainty that threatened to consume her.

Anastasia continued to examine the evidence, each new piece adding another layer to the complex puzzle before her. The strange symbols seemed to call out to her, begging her to decipher their secrets. And in the depths of her soul, Anastasia Asma'u knew that those secrets would redefine her understanding of the world – and herself.

Anastasia Asma'u stood at the edge of the crime scene, her eyes scanning the chaotic aftermath. Shattered glass and debris littered the ground, evidence of a violent struggle that had taken place just hours before. She could see fellow agents already hard at work, collecting samples and questioning witnesses. Despite their best efforts, however, Anastasia couldn't shake the feeling that this case was unlike anything they'd ever encountered before.

"Agent Asma'u," a voice called out, pulling her from her thoughts. She turned to see Agent Michael Davis, a seasoned investigator with an impressive record, approaching her with a furrowed brow. "I've been going over the witness statements and there's something that doesn't add up."

"Go on," she replied, her curiosity piqued.

"Several witnesses reported seeing a figure clad in dark clothing fleeing the scene, but their descriptions don't match," he explained, frustration clear in his voice. "Some say the suspect was tall and lanky, while others claim they were short and stocky."

"Could it be possible that there were two assailants?" Anastasia suggested, her mind racing to make sense of the conflicting information.

"Maybe," Davis conceded, rubbing his chin thoughtfully. "But the security footage shows only one person entering and leaving the building around the time of the murder."

"Curious," Anastasia murmured, her brow furrowing as she considered the implications. "Perhaps the killer used some form of disguise or illusion to alter their appearance."

"Or maybe the witnesses aren't as reliable as we think," Davis countered, skepticism tainting his words.

"Either way, we can't afford to overlook any possibilities," Anastasia insisted, her determination unwavering. "Have the forensics team analyze the security footage for any signs of tampering or manipulation. And let's not forget those strange symbols – we must find out what they mean."

"Of course, Agent Asma'u," Davis agreed, his tone betraying a newfound respect for her tenacity and insight. "I'll get right on it."

As he walked away, Anastasia couldn't help but feel a sense of unease gnawing at the edges of her consciousness. The conflicting witness statements, the odd symbols, the lingering visions of her ancestral homeland – all seemed to be pieces of an intricate puzzle that she was only just beginning to comprehend.

"Hey, Anastasia," called another agent, a young woman with bright red hair named Sarah. "I've got something you might find interesting." She held up a small, clear bag containing a single silver coin, its surface marred by peculiar etchings.

"Where did you find this?" Anastasia asked, taking the bag from Sarah and examining the coin closely.

"Over by that broken window," Sarah replied, pointing to a jagged hole in the glass. "It's not like any currency I've ever seen."

"Neither have I," Anastasia admitted, her fingers tracing the strange markings on the coin. They felt oddly familiar, yet foreign – much like the symbols from the crime scene. "Keep searching for any more of these. They could be important."

"Will do, boss," Sarah said with a nod, before disappearing back into the fray.

Anastasia clutched the mysterious coin tightly, an inexplicable chill running down her spine. The stakes were higher than ever, and the investigation had only just begun. But as the pieces slowly started to fall into place, she knew one thing for certain: she wouldn't rest until the truth was uncovered, no matter how dangerous or unsettling it might be.

With renewed purpose, Anastasia Asma'u dove headfirst into the tangled web of mystery and deception, determined to unravel the secrets hidden within the shadows of Detroit. And as the city's dark underbelly threatened to engulf her, she couldn't help but wonder if the answers she sought would lead her not only to the killer but also to the truth about her own enigmatic past.

Anastasia Asma'u stood at the edge of the crime scene, her eyes drawn to the setting sun as it cast long shadows across the bustling Eastern Market district. The vibrant tapestry of scents and sounds was momentarily pushed to the background as she whispered a quiet prayer for the deceased businessman. She touched her hijab in reverence, feeling both anchored by her faith and shaken by the supernatural elements that had begun to seep into her world.

"Agent Asma'u?" A voice pulled her from her thoughts. It was Agent Thompson, a seasoned investigator who had partnered with her on other high-stakes cases. "We found something new."

"Show me," she replied, tucking the mysterious coin from earlier into her coat pocket.

Thompson led her through the throng of investigators to the shattered window where Sarah had pointed out earlier. He gestured towards a trail of peculiar, crimson footprints leading away from the broken glass. Anastasia squatted down, her brows furrowing as she examined the prints closely.

"Blood?" she asked, looking up at Thompson.

"Seems so," he confirmed. "But lab results show it's not human blood. And it doesn't match any known animal species either."

The implications sent a shiver down her spine, but Anastasia hid her unease behind a mask of professionalism. "Have these footprints been photographed? We need to follow the trail and see where it leads."

"Already done, boss," Thompson assured her. "We're waiting for your lead."

As they followed the enigmatic trail, Anastasia whispered another quick prayer, seeking guidance from Allah. She grappled with the growing strangeness of the case, along with the fleeting visions of her ancestral homeland in Nigeria that seemed to grow more vivid with each passing day.

"Boss, look!" Sarah called out, pointing to a narrow alley where the trail abruptly ended, leaving no sign of the mysterious figure who had left it.

"Where did they go?" Anastasia muttered, her eyes scanning the brick walls and metal dumpsters for any hint of an escape route. The alley was a dead end, yet there was no trace of their quarry.

"Agent Asma'u," Thompson said, his voice tinged with concern. "Do you think this is…"

"Supernatural?" Anastasia finished for him, her voice barely a whisper. She frowned, wrestling with her own doubts and fears. "I don't know, Thompson. But whatever it is, we need to find answers."

"Agreed," he nodded.

As they prepared to leave the alley, Anastasia's hand brushed against a dumpster. Her fingers grazed something cold and metallic, and she felt a sudden jolt of energy surge through her. With a gasp, she pulled her hand away and found another coin similar to the one she had discovered earlier.

"Another one…" she breathed, staring at the strange markings that seemed to pulse beneath her fingertips.

"Boss, are you alright?" Sarah asked, noticing her uncharacteristic reaction.

"Fine," Anastasia replied quickly, pocketing the second coin. "Let's focus on finding more leads."

As the agents dispersed, Anastasia Asma'u couldn't shake the unsettling feeling that the trail had led them to the very edge of reality itself. With a deep breath and another whispered prayer, she steeled herself for the unknown dangers that lay ahead, determined to uncover the truth behind the supernatural undercurrents running through Detroit.

"Ya Allah, guide me," she murmured, her heart heavy with the weight of her responsibilities and the growing sense that her world would never be the same again.

Inciting Incident

Anastasia stood in the middle of her living room, surrounded by the warm glow of soft lamplight. The familiar scent of her mother's homemade incense filled the air, mingling with the earthy aroma of the potted plants that lined her windowsills. She felt a deep sense of comfort within these walls, every piece of furniture and decoration a testament to her rich Nigerian heritage. This was her sanctuary, her refuge from the chaos of the outside world.

Lost in thought, she didn't notice the sudden draft that swept through the room, causing the curtains to billow like ghostly apparitions. It wasn't until she heard an unusual sound, almost like the rustle of feathers, that she looked up to see an enormous golden eagle perched on the back of her sofa. Its feathers shimmered with an ethereal light that seemed alien to the dim room, as if it had brought the sun itself within its plumage.

The eagle's eyes were unlike anything Anastasia had ever seen: large, dark orbs that seemed to hold a depth of wisdom far beyond any mortal creature. They appeared to bore into her soul, and she found herself unable to look away, captivated by their intensity.

"Peace be upon you, Anastasia Asma'u," the eagle spoke, its voice melodic and soothing, yet somehow commanding her full attention. "I am Artiya'il, sent to you as a messenger and guide."

Anastasia stared at the majestic creature, her heart pounding furiously in her chest. The air around the eagle seemed to vibrate with a power she couldn't quite comprehend, and she could feel the hairs on the back of her neck standing on end.

Anastasia blinked, her mind racing to catch up with the reality before her. She studied the golden eagle perched upon her sofa, its very presence defying everything she understood about the world. "This… this can't be real," she stammered, disbelief dripping from every word as her eyes darted around the room, searching for any possible explanation.

"Your disbelief is understandable," Artiya'il replied gently, his dark eyes never leaving hers. "But I assure you, I am quite real. And my message is of great importance."

Anastasia swallowed hard, her throat suddenly dry, and struggled to find her voice again. "What message?" she asked hesitantly, a small part of her desperate to cling onto the semblance of normalcy that had been shattered in an instant.

"Your lineage, Anastasia. You are a descendant of the ancient asasiyyin, the hidden ones who have protected the balance between the mundane and the supernatural for centuries." Artiya'il's words carried a weight that made her chest feel tight, her breath coming in short gasps as she tried to take it all in.

"Impossible," Anastasia whispered, shaking her head vigorously. Her heart raced like a wild animal trapped within her ribcage. This was too much to process, too fantastical to accept. "My family… we were just ordinary people."

"Ordinary on the surface, perhaps," Artiya'il conceded, tilting his head slightly. "But your blood carries the legacy of warriors and guardians, those who have stood against the darkness and maintained the fragile balance between worlds. This power now awakens within you, and you must learn to embrace it."

Anastasia stared at the otherworldly being before her, her mind struggling to comprehend the enormity of what she had just learned. A torrent of emotions swirled within her: shock, disbelief, and a growing sense of awe that threatened to overwhelm her completely. Her hands trembled at her sides, as if they too were trying to grasp the reality of her newfound lineage.

"Wh-what does this mean?" she finally managed to utter, her voice cracking under the strain of her conflicting emotions.

"Your path will not be an easy one, Anastasia Asma'u," Artiya'il replied somberly, his gaze unwavering. "But you are destined for greatness. Your journey has only just begun."

The weight of Artiya'il's words settled heavy on Anastasia's shoulders, as if the truth they carried were a tangible burden. Her breath hitched in her throat, and she struggled to find her voice amid the chaos that now roiled within her.

"Greatness?" she whispered, her hands trembling as she tried to fathom the immensity of what had been laid at her feet. "My whole life, I've known only one path – to serve and protect the people around me through my work with the FBI. But this... this is something else entirely."

"Indeed," Artiya'il replied gently, his golden eyes filled with understanding. "Your previous life was but a prelude to the destiny now unfolding before you. Your skills as an agent will serve you well, but you must also learn to harness the power that now awakens within you."

Anastasia clenched her fists, her nails biting into her palms as she fought to keep the tremors in her hands at bay. Her heart raced, its thunderous beat echoing in her ears as it attempted to outrun the uncertainty that gnawed at her soul.

"Who am I supposed to be?" she asked, desperation lacing her words. "How can I reconcile the person I thought I was with this... this new reality?"

"By embracing the truth of your heritage," Artiya'il said, his voice steady and resolute. "You are both Anastasia Asma'u, the diligent and dedicated agent, and a descendant of the ancient asasiyyin. You do not need to forsake one identity for the other; rather, they are intertwined, each one lending strength to the other."

Anastasia's chest tightened, her mind grappling with the sudden shift in her understanding of the world and her place in it. She closed her eyes, taking a deep breath in an attempt to quell the storm of emotions raging inside her.

"Tell me," she said, her voice barely more than a whisper. "Tell me how I can walk this path. Show me what I need to do."

"Your journey begins with accepting the responsibility that has been bestowed upon you," Artiya'il replied, his gaze never wavering from hers. "You must train and learn the ways of your ancestors, honing both your physical abilities and your newfound powers."

"Where will I find such training?" Anastasia asked, her resolve beginning to solidify as she focused on the tangible task before her.

"Seek out those who share your bloodline and hold the ancient knowledge," Artiya'il instructed. "They will guide you in this new chapter of your life. And remember, Anastasia Asma'u – I will be with you every step of the way."

As the weight of her newfound purpose settled within her soul, Anastasia drew herself up, her trembling hands steadying as she took her first steps toward embracing her destiny.

Anastasia took a deep breath, focusing on the energy that coursed through her veins. It was a sensation she had never experienced before, like an electric current tingling beneath her skin. She closed her eyes, attempting to harness this newfound power.

"Try to feel the energies around you," Artiya'il instructed, his soothing voice guiding her. "Allow your senses to expand, and you will begin to perceive the supernatural beings that dwell within the shadows of this world."

Anastasia concentrated, her mind reaching out tentatively. And then, suddenly, it was as though a veil had been lifted from her eyes. Whispers of energy floated around her, colors and shapes she could barely comprehend. A faint outline of a figure flickered at the edge of her vision, disappearing as quickly as it had appeared.

"Did you see that?" Anastasia asked, breathless with excitement.

"Indeed," Artiya'il replied, a hint of pride in his voice. "That was a minor spirit, one of many who inhabit the hidden realm. You are beginning to see the world as the asasiyyin do."

Anastasia marveled at the reality now revealed to her, her heart pounding with exhilaration and trepidation. "Tell me more about my lineage, Artiya'il. What is the true purpose of the asasiyyin?"

"Your ancestors were the protectors of the balance between the mortal and supernatural realms," Artiya'il explained, his eyes filled with ancient wisdom.

"They possessed unique abilities to sense and combat dark forces, ensuring that neither side overwhelmed the other."

"Then I am meant to be a guardian?" Anastasia asked, grappling with the enormity of her new role.

"Indeed, Anastasia Asma'u. You are destined to inherit their legacy, to walk the path of the asasiyyin and defend the world from the encroaching darkness."

"Darkness?" Her brows furrowed in concern. "What challenges will I face?"

"Many supernatural beings maintain a fragile equilibrium with humanity, coexisting peacefully or driven by their own agendas," Artiya'il said gravely. "However, there are those who seek to disrupt this balance, spreading chaos and destruction. It will be your duty to confront these malevolent forces, and to keep the world from descending into disorder."

Anastasia's resolve grew stronger, her newfound abilities beginning to feel like an extension of herself. She was no longer a mere mortal but an asasiyyin, tasked with safeguarding the delicate harmony between realms.

"Teach me, Artiya'il," she pleaded, determination burning within her. "Help me become the protector I am meant to be."

"Of course, Anastasia Asma'u," Artiya'il replied, his voice filled with reassurance and warmth. "Together, we shall prepare you for the trials ahead."

And so, under the guidance of the celestial messenger, Anastasia embarked on the journey of embracing her destiny – a journey that would test her courage, her faith, and her very essence. But she was not alone; with the wisdom of the ancients at her disposal, she vowed to walk the path of the asasiyyin and protect both the mortal and supernatural realms from the gathering darkness.

Anastasia's heart raced with anticipation, her mind teeming with questions. Artiya'il's revelation of her lineage and the hidden realm had ignited a fire within her that she could no longer contain. "Artiya'il," she began, her voice tinged with both awe and determination. "Tell me more about the hidden realm – how does it differ from our world?"

"Ah, the hidden realm," Artiya'il replied with a knowing smile. "It is a place where the supernatural beings dwell, invisible to human eyes. It exists alongside the mundane world, yet it is an entirely separate plane."

"Can you describe it?" Anastasia asked breathlessly.

"Imagine a vast, ethereal landscape, where time itself flows differently than in our world," Artiya'il said, his voice taking on a dreamy quality as he painted a picture with his words. "Rivers of shimmering light that course through the air like veins of a living being, forests where the trees breathe life into the very soil, and creatures beyond your wildest dreams roam free. The colors are more vibrant, the scents more intoxicating, and the sounds more enchanting than anything you have ever experienced."

Listening to Artiya'il, Anastasia's eyes widened as she tried to envision such a realm. To think that there was an entire world existing in parallel with their own, unseen and unknown to most, was both exhilarating and terrifying.

"Is there a way for me to access this realm, or can I only perceive it?" Anastasia inquired, the curiosity in her eyes shining like stars in a moonless night.

"Your newfound abilities will enable you to glimpse into the hidden realm, though entering it fully may require assistance from other supernatural beings," Artiya'il explained. "But beware, Anastasia Asma'u; not all beings you encounter will be friendly, and some may seek to deceive or harm you."

Anastasia's heart skipped a beat as she considered the potential dangers, but her determination did not waver. "I understand," she said firmly. "But I must learn more about my abilities and this realm if I am to fulfill my role as an asasiyyin."

"Indeed," Artiya'il agreed. "And I shall guide you in your journey, Anastasia Asma'u. Together we will unlock the secrets of your lineage, hone your skills, and prepare you for the challenges that lie ahead."

"Thank you, Artiya'il," Anastasia whispered, her hand trembling as she reached out to touch the luminous feathers of the majestic golden eagle before her.

In that moment, a connection was forged between them – ancient and powerful – as Anastasia took her first steps toward understanding the hidden realm and embracing her destiny as a protector of both worlds.

Anastasia spent the next several days immersed in the mystical teachings of Artiya'il, her mind opening to a world she had never before imagined. She found herself marveling at the ethereal beauty of the hidden realm, its shimmering landscapes and luminescent skies offering a stark contrast to the concrete jungle of Detroit.

"Focus, Anastasia," Artiya'il chided gently, his celestial voice pulling her from her reverie. "In order to protect both worlds, you must embrace your role as an asasiyyin fully."

"I know," she replied, determination sparking in her dark eyes. "It's just… all so overwhelming." Her heart constricted with the weight of this new reality, but she refused to let fear hold her back.

"Your strength lies not only in your newfound abilities, but also in your unwavering faith and devotion to justice," Artiya'il reminded her. "You have been chosen for this path, Anastasia Asma'u. Trust in yourself and in the guidance of the Divine."

Anastasia took a deep breath, feeling the truth of his words settle within her soul. She nodded, steeling herself for the challenges that lay ahead. "I am ready," she declared, her voice steady and resolute.

"Very well," Artiya'il said, his own resolve apparent. "Let us continue our training."

Over the following weeks, Anastasia honed her skills under Artiya'il's watchful gaze, learning to sense the supernatural energies that pulsed around her like a heartbeat, and catching glimpses of hidden beings lurking in the shadows. Her once mundane life was now filled with wonder and danger in equal measure.

"Remember, Anastasia," Artiya'il cautioned one day as they stood on the rooftop of her apartment building, the city's skyline stretching out before them like a testament to man's ambition. "The balance between the worlds is delicate, and you must remain vigilant. There are many who would seek to exploit this power for their own gain."

"Like the jinni king Sakhr, and the water spirit Mami Wata?" Anastasia asked, recalling the tales Artiya'il had shared about other powerful beings in the hidden realm.

"Among others, yes," he replied, his eyes darkening as a hint of sadness flickered across his ethereal features. "But there are also allies to be found, like Zuhra, the celestial being who transforms into Venus. You will need all the help you can get, Anastasia Asma'u."

Anastasia clenched her fists, her resolve hardening like steel. "I will do whatever it takes to protect my city and the people I care about," she vowed, her gaze locked on the horizon.

"Then let us begin the next phase of your training," Artiya'il said, spreading his majestic wings wide, a golden beacon of hope against the darkening sky.

Anastasia stared at the luminous figure before her, an odd sense of peace settling over her heart. She knew that the road ahead would be filled with danger and uncertainty, but she could no longer deny her destiny as a protector of the supernatural world.

With newfound determination, she stepped forward into the unknown, her every thought consumed by the possibilities that awaited her on this extraordinary path. And in that moment, the ordinary life she had once known was left behind forever.

Echos in the Hallway

Anastasia stood at the entrance of her late grandmother's home, the sun casting long shadows on the overgrown lawn. For years, she had avoided this place – a dusty relic of her childhood, filled with memories she couldn't quite grasp. But now, as the weight of Artiya'il's revelations bore down upon her, she knew that the answers she sought lay within these walls.

"Are you sure about this?" Detective Ayo asked, his tone cautious as his deep-set eyes scanned the house. They had formed an unlikely alliance since their encounter with the supernatural, and although he didn't fully understand the extent of her abilities, he had come to respect her drive for truth.

"Something inside is calling me," Anastasia replied, her voice barely a whisper, yet steadfast in its conviction. "I need to know who I am – what I'm capable of."

She took a deep breath, bracing herself for what she might find, and pushed open the door. The hinges creaked loudly, echoing through the empty halls. Anastasia stepped inside, Ayo following closely behind, his skepticism tempered by a newfound curiosity.

The house was a testament to her family's history, every surface covered in a layer of dust, forgotten memories locked away in sepia-toned photographs and yellowing pages of old books. Anastasia felt a strange mixture of reverence and trepidation as she moved through the rooms, her fingers trailing across time-worn surfaces, searching for clues to her supernatural lineage.

In the dim light filtering through the curtains, she spotted a small, leather-bound book resting on a shelf – its worn spine indicating years of use. She reached out to take it, feeling a sudden surge of energy course through her veins. Curious, she carefully opened it to reveal pages filled with delicate calligraphy and intricate diagrams.

"Look at this," she murmured, holding the book up for Ayo to see. "These symbols… they're familiar, but I don't understand them."

"Maybe it's a code of some sort," Ayo suggested, his eyes narrowing as he studied the pages. "Your family might have been part of a secret society or tradition. It could explain your abilities."

Anastasia furrowed her brow in concentration, trying to make sense of the cryptic text. But even as she attempted to decipher the words, a strange feeling began to bubble up within her – a sensation that seemed to tug at the very core of her being.

"Wait," she said suddenly, her voice urgent. "I think I can read this. It's like… something inside me recognizes it."

Ayo raised an eyebrow, his skepticism surfacing once more. "Are you sure? It looks like gibberish to me."

"Trust me," Anastasia insisted, her dark, expressive eyes shining with determination. She turned back to the book, her finger tracing the lines of text as if guided by an unseen force. "This is a record of my family's history… our connection to the supernatural world."

"Can you find anything about your abilities?" Ayo asked, his curiosity piqued.

Anastasia continued to read, the words flowing through her mind like a long-forgotten language. She could feel the power of her ancestors coursing through her veins, the echoes of their voices whispering secrets from beyond the veil. And as she delved deeper into the mysteries of her past, she knew that her journey had only just begun.

"Give me time," she murmured, her gaze never leaving the page. "I'll find the answers we seek. I promise."

The sun hung low in the sky, casting warm hues of orange and gold across the vast Nigerian landscape. Anastasia stood at the edge of a village bustling with activity, taking in the sights, sounds, and scents that surrounded her. The air was thick with the aroma of spices and freshly cooked food, while laughter and conversations filled the atmosphere.

"Welcome home, Anastasia," she whispered to herself, feeling an inexplicable connection to this place – her ancestral homeland.

Wasting no time, she made her way into the heart of the village, determined to immerse herself in the culture and traditions of her ancestors. She exchanged greetings with the locals, their smiles warm and welcoming. They seemed to recognize something in her, a shared heritage that bound them together, despite the distance that had separated her from her roots for so long.

As the day wore on, Anastasia attended traditional ceremonies, observed age-old rituals, and listened to stories passed down through generations. Yet, amidst the vibrant colors and lively celebrations, she couldn't shake the feeling that there was still something missing – the key to unlocking the truth about her supernatural abilities.

It wasn't until the sun dipped below the horizon, and the villagers began to gather around a roaring bonfire that Anastasia found what she was searching for.

"Tonight, we pay homage to our ancestors," an elderly woman announced, her voice strong and commanding. "We seek their guidance and protection as we navigate the ever-changing world around us."

Anastasia watched intently as the flames danced in the night, casting shadows that seemed to take on forms of their own. Her eyes were drawn to a small group of individuals who stood apart from the rest, their expressions solemn and focused.

"Who are they?" Anastasia asked a young man standing nearby.

"Ah, those are the guardians of our ancestral knowledge," he replied, his tone hushed. "They hold the secrets of our past and possess an understanding of the supernatural world."

Anastasia's heart raced with anticipation, knowing that these individuals could be the key to unlocking her own powers. She approached the group cautiously, her dark eyes meeting those of the eldest guardian.

"Please," she began, her voice steady with determination. "I have traveled far to learn the truth about my abilities. I believe that you can help me."

The elder's gaze was piercing, as if he could see straight into her soul. He studied her for a moment before nodding solemnly. "We will share our knowledge with you, Anastasia. But be warned – the path you embark on is not without its challenges."

"Tell me what I must do," she replied, her resolve unwavering.

"First, you must connect with your ancestors, the ones who walked this earth before you," the elder instructed, gesturing towards the bonfire. "Only then can you truly understand the power that lies within you."

Without hesitation, Anastasia stepped closer to the fire, feeling its heat against her skin. She closed her eyes, focusing her thoughts on the generations that had come before her – their struggles, their triumphs, their wisdom. As she did so, she felt an energy surge through her, a connection that transcended time and space.

"Your ancestors are with you, Anastasia," the guardian whispered. "Their strength, their courage, their love… it all flows through you now."

Anastasia opened her eyes, and for the first time since discovering her supernatural lineage, she felt a sense of belonging – a deep understanding of her place in this intricate tapestry of existence.

"Thank you," she said, her voice filled with gratitude. "I am ready to face whatever lies ahead."

With newfound confidence, Anastasia took her first step towards uncovering the truth about her abilities, guided by the wisdom of her ancestors and the knowledge of those who understood the supernatural world.

"Your journey has only just begun," the elder guardian warned, his eyes reflecting the flames of the bonfire. "Remember to keep faith in yourself and the path that has been laid out before you."

Anastasia nodded, ready to embrace the challenges and revelations that awaited her in this delicate balance between worlds.

Anastasia stood before the dusty shelf, her hand hovering over a worn leather-bound tome. The air in the secluded chamber of the Nigerian spiritual archive was thick with the scent of ancient parchment and ink. Her pulse quickened as she sensed the importance of what lay within these pages.

"Take it," urged the elder guardian, his voice echoing softly in the dimly lit room. "Your destiny is entwined with that of the Jinni War, and these texts hold the key to understanding the conflict unfolding in your own city."

She carefully slid the book from its resting place, feeling the weight of history in her hands. As she flipped through the fragile pages, intricate diagrams and cryptic script danced before her eyes. It was all at once overwhelming and tantalizing – a glimpse into a hidden world, just waiting to be deciphered.

"Look closely," the guardian advised, pointing to an ancient map that depicted Detroit's landscape. "The Jinni War is not a mere myth or legend. It is a very real struggle, one that has been waged for centuries, unbeknownst to most humans."

Anastasia studied the markings on the map, noting the subtle symbols indicating supernatural energy beneath the familiar streets of her hometown. She could feel her heart pounding in her chest, as if some vital piece of her identity had been unveiled.

"I must return to Detroit," she declared, her determination igniting like a flame within her. "I have to understand this conflict and find out how I fit into all of this."

"Be cautious, Anastasia," the elder guardian warned. "The path you now walk can be treacherous, but trust in your instincts and the wisdom of your ancestors. They will guide you."

Anastasia nodded, her resolve unwavering. With the ancient texts secured in her bag, she set off on her journey back to Detroit, eager to uncover the hidden secrets of her city.

Upon her arrival, Anastasia wasted no time in seeking out those who might have knowledge of the supernatural occurrences and the Jinni War. She visited the places marked on the ancient map, searching for signs of the conflict and the individuals who had been affected by it.

"Excuse me," she said to a shopkeeper near one such site, her tone both respectful and assertive. "I'm investigating some recent disturbances in this area. Have you noticed anything unusual or unexplainable?"

The man eyed her warily, his gaze flicking from her determined expression to the FBI badge clipped to her belt. After a moment's hesitation, he nodded slowly.

"Maybe I've seen something," he admitted, leaning in conspiratorially. "There's been talk of strange happenings – shadows moving without people, whispers in the wind. Some folks even claim to have glimpsed creatures that shouldn't exist."

Anastasia absorbed his words, her mind racing with the implications. Could these mysterious sightings be connected to the Jinni War? And if so, what role did she play in this clandestine struggle?

"Thank you," she said, extending her hand in gratitude. "Your information could prove invaluable in my investigation."

"Be careful, Agent," the shopkeeper warned as they shook hands. "There are forces at work here beyond our understanding."

Anastasia returned to her apartment, the ancient texts spread before her like a puzzle waiting to be solved. As she delved deeper into the lore surrounding the Jinni War, she knew that her destiny was intertwined with this hidden conflict. She would need all her strength, her cunning, and the guidance of her ancestors to navigate the treacherous path that lay before her. But she was ready. She was Anastasia Asma'u, a woman of faith and determination – and she would not shy away from the challenges that destiny had chosen for her.

The cacophony of Eastern Market surrounded Anastasia as she navigated the maze of stalls, each one brimming with colorful produce and aromatic spices. The vibrant atmosphere filled her senses, a welcome distraction from the weight of her investigation. But as much as she wished to lose herself in the hustle and bustle of daily life, she couldn't shake the feeling that danger lurked just beneath the surface.

"Fresh apples!" called a vendor, thrusting a bushel towards her. "Sweetest in Detroit!"

"Thank you," Anastasia replied politely, taking an apple and tossing a few coins his way. She took a bite, savoring the crisp sweetness that spread across her tongue, and continued her search for answers.

"Excuse me," a voice interrupted her thoughts. She turned to find a man with a mischievous grin and impish eyes regarding her curiously. His small stature and playful demeanor belied an air of both innocence and cunning. "You seem lost, my friend. Perhaps I can help?"

"Actually," Anastasia said, hesitating only briefly before deciding to trust this stranger, "I'm looking for information about some strange occurrences happening around the city. Have you heard any rumors or stories?"

"Ah, the supernatural?" Amir's eyes twinkled with curiosity. "I may have heard a tale or two. Why don't we walk together? There's a tea shop nearby where we can talk."

As they strolled through the market, Anastasia couldn't help but notice how easily Amir navigated the crowd, weaving between stalls and exchanging pleasantries with the vendors. It was almost as if he'd been part of this community for centuries, though she knew that couldn't be possible.

They settled into a corner booth at the tea shop, steamy mugs clutched in their hands. Anastasia glanced around nervously, her instincts screaming that she was being watched. She shook off the feeling, focusing instead on Amir's words.

"Strange things have been happening," he began, his voice barely above a whisper. "Sudden gusts of wind knocking over stalls with no warning, shadows flickering across walls with no source, voices murmuring in empty alleys."

"Could these events be connected to something called the Jinni War?" Anastasia asked, unable to hide the tremor in her voice.

Amir's eyes widened, and for a moment, he looked genuinely surprised. "Why would you ask about such a thing?"

Anastasia hesitated before replying, her heart pounding in her chest. "I believe I may be involved in it somehow. My ancestors left me clues, and my abilities... they're tied to this conflict."

"Then you must tread carefully, my friend," Amir said gravely. "The Jinni

War is a dangerous game, and those who play it risk far more than they realize." He paused, watching her closely. "But if you truly wish to learn more, I'll help as best I can."

"Thank you," Anastasia said, her resolve strengthened by Amir's offer. "I need to understand what's happening, for the sake of both the human and supernatural worlds."

"Very well," Amir agreed, his impish grin returning as he leaned back in his chair. "Let's unravel the secrets of the Jinni War together, and perhaps we'll find a way to restore balance to our intertwined realms."

As they continued their conversation, Anastasia couldn't shake the feeling that Amir was far more than he appeared. But whether he would prove to be an ally or an adversary remained to be seen. For now, she had to trust him – and herself – if she hoped to navigate the treacherous waters of the Jinni War and protect the worlds that teetered on the brink of chaos.

The sun dipped low in the sky, casting long shadows on the streets of Detroit. Anastasia and Amir ventured deeper into the heart of the city, the air buzzing with a palpable energy that seemed to vibrate through her very bones. She sensed the presence of other supernatural beings, their forms hidden behind human facades. It was as if she had stumbled into an entirely new world – one that had been right under her nose for years.

"Amir, can you feel it too?" she asked, her eyes scanning the bustling crowds for any sign of the supernatural.

"Of course," he replied, his impish grin widening. "We are not alone, Anastasia. Many beings walk among us, some powerful allies, others dangerous foes."

As they meandered through the city, Anastasia found herself drawn to a small park nestled between towering skyscrapers. There, she noticed a group of individuals huddled together, their faces etched with worry and fear. They whispered to each other in hushed tones, their eyes darting around nervously.

"Who are they?" she asked, intrigued by their furtive behavior.

"Ah, those are the survivors of a recent skirmish between Sakhr's forces and our own," Amir explained, his voice somber. "They have seen the devastation that the Jinni War can bring."

Anastasia approached the group cautiously, her heart aching for their suffering. She listened as they recounted their stories – tales of destruction and loss, of families torn apart by the conflict between the jinni factions.

"Such power," Anastasia thought, appalled by the sheer scale of the destruction. "How can we hope to restore balance?"

As if reading her thoughts, Amir placed a comforting hand on her shoulder. "It won't be easy, but together, we stand a better chance. Remember, knowledge is power."

Just then, a gust of wind whipped through the park, sending a chill down Anastasia's spine. She turned to see a tall, imposing figure emerge from the shadows of the skyscrapers, his dark eyes fixed on her and Amir.

"Speak of the devil," Amir muttered under his breath. "Sakhr has arrived."

The jinni king strode towards them, his powerful presence drawing the attention of the nearby survivors. As he stopped before Anastasia and Amir, she could sense the centuries of secrets hidden behind his enigmatic gaze.

"Amir," Sakhr said, his voice deep and commanding. "I see you've taken a new apprentice."

"More like a partner, Sakhr," Amir retorted, standing protectively in front of Anastasia. "She seeks knowledge about the Jinni War, and I intend to help her find it."

"Very well," Sakhr replied, his eyes never leaving Anastasia. "But remember, knowledge can be a double-edged sword."

With that cryptic warning, the jinni king vanished as quickly as he had appeared, leaving Anastasia with more questions than answers. She could feel the weight of the responsibility resting on her shoulders, the lives of both the supernatural and human worlds hanging in the balance.

"Amir," she said, determination shining in her eyes. "We need to learn everything we can about the Jinni War – the players, the stakes, and the consequences. Only then can we hope to protect those who cannot protect themselves."

"Agreed," he replied, his mischievous grin returning. "Let's get to work."

The sun dipped below the horizon, casting a dim glow over the streets of Detroit as Anastasia and Amir ventured deeper into the Eastern Market district. Broken glass crunched beneath their feet as they navigated the shadowed alleyways, evidence of the ongoing conflict between the jinni factions. The air was heavy with tension, like a storm brewing on the edge of the world.

"Watch your step, Anastasia," Amir said, hopping nimbly from one patch of broken glass to another. "Wouldn't want you to cut yourself on any of these little reminders of our war."

"Amir," Anastasia whispered urgently, her mind racing with thoughts of the chaos that could erupt if humans discovered the existence of supernatural beings. "We need to find out who's behind this, and how to stop it before it spirals out of control."

"Patience, my friend," Amir replied, his eyes scanning the dark street corners for signs of danger. "We'll get there. But first, we must gather more information."

As they turned onto a bustling market street, Anastasia spotted an elderly woman huddled in the shadows, her fingers wrapped tightly around a set of prayer beads. The woman's eyes seemed to hold ancient wisdom, and Anastasia felt an inexplicable pull towards her.

"Assalamu alaikum," Anastasia greeted the woman, offering a respectful nod.

"Wa alaikum assalam," the woman replied, her voice thin and reedy. She glanced at Amir with suspicion before turning back to Anastasia. "What brings you two to this place?"

"We're investigating the recent disturbances in the city," Anastasia said cautiously. "We believe there's a connection to the supernatural world – specifically, the Jinni War."

The woman's eyes widened in fear, and she clutched her prayer beads even tighter. "You speak of dangerous things, child. The war between the jinni factions has been escalating, and if it continues to do so, it will not be long before the human world takes notice."

"Can you help us?" Anastasia pleaded, her sense of duty burning like a fire in her chest. "We need to find a way to stop this conflict before it's too late."

"Perhaps," the woman replied hesitantly. "But first, you must prove your intentions are pure."

"Ask me anything," Anastasia said without hesitation, her dark eyes filled with determination.

The woman regarded her for a moment, her gaze piercing into Anastasia's soul. Finally, she nodded, her gnarled fingers releasing their grip on the prayer beads.

"Very well," she said. "I will tell you what I know. But remember, child – in this world, there are no easy answers."

As the elderly woman shared tales of ancient battles and hidden alliances, Anastasia listened intently, her mind working tirelessly to piece together the puzzle of the Jinni War. With each new revelation, her resolve only grew stronger.

"I cannot stand idly by while lives are destroyed and worlds collide," she murmured to herself, her thoughts a whirlwind of plans and strategies. "I must do everything in my power to end this conflict and protect both the supernatural and human realms."

"Spoken like a true warrior," Amir teased, but his eyes shone with pride as he looked at Anastasia. "Together, we'll make things right again."

"Indeed," Anastasia agreed, her voice steady and strong. "Let's finish what we started."

Anastasia stood at the edge of the Detroit River, the water's surface reflecting the vibrant hues of the setting sun. The wind tugged gently at her hijab, and she could feel the weight of her decision settling on her shoulders like a heavy cloak. With each new revelation about the Jinni War, the delicate balance between the supernatural and human worlds seemed more precarious than ever. As she gazed across the river, her thoughts swirled like the currents beneath the surface.

"Are you certain this is the path you wish to take?" Artiya'il asked, his ethereal presence a calming force in the face of Anastasia's turbulent emotions. "The journey ahead will not be an easy one."

"Nothing worth fighting for ever is," Anastasia replied, her voice firm with conviction. "I've come too far to turn back now. I'll find a way to stop the conflict and protect both worlds – it's my duty."

Artiya'il studied her for a moment, the wisdom in his eyes tempered by a hint of sadness. "Very well," he acquiesced. "But remember, you need not face these challenges alone."

Anastasia nodded, grateful for Artiya'il's support and guidance. She knew she would need allies if she had any hope of navigating the treacherous web of intrigue that surrounded the Jinni War.

"Thanks, Artiya'il. I know I can count on you," she said softly, her gaze returning to the water.

"Always," he promised, brushing his fingers lightly against her arm in reassurance.

Over the following days, Anastasia immersed herself in her investigation, seeking out individuals who possessed knowledge of the supernatural world and its secrets. Each conversation brought her closer to the truth, but also served as a stark reminder of the danger she faced.

"Be careful who you trust, Anastasia," Detective Ayo warned, his brow furrowed in concern as they met in a dimly lit alley. "There are forces at play here that even I don't fully understand."

"Trust me, Ayo – I'm well aware of the risks," Anastasia replied, her dark eyes meeting his gaze intently. "But the stakes are too high for me to back down now."

As she delved deeper into the mysteries of her past and the world of the supernatural, her determination only grew stronger. Each new discovery fueled her resolve, driving her forward like a ship cutting through stormy seas.

"I will find a way to stop this war," she vowed, her thoughts a kaleidoscope of strategies and plans. "I won't let either world suffer because of it."

"Your heart is true, Anastasia," Artiya'il whispered, his celestial presence a constant source of comfort and guidance. "And it is that strength of spirit that will see you through the challenges ahead."

Anastasia drew in a deep breath, steeling herself for the journey that lay before her. She knew that the path she had chosen would be fraught with danger and uncertainty, but she also understood that it was her destiny to walk it.

"Let's finish what we started," she murmured, her voice steady and resolute.

"Together," Artiya'il agreed, his eyes shining with pride as he looked upon the courageous woman who dared to defy fate and forge her own path.

Dance of the Jinni

Anastasia sat on the edge of her bed, her mind replaying the events of the past few days. The world had changed, or perhaps it was she who had changed - for she could now see things she never thought possible. Shadows flickered at the corner of her eyes, whispers of hidden creatures lingered in her ears, and a growing energy stirred within her. She closed her eyes, focusing on the newfound power coursing through her veins. It was exhilarating, yet frightening all at once.

"Who am I?" she murmured to herself, pondering her place in this mysterious realm that had revealed itself to her. As if in response to her question, a soft light began to fill the room, emanating from a single point near the window. Anastasia opened her eyes and watched in awe as the light intensified, taking the form of a woman.

Zuhra stepped forward, an ethereal figure with a warm, reassuring presence. Her skin glistened as though kissed by the sun, and her long hair flowed like silk around her shoulders. But what struck Anastasia most were her eyes - pools of liquid gold that seemed to contain the wisdom of the ages. They held a quiet understanding, as though they had seen every secret and sorrow the world had ever known.

"Peace be upon you," Zuhra said softly, her voice resonating with a celestial harmony. "I am here to guide you."

Anastasia blinked, her heart pounding in her chest. The very air around

Zuhra shimmered with a gentle radiance, and Anastasia felt a sense of calm settle over her. This otherworldly being was the answer she sought, the key to unlocking the mysteries of her own existence. And so, with a deep breath, Anastasia took a step closer to Zuhra, ready to embrace her destiny.

Anastasia found herself in a small, secluded park tucked away within the bustling city. The sunlight filtered through the leaves of ancient trees, casting dappled patterns on the grassy ground. A gentle breeze rustled the foliage above as she sat on a weathered bench, her thoughts racing with the revelations she had recently encountered.

The air around her seemed to vibrate, and Anastasia sensed a presence approaching. She looked up and saw Zuhra, the radiant figure from before, gliding towards her with an otherworldly grace. Her golden eyes locked onto Anastasia's, and she felt a warmth wash over her, calming her turbulent thoughts.

"Peace be upon you, Anastasia," Zuhra greeted, her melodic voice echoing like a tender lullaby. "I see that you've been reflecting on your recent experiences."

"Indeed," Anastasia replied, her voice barely more than a whisper. "I never knew such things existed, and now… I'm a part of it all."

Zuhra settled beside Anastasia on the bench, her warm smile inviting trust. "Do not fear what you do not yet understand," she said gently. "I have been witness to countless ages and have guided many like you who possess hidden gifts. You are not alone in this journey."

Anastasia studied Zuhra's composed demeanor, sensing the depth of knowledge and experience she held within her. The celestial being seemed to radiate an aura of wisdom and patience, traits that reassured Anastasia even as they awed her.

"Will you guide me too?" Anastasia asked hesitantly, her fingers nervously entwined in her lap.

"Of course," Zuhra replied, her voice filled with kindness. "We shall discover the extent of your abilities together, and I will teach you how to harness them for the greater good."

Anastasia's heart swelled with gratitude and determination, her resolve to embrace the unknown strengthened by Zuhra's presence. She took a deep breath and met the celestial being's gaze, ready to embark on a journey into realms unseen.

"Then let us begin," Anastasia said, steeling herself for the challenges that lay ahead. Zuhra nodded, her eyes shimmering with pride, as they prepared to delve into the mysteries of the supernatural world together.

The sun dipped below the horizon, casting long shadows across the city park. Anastasia sat on a wooden bench beneath an ancient oak tree, her legs crossed and her hands folded in her lap. The fading light cast a warm glow on Zuhra, who seemed to absorb it, making her appear even more radiant than before.

"Long ago," Zuhra began, her voice melodic as she wove together the threads of history, "the supernatural world was unknown to most humans. But there were those among us, the asasiyyin, who could sense its presence and interact with its inhabitants."

Anastasia listened intently, her eyes wide with fascination. This was the knowledge she had craved for so long, the missing pieces of her own fragmented understanding of the world around her.

"Over time, however, the asasiyyin became fewer and fewer," Zuhra continued. "Some lost their way, others succumbed to the temptations of darker powers. And now, there are very few left who can truly protect the balance between our worlds."

"Is that what I am?" Anastasia asked, her voice barely audible. "A descendant of the asasiyyin?"

"Indeed, you are," Zuhra confirmed, her gaze steady upon Anastasia's face. "Your bloodline has been entrusted with this power for generations, though it may have lain dormant until now."

Anastasia's mind raced as she tried to absorb this new information. She thought of her family, of the inexplicable incidents from her past that now seemed to make sense. A mixture of awe and confusion washed over her as she considered the implications of her heritage.

"But... how am I supposed to protect the balance?" she asked, her voice shaky with a combination of excitement and fear. "I don't know anything about this world, or the creatures within it."

"Your knowledge will come in time," Zuhra reassured her. "I will teach you what you need to know, and your instincts will guide you as well. The power within you is strong, and it will only grow stronger as you learn to embrace it."

Anastasia took a deep breath, her chest rising and falling with the weight of her newfound responsibilities. She was no longer just an ordinary young woman living in a bustling city; she was a guardian of worlds, a protector of the balance between light and dark.

"I'm ready," she said, her voice firm with determination. "Teach me everything I need to know. I won't let my ancestors down."

"Very well," Zuhra replied, her eyes shining with pride. "We shall begin by learning how to see the unseen, to sense the energies that surround us."

Anastasia nodded, her resolve solidifying within her. This was her destiny, her purpose. And with Zuhra's guidance, she would rise to meet it.

The sun dipped below the horizon, casting a warm glow over the quiet park where Anastasia stood. She took in a deep breath, feeling the cool evening air fill her lungs as she prepared for her first lesson under Zuhra's guidance. Her heart raced with anticipation, her thoughts swirling with images of unseen worlds and hidden beings.

"Close your eyes," Zuhra instructed softly, standing beside Anastasia. "Focus on your breathing. Let your mind become still, like the surface of a calm pond."

Anastasia obeyed, shutting out the world around her to focus on the rise and fall of her chest. Gradually, her racing thoughts began to slow, replaced by a sense of inner calm.

"Good," Zuhra murmured. "Now, reach out with your senses. Feel the energies that surround you, the pulse of life in every living thing."

At first, Anastasia felt nothing. But as she concentrated, she gradually became aware of a faint hum beneath the surface of the world, like the faintest whisper of a breeze rustling through the leaves. It was a sensation she had never experienced before – a presence that had always been there, just beyond her perception.

"Can you feel it?" Zuhra asked.

"Yes," Anastasia whispered, awestruck. "It's… incredible."

"Those are the energies of the supernatural world," Zuhra explained. "With practice, you will learn to see the hidden beings that dwell among us, to understand their nature and their intentions."

Over the following weeks, Anastasia practiced tirelessly under Zuhra's watchful eye, honing her ability to detect the subtle energies that permeated the world around her. Each day brought new discoveries, as she learned to sense the presence of supernatural creatures and discern their true natures.

One afternoon, as they sat on a park bench watching the world go by, Anastasia felt a sudden surge of energy nearby. Her heart skipped a beat as she turned to Zuhra.

"Something's here," she said, her voice tense with excitement. "I can feel it."

"Very good," Zuhra replied, her eyes twinkling with approval. "Now, try to see it."

Anastasia focused on the sensation, allowing her eyes to drift out of focus. Slowly, an ethereal figure began to take shape before her – a shimmering, otherworldly being that seemed to flicker in and out of existence like a mirage.

"Can you see it?" Zuhra asked, her voice hushed with anticipation.

"Yes," Anastasia breathed, her eyes widening as she beheld the creature for the first time. "It's beautiful."

"Remember this moment, Anastasia," Zuhra advised. "The world you see now is the one you were born to protect. And every day, your powers will grow stronger."

As the weeks passed, Anastasia's skills continued to develop under Zuhra's guidance. She learned to see the hidden beings that populated the city, from the mischievous sprites that danced through alleyways to the solemn guardians who watched over sacred spaces.

With each new discovery, Anastasia's confidence grew. She no longer questioned her abilities or her place in the supernatural world; instead, she embraced her role as a descendant of the asasiyyin, determined to fulfill her destiny.

"I never imagined I could do these things," she marveled one evening as she and Zuhra stood atop a rooftop, gazing out at the city below. "Thank you for showing me what I am capable of."

"Your journey has only just begun, Anastasia" Zuhra replied, her eyes warm with pride. "Together, we will face many challenges – but I have no doubt that you will rise to meet them all."

Anastasia nodded, her eyes shining with determination. She knew the path ahead would not be easy, but with Zuhra by her side, she felt ready to face whatever the future held.

The sun dipped below the horizon, painting the sky with a symphony of colors as Anastasia and Zuhra walked along the riverbank. The air was alive with the sounds of laughter and music from nearby cafés, while the scent of roasting chestnuts wafted by on a gentle breeze. Anastasia closed her eyes for a moment to take in the myriad sensations, feeling the energy of the city coursing through her veins.

"Remember," Zuhra said gently, "to truly understand the supernatural world, you must learn to listen not just with your ears, but with your heart and soul."

Anastasia nodded, focusing her attention on the flow of hidden energies around them. She sensed the subtle vibrations of elementals playing in the water's depths and the protective aura of a benevolent spirit residing in an ancient oak tree.

"Zuhra, how do I know when I should intervene with these beings? What if my actions disrupt the balance?" Anastasia asked, her brow creased with concern.

"Ah, that is where wisdom comes into play," Zuhra replied, her celestial eyes reflecting the shimmering twilight. "You must learn to discern when your presence is needed and when it is best to let events unfold naturally. Trust your instincts, and they will guide you."

As they continued their walk, Anastasia couldn't help but notice the way the shadows seemed to dance and whisper along the cobblestone streets. She felt a twinge of unease, wondering what secrets might lie hidden within the darkness.

"Zuhra, do you ever feel… afraid?" she ventured hesitantly.

"Of course," Zuhra admitted, her voice soft yet steady. "But fear is a natural response to the unknown. Embrace it, and let it fuel your determination to learn more, to grow stronger."

Anastasia took a deep breath, considering Zuhra's words. She knew that she still had much to learn, but with each step, the supernatural world seemed to reveal more of its secrets to her. The thought was both exhilarating and terrifying.

"Always remember," Zuhra added, "that you have a purpose in this realm – to protect it and maintain harmony between the seen and unseen. You are a bridge between worlds, Anastasia."

As they reached the end of the riverbank, the last traces of sunlight vanished, giving way to a sky filled with twinkling stars. Anastasia marveled at their beauty, feeling a sense of wonder and responsibility wash over her.

"Thank you, Zuhra," she said quietly, her voice filled with gratitude. "With your guidance, I will do my best to honor my lineage and fulfill my destiny."

Zuhra smiled, her eyes shining like the stars above. "I have no doubt that you will, Anastasia. Together, we will face the challenges that lie ahead, and you will emerge stronger and wiser than before."

Anastasia gazed at the cityscape before her, its lights shimmering like a sea of fireflies. The air was thick with the scent of jasmine and the distant sounds of laughter from late-night revelers. She closed her eyes, allowing herself to fully experience the supernatural energies that coursed through every corner of the city. It was an overwhelming sensation, like dipping her fingers into a pool of warm honey.

"Feeling the energies around you is only the beginning," Zuhra said gently, placing a hand on Anastasia's shoulder. "With practice, you'll learn to distinguish between different types of beings and even sense their intentions."

Anastasia opened her eyes and looked at Zuhra, determined to learn all she could from her mentor. "I am grateful for your guidance, Zuhra. I promise to fulfill my role as a protector of this world – our world – and to use my abilities to maintain harmony between the seen and unseen."

Zuhra's smile was radiant, filling Anastasia with warmth and reassurance. "Your commitment is admirable, Anastasia. But remember, this journey will not be without its trials. You must steel yourself for the challenges that lie ahead."

The wind picked up, causing Anastasia's hair to dance wildly about her face. A shiver ran down her spine as she sensed a presence she had never felt before – something powerful, ancient, and unfathomable.

"What lies ahead?" she asked, her voice barely audible above the howling wind.

Zuhra looked out towards the horizon, her eyes narrowing slightly. "You will face adversaries who seek to disrupt the balance of our world. Some may appear as friends, others as fearsome creatures of nightmares. But know that within you lies a strength greater than any foe."

As the wind began to subside, Anastasia clenched her fists, feeling a surge of determination course through her veins. "I am ready, Zuhra. Whatever challenges I may face, I will not falter."

"Good," Zuhra replied, her gaze returning to Anastasia's face. "But do not forget that you are not alone in this fight. I am here to guide you, and together, we will ensure the safety of our world."

As they stood there, surrounded by the pulsating energy of the city, Anastasia felt a newfound sense of purpose. The road ahead would be filled with danger and uncertainty, but with Zuhra by her side, she knew she could face whatever lay in store.

"Let us begin," she said, her voice steady and resolute.

"Indeed," Zuhra agreed, a gleam of anticipation in her eyes. "Together, we will shape your destiny and safeguard the future of the supernatural world."

A Delicate Balance

Anastasia stood at the entrance of the dimly lit alleyway, her heart pounding in her chest. She glanced down at her hands, which trembled with a mix of anticipation and nervousness. Taking a deep breath, she focused on steadying herself, reminding herself that Artiya'il had chosen her for this moment. This was her first test, her first venture into the supernatural world, and she couldn't afford to fail.

"Remember what I taught you," whispered Amir, the impish genie hovering just beside her ear. "Trust in your instincts, and your lineage will guide you."

"Right," Anastasia murmured under her breath. She could hear the faint rustling of newspaper and the quiet sniffles of the homeless population huddled together in the shadows of the alley. The ghoul had been terrorizing these innocent people, and it was up to her to stop it. "I won't let them down."

"Good," Amir smiled, his tiny hand patting her shoulder before he vanished from sight.

Anastasia cautiously stepped deeper into the alley, her senses heightened and every nerve in her body tingling. The air seemed thick with an unseen tension, heavy with the weight of fear and desperation. The scent of decay wafted through the air, and she knew instinctively that the ghoul was nearby.

"Please," a frail voice whimpered from behind a pile of discarded boxes. A dirty, trembling hand reached out towards Anastasia, pleading for help. "Please save us."

"Stay calm," Anastasia whispered reassuringly. "I'm here to help."

The hand withdrew, as if reassured by her presence. Anastasia could feel the eyes of the homeless victims upon her – wary, frightened, but also hopeful. They had suffered so much at the hands of the ghoul, and now it was up to her to end their nightmare.

"Alright, you monstrous fiend," she muttered under her breath. "You've tormented these people long enough."

Anastasia's heart raced as she continued her search for the ghoul, her every sense focused on detecting any sign of its presence. She knew what she had to do – it was time for her to tap into her supernatural powers and face the beast head-on. But would she be strong enough?

"Remember your lineage," she whispered to herself, repeating Amir's advice like a mantra. "I am a protector. I am the one chosen to maintain the balance between worlds."

With that thought in mind, Anastasia took a deep breath and pushed forward, steeling herself for the battle ahead.

Anastasia crept deeper into the dimly lit alley, her heart pounding in her chest as she tried to steady her breathing. The stench of decay hung heavy in the air, a putrid miasma that mixed with the scent of damp garbage and despair. She knew that somewhere nearby lurked the ghoul that had been terrorizing the homeless population, and it was her duty to stop it.

"Focus," she whispered to herself, her eyes scanning the dark recesses of the alley. "You can do this."

And then she saw it – the ghoul, crouched behind a pile of rotting trash like some twisted abomination birthed from the filth. Its decaying flesh hung loosely from its emaciated frame, a grotesque tapestry of peeling skin and exposed bone. The creature's eyes glowed like burning coals in the shadows, two pools of malevolent crimson that seemed to bore into Anastasia's very soul. And its claws… those hideous, elongated talons that dripped with the blood of its victims, eager to rend and tear at living flesh once more.

"By Allah, what have you become?" Anastasia muttered, her voice barely audible.

"Is it here?" a shaky, disembodied voice asked from behind her.

"Stay back," Anastasia warned without turning around, knowing that the homeless victims were watching her. She needed to protect them, but first, she had to face her own fears.

"Alright, you monstrous fiend," she said, taking a cautious step forward. "Let's end this."

"End me?" the ghoul rasped, its voice a guttural hiss that sent chills down Anastasia's spine. "How deliciously naive."

"Keep your distance," Anastasia demanded, feeling the surge of energy within her as she prepared to tap into her supernatural powers. She could feel her ancestors guiding her, their strength bolstering her own.

"Such a pretty girl," the ghoul mocked, its voice dripping with malicious intent. "You think you can stand against me? The hunger… it never ends."

"Enough!" Anastasia shouted, her resolve hardening. "I am Anastasia Asma'u, protector of the innocent and defender of the balance between worlds. You will not harm another soul."

Anastasia's heart raced as she closed the distance between herself and the ghoul, her senses heightened and her body ready for combat. She had faced many challenges in her life, but none quite like this. As she prepared for the battle ahead, she knew that there was no turning back – her journey as a protector of the supernatural world had only just begun.

Anastasia's eyes darted around the dimly lit alley, taking in the shivering figures huddled against the cold brick walls. The homeless victims of the ghoul's terror were a pitiable sight; their faces etched with desperation and fear. Some clutched tattered blankets around their shoulders, while others simply stared blankly into the darkness, their hopelessness palpable.

"Please, help us," a frail woman whispered, her voice trembling as she reached out to Anastasia with a bony, dirt-streaked hand. "It comes at night, and we…we can't escape it."

"Stay close together and don't make any noise," Anastasia instructed them firmly, her heart pounding in her chest. "I'll do my best to protect you."

"Is it true?" a young man asked, his voice quavering. "Are you really going to fight it?"

"Trust me," Anastasia reassured him, trying to sound more confident than she felt. "I won't let it harm you or anyone else ever again."

"May Allah bless you for your bravery," an elderly man murmured reverently, his eyes shining with gratitude.

"Thank you," Anastasia replied softly, offering him a determined nod before turning to face her enemy.

The tension in the air was nearly suffocating as Anastasia scanned the shadows for any sign of the ghoul. Her muscles tensed, ready to spring into action, while her mind raced with thoughts of what could happen if she failed. She couldn't let these people down; their lives depended on her.

"Come out and face me, you coward!" Anastasia shouted defiantly, her voice echoing through the narrow alley.

A low growl emanated from the darkness, sending a shiver down Anastasia's spine. Her breath caught in her throat as the ghoul stepped out of the shadows, its glowing red eyes fixed on her and its decaying flesh barely clinging to its grotesque form.

"Ah, the brave protector," it sneered, its voice a guttural hiss. "I've been waiting for you."

"Your reign of terror ends tonight," Anastasia declared, her voice steady despite the icy fear that gripped her heart.

"Bold words from someone so inexperienced," the ghoul taunted, its claws scraping against the asphalt as it approached her. "But I'm eager to see what you're capable of."

Anastasia swallowed hard, trying to push past her own uncertainty and focus on the task at hand. She was their only hope – she couldn't afford to fail. With a deep breath, she readied herself for the battle that would change her life forever.

"Let's do this," she whispered, steeling herself as the ghoul advanced, the weight of her newfound responsibilities bearing down on her.

The ghoul lunged at Anastasia with lightning speed, its claws slashing through the air like razor-sharp knives. Her instincts kicked in, and she narrowly dodged the attack, feeling the icy wind as the creature's talons grazed past her face.

"Is that all you've got?" Anastasia taunted, trying to mask her own fear.

The ghoul snarled, baring its rotting teeth as it circled her. "You'll regret those words," it hissed, its glowing red eyes promising a gruesome end.

"Enough!" Anastasia shouted, her voice ringing out with confidence she didn't quite feel yet. She knew now was the time to tap into her supernatural powers, to channel the energy coursing through her veins and summon the strength necessary to defeat this monster.

Closing her eyes for a brief moment, Anastasia focused on the power within her, the ancient lineage of celestial beings that she had inherited. She felt a warm sensation surge through her body, igniting her limbs with newfound strength. Opening her eyes, she stared down the ghoul with determination.

"Let's see how you handle this," she said, her voice filled with resolve.

The ghoul sneered, unimpressed by her bravado. "Your powers won't save you," it growled, lunging at her once more.

Anastasia deftly sidestepped the attack, feeling the thrum of energy beneath her skin, empowering her movements. With newfound agility, she countered the ghoul's assault, landing a powerful blow to its decaying form. The creature stumbled back, surprise flickering across its grotesque features.

"Impossible!" it snarled, anger clouding its eyes.

"Get used to it," Anastasia retorted, her heart pounding as she reveled in the realization that she could stand against this nightmare.

The ghoul roared, its fury palpable as it charged at her again. But this time, Anastasia was ready. She allowed her supernatural instincts to guide her, dodging the creature's attacks with a grace and speed that would have been impossible just moments ago.

"Your time is up," she whispered, feeling the energy within her build to a crescendo, ready to be unleashed.

"Never!" the ghoul spat, rage twisting its already terrifying visage.

Anastasia knew there was no room for doubt – not when lives hung in the balance. She had to trust herself, her powers, and her purpose. And so, with a fierce battle cry, she tapped into the very core of her newfound strength, preparing to banish the ghoul once and for all.

The ghoul's claws whistled through the air, narrowly missing Anastasia's face as she ducked and weaved around its strikes. Her heart thundered in her chest, the adrenaline coursing through her veins with every calculated dodge and counterattack.

"Is that all you've got?" she taunted, gritting her teeth as she swung a powerful kick at the creature's abdomen. It staggered back, momentarily winded, but quickly recovered, baring its fangs in a snarl.

"Your arrogance will be your downfall," it hissed, lunging forward once more.

Anastasia knew this was only the beginning of her battle, but with each clash of power, she could feel her confidence growing. The energy inside her surged, urging her to push past her limits. She couldn't let the innocent people in the alley fall victim to this monster.

"Never underestimate me," she spat, locking eyes with the ghoul as they circled each other like predators.

"Enough!" the ghoul roared, its decaying flesh quivering with rage. It swiped at her again, but Anastasia anticipated the move, using her heightened senses to evade the blow. She spun on her heel, landing a solid punch against the creature's jaw. Its head snapped to the side, giving her the opportunity to follow up with a quick series of jabs.

"Pathetic," she muttered, her breath coming in ragged gasps as she prepared for the ghoul's next attack.

"Silence, worm!" the ghoul screeched, its red eyes ablaze with fury. It lunged at her with renewed determination, its claws slicing through the air like sharpened steel.

But Anastasia was ready. With a fluidity she never imagined possible, she parried the creature's blows, responding with her own fierce attacks. It was as if the battle had awakened something within her, a primal force that thrived on the chaos and danger.

The ghoul's relentless onslaught kept coming, but Anastasia didn't shy away from the challenge. She could feel the weight of responsibility settling on her shoulders as she fought to protect the vulnerable people huddled in the shadows. Their lives depended on her ability to harness her newfound powers, to banish the evil that threatened their very existence.

"Enough!" she screamed, her voice echoing through the alley as she unleashed a torrent of energy at the ghoul.

"Impossible," it whispered, its body contorting and writhing under the assault.

Anastasia watched the creature with steely determination, refusing to let up even as it howled in pain. This was her duty, her purpose – and she would not falter.

"Your reign of terror ends now!" she shouted, delivering one final, devastating blow that sent the ghoul crashing against the brick wall behind it.

Anastasia's breath came in sharp, ragged gasps as she faced the ghoul, her heart pounding against her ribcage. She knew it was time to put an end to this nightmare. The terror-stricken faces of the homeless victims hiding in the alley served as a constant reminder of what was at stake.

"Your time is up, abomination," Anastasia hissed, drawing upon her supernatural powers. A warmth spread through her veins, making her feel alive and powerful. She raised her hands, palms outstretched, and focused all her energy on banishing the ghoul.

"By the power of the celestial beings that guide me, I command you to return to the darkness from whence you came!" she shouted, her voice ringing with authority.

The ghoul snarled, its glowing red eyes widening in shock as it realized what was happening. It tried to lunge at Anastasia one last time, but she held her ground, her determination unwavering.

"Leave this place and never return!" Anastasia cried out, unleashing a burst of energy that surged towards the ghoul.

"NOOOO!" the creature screamed as the force engulfed it. Its decaying flesh seemed to dissolve, its elongated claws crumbling into dust. With a final, guttural moan, the ghoul vanished into thin air, sent back to the realm it belonged to.

In that moment, silence fell over the alley. Anastasia's chest heaved as she struggled to catch her breath, her body still coursing with adrenaline. The fear that had gripped her earlier now gave way to a sense of accomplishment and relief. She had done it—she had protected the innocent lives huddled in the shadows.

"Is…is it gone?" one of the homeless victims whispered, peeking out from behind a dumpster.

"Yes," Anastasia replied, offering a reassuring smile. "You're safe now."

"Thank you," the man said, awe and gratitude in his eyes. The other victims echoed his sentiment, their relief palpable.

Anastasia nodded, still processing everything that had just happened. She had triumphed over the ghoul, and with her newfound powers, she had saved these people from a terrible fate.

"Remember, there is more to the world than what meets the eye," Anastasia warned the small crowd. "Be careful out here."

"Thank you, miss," an older woman whispered, clutching a tattered shawl around her shoulders. "May God bless you."

"God willing," Anastasia murmured, her heart swelling with pride. She knew this was just the beginning of her journey as a protector of the supernatural world, but for now, she had made a difference—and that was worth celebrating.

Anastasia stood in the now-quiet alley, the stench of the ghoul's decaying flesh still lingering in the air. The homeless victims had dispersed, leaving her alone with her thoughts. The night sky above seemed to hold a new kind of darkness—one that was both foreboding and full of potential.

"Amir," she whispered, seeking comfort from her mischievous impish companion, who materialized by her side, his eyes glinting with curiosity.

"Quite a show you put on there, Anastasia," he grinned, looking around at the wreckage left behind.

"Was it enough?" she asked softly, her voice tinged with uncertainty. "I've barely begun to understand my powers—my destiny."

"Of course it was enough," Amir replied, his tone sincere. "You saved those people tonight. You're learning, Anastasia. But this…this is just the beginning."

Anastasia considered his words, staring into the darkness that seemed to stretch into infinity. She thought about Artiya'il, the celestial messenger who had revealed her true lineage, and what he had told her about her purpose in this world. A protector, a guardian against the shadows that threatened to consume humanity.

"Amir," she said quietly, "what lies ahead for me? What challenges will I face?"

The genie looked thoughtful for a moment, his playful demeanor giving way to a more serious expression. "I cannot say for certain, Anastasia. But know this: as you grow stronger, so too will the forces that seek to oppose you. You will be tested, time and again. And through these trials, your path will become clear."

"Then I must be ready," she declared, determination burning in her dark eyes. "I cannot falter in my duty to protect the innocent. My journey has only just begun, and I will not waver."

"Ah, spoken like a true warrior," Amir smiled, his impish grin returning. "You'll always have me by your side, Anastasia. Together, we'll face whatever comes next."

"Thank you, Amir," she said softly, grateful for his unwavering support.

Anastasia took one last look at the alley, her mind already racing ahead to the challenges that awaited her. The supernatural world was vast and full of unknowns, but she was ready to embrace her destiny and forge her own path through the darkness. With a newfound sense of purpose, she stepped out of the shadows and into the night, her journey as a protector of the supernatural world only just beginning.

Anastasia stepped out of the alleyway, her heart still pounding from the adrenaline of her first supernatural confrontation. The cold night air was a welcome relief on her heated skin, and she took in a deep breath, steadying herself. She could feel the weight of her new responsibilities settling on her shoulders like a heavy cloak. The world around her had transformed, revealing hidden dangers and ancient powers that demanded her attention.

"Amir," she whispered, trying to keep her voice steady. "What can we expect next? I know there'll be more challenges ahead."

The small genie appeared at her side, his mischievous eyes clouded with concern. "There's no telling, Anastasia. But you have faced your first test with courage and skill. That bodes well for the path ahead."

She looked towards the cityscape, the bright lights casting long shadows across the streets. Within those shadows, she knew there were secrets waiting to be uncovered - secrets that could change the course of her life forever.

"Tell me about the others," she asked quietly, her thoughts turning to the supernatural beings who shared her world. "The ones who walk among us, unseen."

Amir hesitated for a moment before replying. "There are many, Anastasia. Some benevolent, some malevolent, and some who walk the line between both worlds. You will encounter them all in time, and you must learn to discern friend from foe."

As they walked down the moonlit streets, Anastasia felt a strange exhilaration mixed with her apprehension. Her life had taken an unexpected turn, and while she couldn't predict what lay ahead, she knew it would be a journey unlike any other.

"Will I always be fighting?" she asked Amir as they turned a corner, her voice barely audible above the distant sounds of the city.

"Perhaps not always," he replied thoughtfully. "But you must be prepared for the times when violence is the only recourse, and know when to use diplomacy instead. The balance between the two will be crucial to your success."

Anastasia nodded, her resolve strengthening with each step they took. Her mind raced with questions about the supernatural world she was now a part of, but she knew that answers would come with time and experience. For now, she had to focus on honing her skills and learning more about her newfound abilities.

"Then let's begin," she said decisively, her eyes filled with determination. "I'm ready to face whatever challenges lie ahead."

Amir smiled at her, his impish grin returning. "Very well, Anastasia. Let us embark on this journey together, and may we find the wisdom and strength we need along the way."

As they continued through the city streets, Anastasia could feel the energy within her stirring, a potent force waiting to be unleashed. She knew that the path ahead would be fraught with danger and uncertainty, but she also knew that she had the power to shape her own destiny.

And so, beneath the watchful gaze of the moon, Anastasia Asma'u set forth on her journey into the unknown, ready to embrace all the challenges and revelations that awaited her in the vast, untamed realm of the supernatural.

Detective Ayo

Anastasia stood at the edge of the city, gazing out at the sprawling metropolis that stretched out before her like a living organism. She knew she couldn't maintain the delicate balance between the human and supernatural worlds on her own - not for long, at least. Her thoughts swirled with the realization that she needed allies, beings who understood the complexities and dangers that lurked within the shadows, just as she did.

"Harut," she whispered, the name slipping from her lips like a secret incantation. He was an enigmatic figure, spoken of in hushed tones among the supernatural community. A fallen angel with a mysterious aura and an air of danger that seemed to follow him wherever he went. It was said that his dark eyes held secrets as ancient as the stars themselves, and that his intentions were as difficult to discern as smoke in a storm. Anastasia knew that if anyone could help her navigate this world of darkness and deceit, it was Harut.

He was rumored to possess knowledge of celestial weapons, powerful artifacts that could shift the balance of power between humans and supernaturals. And though many had sought him out, few had ever managed to find him. It was whispered that he made his residence in an abandoned church, hidden away in some forgotten corner of the city.

"An elusive ally is better than none at all," Anastasia murmured to herself as she began her search, her heart pounding with anticipation. Somehow, she could sense that finding Harut would be both a blessing and a curse. But it was a risk she was willing to take. After all, maintaining the balance between two worlds was never meant to be easy.

"Excuse me," Anastasia asked a passing stranger, "do you know where I could find an abandoned church?"

"Abandoned church?" The man gave her a dubious look. "I don't know about that. But there's an old church not too far from here, down that alley and to the left."

"Thank you," Anastasia replied, a small smile playing on her lips. She continued onward, following the man's directions.

As she walked, her thoughts returned to Harut. His reputation preceded him, but Anastasia knew better than to trust rumors alone. If she was going to forge an alliance with this enigmatic figure, she would have to tread carefully. For now, though, she focused on finding the abandoned church - and the mysterious, dangerous angel who called it home.

The abandoned church loomed before Anastasia, a crumbling monument to a forgotten past. Darkened windows stared out like the empty eyes of a skull, and ivy snaked its way up the ancient walls, as if trying to strangle the last remnants of life from the building. A sense of foreboding weighed heavy in the air, making it difficult for Anastasia to breathe.

"Is this where I'll find you, Harut?" she whispered, her voice barely audible over the wind's eerie howl.

She hesitated at the church's threshold, her hand hovering over the rusted iron door handle. Deep down, she knew that crossing this line would irrevocably change her path, binding her fate to that of the enigmatic angel. But maintaining the balance between the human and supernatural worlds was her responsibility, and she needed all the help she could get. With a deep breath, she pushed open the door.

Inside, shadows clung to every corner, hiding secrets and whispers of things best left unseen. The air was stale, thick with the scent of decay. Anastasia's footsteps echoed through the nave, sending an involuntary shiver down her spine. She felt as though she were trespassing in a crypt, disturbing the slumber of the dead.

"Harut," she called out, her voice wavering slightly. "I've come seeking your help."

"Many have sought my aid, child," a voice answered from the darkness, smooth as silk yet laced with an underlying menace. "What makes you think I'll grant it to you?"

Anastasia swallowed hard, squaring her shoulders. "I am tasked with maintaining the balance between our world and the supernatural realm. And I believe your knowledge of celestial weapons could be invaluable in achieving that goal."

"Ah," Harut's voice grew closer, his form materializing from the shadows like a phantom. His dark eyes seemed to pierce her very soul, and Anastasia felt a wave of unease wash over her. Despite the power she wielded, she was but a mortal in the presence of an ancient being.

"An admirable quest," he mused, circling her like a predator sizing up its prey. "But what's in it for me?"

"Protection," Anastasia replied hesitantly, watching his every move. "And a chance to use your knowledge for the greater good."

"An intriguing proposition." Harut stopped in front of her, tilting his head as if considering her words. "Very well, I shall assist you. But remember, alliances can be as fragile as glass."

Anastasia nodded, trying to suppress the feeling of dread that clawed at her chest. She knew that trusting Harut would be a gamble, that his intentions were difficult to discern. But as they stood together in the heart of darkness, she couldn't help but hope that the alliance they forged would light their way through the shadows of the supernatural realm.

Anastasia cautiously followed Harut out of the abandoned church, the weight of their tentative alliance pressing upon her. The sun had nearly set, casting long shadows across the cityscape like grasping fingers. As they walked, she couldn't help but wonder what other supernatural forces lurked within the human world.

"Before we go further, we need to establish some ground rules," Anastasia said, her voice firm despite her inner turmoil. "We must be honest with each other and work together. We can't allow personal ambitions to cloud our judgment."

"Agreed," Harut replied, his tone unreadable. "But we must also respect each other's boundaries. There are secrets I hold that you may not be ready to learn."

"Fair enough," she conceded, her eyes narrowing in suspicion. "But if those secrets endanger our mission or the balance between worlds, I expect you to reveal them."

"Understood," he replied, a hint of amusement lingering on his lips. "Now, there is another ally you should consider. They are elusive beings, capricious yet invaluable in their insights."

"Who are they?" Anastasia inquired as they turned a corner, entering one of the city's many parks. The once lush garden now lay shrouded in twilight, its beauty hidden beneath an eerie veil.

"Irshi," Harut whispered, his gaze scanning the shadowy foliage. "They know the secrets of this city better than anyone else. But beware, they are unpredictable and mischievous."

As if summoned by Harut's words, a flutter of movement caught Anastasia's eye. A small creature emerged from the underbrush, its features shifting like quicksilver. One moment it appeared as a delicate fairy with iridescent wings, the next as a fanged imp with glowing eyes.

"Ah, Irshi," Harut greeted the being with a nod. "We come seeking your wisdom and guidance."

"Interesting," the Irshi replied, its voice a chorus of whispers. "And what do I gain in return?"

"Protection, as we offer each other. And perhaps some amusement along the way," Harut suggested, a sly smile playing on his lips.

"Very well," the Irshi agreed, settling into a more stable form – that of a lithe, cat-like creature with a mischievous grin. "I shall join your alliance, but remember: I am beholden to none."

Anastasia studied the mercurial being, aware that their alliance now included an unpredictable element. Yet she couldn't deny the potential advantage of having the elusive Irshi on their side.

"Welcome, Irshi," Anastasia said cautiously, feeling both excitement and trepidation at the path before them. With her newfound allies by her side, they would delve deeper into the supernatural realm, navigating its intricate politics and dangerous factions, all in the name of maintaining balance between worlds.

The sun dipped below the horizon, casting a warm glow over the trees and flowers of the city's many parks and gardens. Anastasia found herself drawn to these ethereal havens, where the boundary between the human and supernatural worlds seemed at its thinnest. She walked along a cobblestone path, marveling at the vibrant colors of the flora surrounding her. The air was perfumed with the scent of roses, lavender, and the faintest hint of something more – a whisper of enchantment that lingered on the breeze.

"Such a beautiful place," Anastasia murmured to herself, feeling an inexplicable pull towards the verdant heart of the garden. She ventured off the path, her footsteps muffled by the lush grass beneath her feet. It was here, amid the tangled foliage and the soft sighs of wind through leaves, that she first encountered Irshi.

"Hello," came a lilting voice from above. Anastasia glanced up, startled to see a pair of gleaming eyes peering down at her from the branches of a nearby tree. The creature perched there seemed to be in a constant state of flux, its form shifting like shadows upon water. One moment it resembled a bird with shimmering feathers, the next a mischievous-looking sprite with delicate wings.

"Who are you?" Anastasia asked cautiously, taking a step back as the being flitted down from the tree to land gracefully before her.

"Ah, I have been called many names," it replied, settling into the form of a slender, green-skinned figure with pointed ears and a playful smirk. "But you may call me Irshi."

Anastasia hesitated, aware of the unpredictable nature of the creature before her. However, she could not deny the potential value of such a shape-shifting ally in her quest to maintain balance between worlds.

"Harut has mentioned you," she said, watching as Irshi's eyes sparkled with curiosity. "He believes you can provide valuable insight and assistance in our mission."

Irshi tilted their head, considering the proposition. "And what do I gain from aiding you?" they asked, their voice a melodic mixture of tones.

"An alliance," Anastasia replied, aware that her words held both promise and risk. "Protection and support from those who share your goal of maintaining balance."

"Interesting," Irshi mused, their form rippling like water before solidifying into a sinuous, cat-like creature with luminous eyes. "Very well, I shall accept your offer – for now. But remember, my loyalty is as mutable as my form."

Anastasia nodded, noting the mercurial nature of her new ally. Despite the inherent uncertainty that came with partnering with such an enigmatic being, she couldn't help but feel a sense of exhilaration, knowing that their combined strengths would aid her in navigating the treacherous landscape of supernatural politics and power struggles.

"Then let us begin," she said firmly, her heart pounding with determination. Together, they would traverse the shadowy realms between worlds, forging alliances and facing challenges beyond imagination – all in the name of preserving the delicate balance that held their worlds together.

In the twilight of the city park, Anastasia met Harut and Irshi amidst the rustling leaves of ancient trees and the songs of hidden nocturnal creatures. The ethereal glow of moonlight filtered through the canopy above, casting dappled shadows on the trio as they gathered around an old stone bench encrusted with moss and lichen.

"Let us discuss the terms of our alliance," Anastasia began, her eyes flicking between Harut's inscrutable gaze and Irshi's ever-changing form. "We must be clear on what we offer one another and what we expect in return."

"Agreed," Harut replied, his voice a deep, resonant thrum. He leaned back against a gnarled tree trunk, the shadows seeming to cling to him like a second skin. "I can provide knowledge of celestial weapons and guidance within the supernatural realm."

"An invaluable resource," Anastasia acknowledged, aware of the power Harut's expertise could yield. "And you, Irshi?"

"Information," Irshi answered, their form shifting from sinuous feline to an elegant, otherworldly figure with elongated limbs and iridescent wings.

"I know the secrets whispered in every corner of this city, and I can traverse both the human and supernatural realms with ease."

"Then let me be plain: I seek to maintain the balance between our worlds, to prevent chaos and destruction," Anastasia said, her voice resolute. "If you commit to this cause, I pledge my loyalty and protection in return."

"Balance is a delicate thing, Anastasia," Harut warned, dark eyes narrowing. "You must be prepared to make difficult choices. Sometimes, sacrifices are necessary."

"Indeed," Irshi chimed in, their voice a lilting song. "But it is also true that there are forces which seek to disrupt the equilibrium. We must be vigilant against those who would exploit the vulnerabilities of our world."

Anastasia's mind raced, her thoughts spinning with the implications of their alliance and the potential paths that lay ahead. She weighed Harut's caution against Irshi's enthusiasm, attempting to find the delicate balance between pragmatism and optimism.

"Then we are agreed," she said finally, her heart a tight knot of determination. "We will work together, sharing knowledge and resources, to preserve the fragile harmony between worlds."

"Very well," Harut murmured, his voice an ominous rumble. "But tread carefully, Anastasia. The politics of the supernatural realm are complex and treacherous. One misstep could lead to disaster."

"Which is precisely why I need allies," Anastasia replied, her gaze steely as she looked into the depths of Harut's eyes. "Together, we can navigate these challenges and uphold the delicate balance that keeps both our worlds from collapsing into chaos."

"Indeed," Irshi added, their form shifting to resemble a flock of iridescent birds swirling around Anastasia. "With our combined strengths, we shall confront the unknown and ensure the preservation of all that we hold dear."

As the echoes of their words faded into the night, Anastasia felt the weight of her decision settle upon her shoulders. There was no turning back now. With a sense of both excitement and trepidation, she stood firm, resolved to face whatever lay ahead in this next phase of her journey, armed with her newfound allies at her side.

Anastasia watched the shadows dance across the walls of Harut's abandoned church, reflecting the flickering light of a single candle. The atmosphere was heavy with an unspoken tension that seemed to seep into every corner of the room. Seated at a makeshift table, she tried to focus on the conversation between her new allies but found it increasingly difficult as the power dynamics between them played out before her eyes.

"Your assistance is appreciated, Irshi," Harut said, his voice dripping with condescension. "But do not forget your place in this alliance."

Irshi scoffed, their form briefly shifting into a snarling wolf before settling back into their human guise. "Oh, I know my place, fallen angel. It's right beside Anastasia, offering insights and support that you could never hope to provide."

"Enough," Anastasia interjected, her tone firm yet weary. "We are all here for the same purpose – to maintain balance between the realms. We must learn to work together if we are to succeed."

Harut inclined his head, a shadow of a smile playing on his lips. "Of course, my dear. But one cannot help but acknowledge the hierarchy within our world. Some factions will be more… challenging to deal with than others."

"Which is why I need both of you by my side," Anastasia said, her gaze flicking between Harut and Irshi. "Your unique skills and knowledge will be invaluable when dealing with the complexities of the supernatural realm."

"Very well," Harut agreed, his eyes narrowing slightly. "But remember, Anastasia, trust must be earned. And in our world, loyalty is often a fleeting thing."

"Trust goes both ways," she reminded him, her voice steady and strong. "I am willing to put my faith in both of you, but you must also have faith in me."

"Agreed," Irshi chimed in, their form shifting to that of a majestic peacock. "We will stand by your side and face the challenges ahead, but you must be prepared for the treacherous nature of our world."

Anastasia nodded, her heart pounding with an uneasy mixture of anticipation and dread. She knew that forging these alliances was a necessary step in her journey but couldn't shake the feeling that she was diving headfirst into a world filled with danger and deceit.

"Then let us begin," she said, her voice resolute. "Together, we will navigate the murky waters of the supernatural realm and do whatever it takes to maintain the balance between worlds."

"Indeed," Harut murmured, his dark eyes meeting hers with a mixture of curiosity and admiration. "May our alliance prove to be a formidable force against those who seek to disrupt the harmony we strive to protect."

"Here's to new beginnings," Irshi added, their form shimmering like a mirage before solidifying into a strong, resolute figure by Anastasia's side.

As the three of them stood together, united in purpose and determination, Anastasia felt a surge of excitement course through her veins. The road ahead was fraught with danger, but she knew she could not face it alone. With the support of her newfound allies, she was ready to embark on this next phase of her journey, whatever the cost.

Whispers of Witches

Anastasia's office was shrouded in darkness, the only light coming from the glow of her computer screen as she poured over files and case notes, her determination to uncover the traitor within the FBI burning like a fire in her chest. Time was running out, and she couldn't shake the nagging feeling that whoever they were, they were getting closer to their goal.

"Special Agent Anastasia," called her colleague Mike from the doorway, his voice startling her out of her intense focus. "There's a meeting in five minutes."

"Thanks, I'll be there," she replied, her mind already racing with the prospect of using her supernatural abilities to detect lies and hidden intentions among her colleagues.

In the conference room, agents gathered around the large table, discussing recent developments and sharing updates on ongoing cases. But for Anastasia, this was an opportunity to search for clues that might reveal the identity of the traitor in their midst.

As she sat down, her senses heightened, she focused on the words of her fellow agents, listening carefully for any sign of deception. Quietly, she whispered a prayer under her breath, invoking the guidance of Artiya'il, the celestial messenger who had shown her the path to embracing her supernatural lineage.

"Everyone, please settle down," said Agent Rogers, bringing the room to order. "Let's begin with the latest update on the Awar case."

As her colleagues spoke, Anastasia subtly scanned their faces, looking for any hint of guilt or duplicity. She could feel the energy in the room, the swirling currents of emotions and intent that she had come to recognize as her own unique gift.

"Agent Johnson," she asked during a lull in the conversation, "can you confirm the location of the surveillance equipment? You mentioned last week it was moved to a new site."

"Uh, yeah," Agent Johnson stammered, looking uncomfortable under her scrutiny. "It's now in place near the suspect's workplace."

Anastasia's instincts sounded a silent alarm, sensing the hesitation and unease within the agent's response. Was he hiding something? She couldn't be sure, but it was enough to raise her suspicions.

"Great," she said, forcing a smile. "We'll need to keep a close eye on that area."

She continued to engage with her colleagues, asking questions and probing for information, all the while using her abilities to detect even the smallest hint of deception. It was mentally exhausting, trying to maintain her composure while sifting through the tangled web of emotions and intentions surrounding her.

With each passing moment, her determination only grew stronger, fueled by the knowledge that the traitor was out there, threatening not only the safety of her fellow agents but also the delicate balance between the human and supernatural worlds.

And Anastasia would stop at nothing to bring them to justice.

The incessant hum of the fluorescent lights above seemed to vibrate in sync with the tension that filled the air. Anastasia glanced at her watch, noting how the minutes seemed to crawl by. She knew she needed to act quickly if she was going to find answers and root out the traitor among them.

"Agent Nakamura," she called out as a fellow agent walked past her office door. "Do you have a moment?"

"Sure, Anastasia, what's up?" he replied, stepping into her office, his eyes betraying a mix of curiosity and concern.

Anastasia studied him closely, examining every nuance of his expression as she posed her question. "I was wondering if you noticed anything unusual during our last operation. Anyone acting… out of character?"

Agent Nakamura hesitated for a fraction of a second before responding. "Well, now that you mention it, I did see Agent Johnson lingering around the surveillance van for longer than usual."

"Interesting," Anastasia murmured, feeling the seed of suspicion take root within her chest. She nodded her thanks, knowing she would need to tread carefully from here on out.

As the day drew to a close, Anastasia found herself alone in her office, the weight of her suspicions resting heavily on her shoulders. She closed her eyes and whispered an invocation under her breath, summoning her supernatural allies: Artiya'il, Amir, and Sakhr.

"Peace be upon you," Artiya'il said gently, materializing before her, his celestial aura soothing her frayed nerves.

"Hello, friend!" Amir chimed in, appearing beside Artiya'il with his trademark impish grin.

"Speak your mind, Anastasia," Sakhr commanded, his authoritative presence demanding her full attention.

"I suspect there's a traitor within our ranks," she began, her voice low and urgent. "Someone who may be working with Awar and endangering both the human and supernatural worlds. I need your guidance to unmask them."

"Your abilities to detect lies and hidden intentions have served you well," Artiya'il observed, his eyes reflecting empathy and wisdom. "You must trust in yourself and continue to use your gifts."

"Remember, though," Amir added, his tone more somber than usual, "not everyone is as they seem. Keep an open mind and consider all possibilities."

"Indeed," Sakhr agreed, his voice deep and resonant. "The line between ally and enemy can often blur. You must remain vigilant and steadfast in your pursuit of justice."

Anastasia absorbed their words, her resolve hardening within her. She knew that uncovering the truth would be a difficult and dangerous task, one that might very well put her own life at risk. But the stakes were too high for her to back down now.

"Thank you, my friends," she whispered, determination shining in her dark, expressive eyes. "I will do whatever it takes to protect both worlds."

"May the Almighty guide you on your path," Artiya'il said softly before vanishing along with Amir and Sakhr, leaving Anastasia alone once again in the dimly lit office.

She clenched her fists, feeling the fire of purpose ignite within her soul. The traitor would be found, no matter the cost. And Anastasia would be the one to bring them to justice.

Anastasia's heart raced as she stood at the edge of a dimly-lit hallway, her eyes scanning for any signs of movement. It was well past midnight, and the FBI building was eerily quiet. Her heightened senses, a gift from her supernatural lineage, allowed her to hear the faint hum of the air conditioning and the distant click of a keyboard. She was about to embark on a covert investigation, one that could change the course of her life forever.

Her mind wandered to Detective Ayo, whose skeptical yet inquisitive nature had led him to join forces with Anastasia in this dangerous pursuit. Despite their differences in beliefs and backgrounds, they had formed an unlikely alliance, built on trust and a mutual desire for justice. Anastasia smiled inwardly, recalling their latest late-night strategy session over cups of strong coffee and worn case files.

"Promise me you'll be careful," Ayo had said, his deep-set eyes revealing a hint of concern.

"I promise," she had replied, feeling grateful for his support. "And I'll keep you informed every step of the way."

Now, as she stealthily made her way down the dark corridor, Anastasia couldn't help but feel the weight of that promise. She knew the risks involved in investigating her own colleagues, but she also understood the importance of unmasking the traitor within their ranks. With each step, she reminded herself of her purpose: to protect both the human and supernatural worlds, no matter the cost.

Suddenly, a door creaked open further down the hall, and Anastasia pressed herself against the wall, her breath caught in her throat. A figure emerged, carrying a stack of files and moving with purpose. Anastasia watched intently, using her ability to detect lies and hidden intentions to discern whether this person was involved in the betrayal.

"Late night, Agent Matthews?" she whispered, taking a calculated risk as she stepped into the dim light.

"Jesus, Anastasia," he hissed, nearly dropping his files. "You scared me half to death."

"Sorry," she replied, her eyes never leaving his face. "I didn't mean to startle you."

"Can't sleep, huh?" Matthews asked, trying to regain his composure. "Me neither. There's just too much work to do."

"Indeed," Anastasia agreed, searching for any signs of deception in his words and demeanor. But Matthews seemed genuinely focused on his work, not betraying any hidden intentions.

"Stay safe out there, Anastasia," he said, offering a weary smile before disappearing down another corridor.

"Thank you," she murmured, watching him leave. Although Matthews' late-night activities appeared innocent, Anastasia knew she couldn't afford to overlook anyone. She continued her covert search, gathering bits and pieces of evidence that slowly began to form a bigger picture.

As the night wore on, she sent periodic updates to Ayo, who responded with his own insights and words of encouragement. Their shared determination only served to strengthen their bond, cementing their status as steadfast allies.

"We're getting closer," Ayo texted her after one such update. "I can feel it."

"Me too," Anastasia replied, the fire of resolve burning brightly within her. "We won't stop until we uncover the truth."

With each new piece of evidence, the puzzle of the traitor's activities became clearer. And as the sun began to rise over the city, Anastasia knew one thing for certain: whoever the traitor was, they would soon be exposed. And together, she and Ayo would bring them to justice.

Anastasia's heart raced as she approached the door of Agent Johnson's office, her hands damp with sweat. The shadows from the dim hallway cast eerie shapes on the frosted glass, heightening her sense of unease. She could feel the weight of the evidence she had collected bearing down on her, and she knew this confrontation was inevitable.

"Agent Johnson, may I speak with you?" Anastasia asked, her voice steady despite the turmoil inside her.

"Of course," he replied, his tone light but with an undercurrent of tension that only heightened Anastasia's suspicions. She stepped into the cramped office, the stale air heavy with the scent of old coffee and paper. Johnson leaned back in his chair, feigning nonchalance, but Anastasia could see the muscles in his jaw tighten.

"Cut the act, Johnson. I know what you've been doing." Anastasia locked her gaze onto his, silently calling upon her supernatural abilities to discern the truth. "You're the traitor."

He scoffed, but his eyes betrayed a flicker of fear. "I don't know what wild conspiracy theory you've cooked up, but you're way off base, Anastasia."

"Am I?" Anastasia challenged, laying out the evidence before him – intercepted messages, clandestine meetings, and damning financial transactions. "This all points directly to you."

Johnson's face paled as he glanced at the papers, his facade crumbling. He sighed, dropping the pretense. "Fine, you got me. But you have no idea what's really going on."

"Then enlighten me," Anastasia insisted, her fists clenched at her sides, ready for any sudden moves or attempts at escape.

"Alright." Johnson swallowed hard. "It's not greed or power that drove me to do this – it's fear. Awar is a force beyond our comprehension, and he's been pulling the strings all along. He has connections in every corner of the supernatural world, and he's got plans for Detroit."

"Plans? What kind of plans?" Anastasia asked, her heart pounding in her chest as she processed this revelation.

"Complete domination." Johnson's voice trembled, his eyes wide with terror. "He wants to control both the human and supernatural worlds – and he'll destroy anyone who stands in his way."

"Then why didn't you tell us? Why betray your own team?" Anastasia demanded, anger and confusion swirling within her.

"Because I had no choice!" Johnson exclaimed, desperation etched on his face. "Awar threatened my family. He said if I didn't help him, they'd suffer unimaginable pain. I did what I had to do to protect them."

Anastasia's mind raced as she weighed the truth of his words against the gravity of his betrayal. She understood the instinct to protect one's family, but at what cost?

"Johnson," she said quietly, steeling herself for the difficult path ahead, "you're going to help me bring Awar down. We will find a way to keep your family safe, but we cannot let him win."

"Alright," he whispered, resignation lacing his voice. "I'll do everything I can to help you stop him."

Anastasia nodded firmly, her resolve unwavering. The stakes had never been higher, but she was determined to see this through – no matter the consequences.

Anastasia sat at her desk, the dim lamplight casting a warm glow over her cluttered workspace. Her fingers tapped anxiously on the worn surface, betraying her inner turmoil. She had always been driven by a fierce sense of justice, but the revelation of Johnson's betrayal had shaken her to her core. How could she trust anyone in her own organization if even one of them had turned against her?

"Damn it," she muttered under her breath, her dark eyes brimming with frustration. As an agent of both the human and supernatural worlds, she had always treaded a delicate line between her two identities. But now, that balance seemed more precarious than ever. If the FBI had been infiltrated, what did that mean for her celestial allies? And what of her role as a guardian, sworn to protect both realms from harm?

"Are you alright, Anastasia?" Detective Ayo's voice cut through her thoughts, his deep-set eyes filled with concern.

She hesitated, unsure of how much to reveal. "There's just...a lot going on right now," she admitted, her voice catching slightly. "I'm not sure I can handle it all."

"Hey," Ayo said softly, leaning across her desk. "You're not alone in this. Whatever you're facing, we'll face it together."

Anastasia looked into Ayo's eyes, seeing the sincerity and strength reflected there. It was a comfort to have someone who believed in her, even when she didn't believe in herself. But could she really entrust him with the full weight of her dual identity?

"Thank you, Ayo," she said, allowing a small smile to touch her lips. "But I can't help but feel like…like I'm failing. What if I can't protect everyone? What if I can't stop Awar?"

"Nobody expects you to be perfect, Anastasia," Ayo replied, his voice steady and reassuring. "But I do know one thing – you're the strongest person I've ever met. And if anyone can stop Awar, it's you."

Anastasia sighed, her moment of vulnerability giving way to determination. She couldn't afford to wallow in self-doubt; there was too much at stake. Her fingers curled into fists, nails digging into her palms as she steeled herself for the battles to come.

"Alright," she said, her voice laced with resolve. "Let's get to work."

Together, they dove into the case files, searching for any clues that might lead them closer to Awar. The world around them seemed to fade away, leaving only the flickering lamplight and the relentless pursuit of justice. For Anastasia, it was a reminder that though the road ahead was treacherous, she wouldn't have to walk it alone.

The sun dipped below the horizon as Anastasia and Detective Ayo stood on the rooftop of a dilapidated building, peering through binoculars at the dark windows of a warehouse. Anastasia could sense the energies shifting, her supernatural instincts prickling at the back of her neck. The traitor they were hunting was close, she could feel it.

"Are you sure this is the place?" Ayo whispered, his breath fogging up in the cold air.

Anastasia nodded, her eyes never leaving the warehouse. "This is where the evidence led us. I can feel their presence."

"Alright, let's be careful," Ayo warned, his hand resting on the grip of his gun.

As they moved closer to the warehouse, Anastasia felt a growing sense of unease. Each step forward increased the risk, but she couldn't turn back now. Too many lives depended on her ability to bring this traitor to justice.

"Wait," Anastasia said suddenly, her voice barely audible. She closed her eyes, focusing on the energy surrounding them. Her hands trembled with the effort, but she pushed through it, determined to locate the traitor. "There."

"Where?" Ayo asked, scanning the area.

"Third floor, fourth window from the left," Anastasia replied, pointing with unwavering certainty. "That's where they are."

"Okay, let's go," Ayo said, determination etched on his face. He knew the risks, but he trusted Anastasia implicitly. Together, they made their way inside the warehouse, moving stealthily up the stairs.

As they reached the third floor, Anastasia could feel the tension in the air like a physical weight. Every creaking floorboard seemed amplified, every shadow loomed larger. It felt as if they were walking into the lion's den, but she refused to let fear dictate her actions.

"Stay close," Anastasia whispered as they approached the door. "We don't know what we're dealing with."

"Always," Ayo replied, his voice steady despite the pounding of his heart.

With a deep breath, Anastasia kicked open the door and burst into the room, gun raised and ready for action. The traitor was there, just as she had sensed – a figure hunched over a table covered in maps and documents. They looked up, their eyes wide with shock and betrayal.

"Put your hands where I can see them!" Anastasia commanded, her voice unwavering despite the turmoil inside her. "You're under arrest."

"Please, it's not what you think," the traitor stammered, but Anastasia could sense the lie beneath their words. She knew she was risking everything by confronting them – her safety, her reputation, her very identity – but she refused to back down now. The truth was within reach, and she would drag it into the light, no matter the cost.

The room was dimly lit, casting sinister shadows along the walls and onto the traitor's face. Anastasia kept her gun trained on them, her finger itching to pull the trigger but holding back. The air was thick with tension, and she could sense Ayo's uncertainty behind her.

"Start talking," Anastasia demanded, her voice sharp and cold. "What were you doing in here?"

"I... I can't say," the traitor replied, their voice trembling.

"Wrong answer." Anastasia stepped forward, feeling the power of her supernatural abilities surging through her veins, sharpening her senses and heightening her instincts. She focused her gaze on the traitor, searching for any indication of their true intentions.

"Look, you don't understand," the traitor insisted, desperation creeping into their voice. "I'm trying to protect all of us. This is bigger than you think."

"Then enlighten me," Anastasia spat, taking another step closer. She could feel the weight of what was at stake pressing down on her, and she knew that every second counted. If she didn't unravel this mystery soon, the consequences would be grave for both the human and supernatural worlds.

"Okay, okay," the traitor said, finally relenting. They began to explain a convoluted scheme involving an alliance between Awar and a shadowy figure from within the supernatural community. As they spoke, Anastasia felt a sinking sensation in her chest – it sounded as if the betrayal ran deeper than she could have ever imagined.

"Who are you working with?" Anastasia asked, her voice barely a whisper.

The traitor hesitated, their eyes darting around the room as if seeking escape. "I can't tell you. You don't know what they're capable of."

"Neither do you," Anastasia retorted, her voice laced with venom. "But I will find out. And when I do, you'll wish you had told me the truth."

"Enough!" Ayo interjected, stepping forward and placing a hand on Anastasia's shoulder. "We need to get them back to headquarters for questioning."

"Fine," Anastasia agreed begrudgingly, keeping her gun trained on the traitor as they began to move towards the door.

As they stepped into the hallway, a sudden explosion rocked the building, sending debris flying through the air and knocking the trio off their feet. The walls shook violently, and the ceiling began to crumble around them.

"Go! Get out of here!" Anastasia shouted, struggling to her feet and pushing

Ayo and the traitor ahead of her. They stumbled through the crumbling building, dodging falling debris and choking on the thick dust that filled the air.

Just as they were about to reach the exit, a massive chunk of concrete crashed down in front of them, blocking their path. They were trapped.

"Find another way out!" Anastasia ordered, her heart pounding in her chest as she frantically searched for an escape route. But with each passing second, the building seemed to crumble further, sealing their fate.

"Wait," the traitor said suddenly, their voice barely audible above the chaos. "I can help us. But you have to promise to let me go."

Anastasia hesitated, torn between her duty and her desperation to survive. The choice she made now would define her future – but could she really trust a traitor with their lives?

Shadows and Allegiances

Anastasia's fingers flew across the keyboard, her eyes scanning articles and ancient texts about jinn and genies. She had spent hours poring over historical accounts, trying to understand their motivations and find potential common ground for peace negotiations. Her brow furrowed as she sifted through the endless troves of information, searching for the right path towards peace.

"Seems like they've been at odds since the beginning of time," she muttered under her breath. Her head ached from the strain of reading so many conflicting accounts. Surely there had to be something, some shared experience or grievance that could bring them together.

A sudden chime from her phone startled Anastasia out of her thoughts. She glanced down at the screen, seeing a message from Amir: "Good evening, Anastasia. What can I do for you?"

"Amir," she typed quickly, her heart pounding with anticipation, "we need to talk. It's important."

"Of course! Where would you like to meet?" came his prompt reply, accompanied by a playful genie emoji.

"Your place, if that's alright. And please, be serious. This is urgent." Anastasia pressed send and held her breath. The fate of both the supernatural and human worlds hung in the balance. She couldn't afford any distractions.

"Alright, alright, I'll behave," Amir agreed reluctantly. "See you soon."

Closing her laptop, Anastasia took a deep breath and gathered her belongings. She needed to convince Amir that reaching out to Sakhr was not only necessary but crucial in preventing the exposure of the supernatural world to humans. She knew it would be no easy task. Amir was mischievous and cunning, often more interested in playing tricks than engaging in serious discussions.

As Anastasia approached Amir's home, she rehearsed what she planned to say, hoping to appeal to his sense of responsibility. His front door opened before she even had the chance to knock, revealing Amir's impish grin and twinkling eyes.

"Welcome, Anastasia! What brings you here on such short notice?" he asked, feigning innocence.

"Thank you for seeing me, Amir." She stepped into his home, her eyes scanning the room for any signs of mischief. "We need to discuss a possible peace negotiation with Sakhr."

Amir raised an eyebrow, his playful demeanor appearing to falter for a moment. "You've been doing your research, haven't you? But what makes you think that now is the time for peace?"

"Because," she began, her voice steady and determined, "if we don't find a resolution soon, our world might be exposed to humans. And if that happens, everything we hold dear will be in jeopardy."

"Ah, I see." Amir's eyes darkened as he considered her words. "Very well. I'll hear you out."

"Thank you," Anastasia replied, nodding solemnly. "I know this won't be easy, but it's essential for the survival of both our worlds."

As they sat down to discuss their options, Anastasia knew that the road ahead would be fraught with challenges. But she also knew that the consequences of failure were too great to ignore.

Though Amir had agreed to discuss the matter, Anastasia could sense his skepticism. They settled into a cozy corner of Amir's living room, where antique tapestries and trinkets adorned the walls, creating an atmosphere of centuries-old wisdom. The scent of rich spices filled the air.

"Peace with Sakhr?" Amir scoffed, crossing his legs with a fluid grace that belied his stature. "You truly believe it's possible?"

Anastasia looked into his mischievous eyes, searching for any hint of understanding. She knew she had to tread carefully. "I do," she replied, her voice steady but gentle. "But I need your help, Amir."

"Help?" His impish grin returned, bolder than before. "Why would I want to help broker peace with someone who seeks only power and control? Sakhr is a threat to us all, Anastasia. He must be challenged, not appeased."

"Challenging him will only lead to more conflict," she countered. Her heart raced as she considered the delicate balance between their worlds. "And it's not just about us, Amir. Innocent humans are at risk, too."

Amir's laughter rang through the room, echoing off the walls adorned with ancient relics. "Humans?" he snorted. "They've been meddling with our world for centuries. Why should we worry about them now?"

"Because they're changing, Amir." Anastasia leaned forward, her hands clasped tightly in her lap. "Their technology, their knowledge—it's all growing at an alarming rate. If our existence is discovered, it won't simply be meddling anymore. They'll hunt us down, enslave us, or worse."

Her words hung heavily in the air. Amir's grin faded, replaced by a thoughtful frown. He leaned back, his fingers tapping rhythmically against the armrest. "And you believe that peace with Sakhr is the key to preventing this exposure?"

"His power and influence cannot be denied," she admitted. "But if we can find common ground, we might be able to work together for the good of our worlds."

Amir sighed, his gaze drifting toward the window where moonlight cast eerie shadows on the floor. "You always did have a way of making me see reason, Anastasia." He turned back to her, his eyes filled with a mixture of resignation and determination. "Very well. I will consider your proposal."

"Thank you, Amir." Relief washed over her, though she knew their journey had only just begun. "I promise you, this path may not be easy, but it is the best chance we have at preserving the delicate balance between our worlds."

"Then let us hope," Amir murmured, his impish grin returning, albeit with a hint of solemnity, "that you are right."

Anastasia took a deep breath, the air laden with the scent of old parchment and burning candles. The ancient tomes that lined the walls of her study seemed to whisper secrets from their worn pages as she contemplated her next move. She knew proposing a neutral meeting ground would be a delicate task, one that could set the course for the future of the supernatural world.

"Amir," she began softly, feeling the weight of her responsibility settle onto her shoulders. "For this negotiation between you and Sakhr to have any chance of success, we must find a location where both parties can feel at ease. A place that neither of you holds dominion over."

"Neutral ground, then?" Amir asked, his eyes flickering like candlelight as he considered her words. "It won't be easy, Anastasia. We're creatures of pride, jinn and genies alike."

"True," Anastasia conceded. "But it is crucial for the sake of our world that you both come together to find common ground." Her gaze met his, her determination unwavering. "We cannot let our pride dictate the fate of countless lives."

Amir's brow furrowed in thought, his expression a mix of reluctance and understanding. "Very well," he agreed after a moment of silence. "Propose a suitable venue, and I will attend."

"Thank you, Amir," Anastasia replied, her heart swelling with gratitude and resolve.

She turned her attention to the task of contacting Sakhr, the mighty jinni king. With the urgency of the situation heavy on her heart, she gathered her thoughts and whispered an ancient incantation. The air around her shimmered, a portal opening before her like a rippling pool of water.

"Sakhr!" she called into the vortex, her voice echoing through the spaces between worlds. "I implore you to hear my plea!"

The portal quivered, and within moments, Sakhr's ominous presence filled the room. His regal bearing was unmistakable, and his dark eyes seemed to pierce her very soul. "Anastasia," he said, his voice low and imposing. "This had better be important."

"Indeed it is, Your Majesty," she replied, forcing herself to maintain eye contact despite her nerves. "I come bearing a proposal, one that could preserve the delicate balance between our worlds."

"Speak quickly, then."

"Amir has agreed to meet with you on neutral ground," Anastasia explained, her voice steady even as her heart raced in her chest. "A place where both of you can lay aside your grievances and discuss how best to coexist without endangering the secrecy of our world."

"Amir?" Sakhr's eyes flashed with intrigue. "The genie believes we can find common ground?"

"Both of you hold great power and influence in our realm," Anastasia replied, her confidence growing with each word. "But if we continue down this path of conflict, we risk exposing our existence to the humans. The consequences could be catastrophic."

Sakhr studied her for a long moment, his expression unreadable. Then, with a slow nod, he said, "Very well, Anastasia. I will entertain this notion of peace, for now. But know this: My patience has its limits."

"Understood, Your Majesty." Relief washed over her, though she knew the hardest part still lay ahead. "I promise that your faith in me will not be misplaced."

"See that it isn't." And with that, Sakhr vanished back through the portal, leaving Anastasia alone in her study once more.

She allowed herself a single moment of quiet triumph before turning her mind to the monumental task at hand: finding a neutral location, and preparing herself mentally and emotionally for the meeting that would determine the fate of their worlds.

Anastasia stood at the edge of an ancient bridge, its once-gleaming stone now worn smooth by time and countless footsteps. The bridge spanned a churning river, separating the mundane world from the supernatural. It was here that she would bring Amir and Sakhr together, hoping that the meeting ground would be as neutral as its symbolism.

"Your Majesty," Anastasia spoke into the swirling ether, summoning Sakhr to her side. In a whirlwind of smoke, the powerful jinni king materialized before her, his regal bearing and dark eyes demanding respect.

"Speak, Anastasia," Sakhr commanded, his tone laced with wariness.

"Your Majesty, I have found a location for your meeting with Amir." She gestured to the bridge, her heart pounding in anticipation of his response. "Here, where the worlds meet but do not cross, you both will have equal footing."

"An interesting choice," Sakhr admitted, studying the bridge with a piercing gaze. "But remember this, Anastasia: I will not tolerate any disrespect or attempts to undermine my authority during our negotiations."

"Of course, Your Majesty," Anastasia reassured him, her mind racing with potential ways to navigate the delicate conversation ahead. "I understand the importance of maintaining respect between all parties involved."

"Very well," Sakhr conceded, though his expression remained guarded. "When shall this meeting take place?"

"Under the next full moon, Your Majesty," she replied, knowing that the celestial event would provide ample energy to facilitate their negotiations. "That should give us enough time to prepare."

"Fine," Sakhr said, his voice heavy with reluctance. "I will be there. But know this, Anastasia: if I sense any deception or ulterior motives, I will not hesitate to end this farce."

"Understood, Your Majesty," Anastasia affirmed, bowing her head in deference. "I promise you that my only goal is to find a peaceful resolution for the sake of our realms."

"See that it is," Sakhr warned before dissolving into smoke once more, leaving Anastasia alone on the bridge.

She stood there for a moment, taking deep breaths to steady her resolve. Then, she turned her gaze to the sky, where the moon was steadily waxing toward fullness. The weight of her responsibility hung heavily over her as she began to plan every detail of the meeting.

"Amir," she whispered into the wind, feeling the familiar fluttering of his presence. "It's time for us to prepare."

Anastasia stood before the ancient mirror in her dimly lit chamber, her hands trembling as she carefully braided her hair. The flickering candles cast shadows that danced around the room like restless spirits, mirroring the turmoil within her thoughts.

"Peace," she whispered to herself, reaching for an amulet that hung from a silver chain around her neck. The cold metal warmed beneath her fingers as she channeled her inner strength, reminding herself of the importance of her role as mediator between Amir and Sakhr. She could not afford to let her emotions cloud her judgment or interfere with her ability to bring about a resolution.

Closing her eyes, Anastasia took several deep breaths, allowing the familiar scent of sandalwood incense to fill her senses and calm her nerves. Her heart rate steadied, and her mind cleared as she focused on her purpose: protecting the delicate balance between the supernatural and human worlds.

She opened her eyes to find Amir standing in front of her, his impish grin shining through the darkness. "Are you ready?" he asked, mischief playing in his eyes. Despite his playful demeanor, Anastasia knew he understood the gravity of the situation.

"Let us begin," she replied, her voice steady and determined.

The full moon above cast its silvery glow upon the neutral ground as Anastasia, Amir, and Sakhr gathered beneath the ancient oak tree. Its gnarled branches stretched high above them, seeming to cradle the luminous orb in the sky.

"Thank you both for agreeing to meet," Anastasia began, addressing Amir and Sakhr equally. "It is my hope that through open dialogue, we can find a way to coexist peacefully without endangering the secrecy of our world."

"Speak your grievances," she urged, looking first to Amir. His small stature belied the power he held, and Anastasia knew his perspective was crucial to finding a resolution.

"Your Majesty," Amir addressed Sakhr with a respectful nod, "I understand the importance of your rule, but I see too many suffering under the weight of your authority. We must be willing to adapt, to find new ways of maintaining our world without causing undue harm to those who dwell within it."

Anastasia then turned her gaze to Sakhr, his regal bearing and dark, knowing eyes demanding respect. "And you, Your Majesty? What are your concerns?"

Sakhr's voice was deep and commanding as he replied, "My rule has kept order for centuries. Change brings chaos, and chaos endangers us all. If the supernatural world were exposed, chaos would reign – both in our realm and the human world."

"Both of you have valid points," Anastasia acknowledged, her voice even and steady. "But we must find a middle ground. A way for tradition and adaptation to coexist without tipping the balance."

Amir and Sakhr locked eyes, each attempting to gauge the other's willingness to compromise. The tension between them was palpable, like the charged air before a storm. As their mediator, Anastasia knew she had to steer the conversation toward common ground, lest they become lost in the tempest of their grievances.

"Let us find that balance together," she urged, her words soft yet firm. "For the sake of our realms and the lives that depend on our actions. We cannot afford to let our differences divide us any longer."

Anastasia focused on the tension in the room, feeling the air crackle with the intensity of Amir and Sakhr's opposing energies. She closed her eyes for a moment, drawing on her supernatural gifts to detect any undercurrents of deceit or hidden intentions within their words.

"Amir," she began, reopening her eyes and addressing the genie directly. "You speak of change and adaptation. What specific actions do you propose that would keep our world safe while also embracing the future?"

Amir's impish grin faded as he considered his response, his mischievous eyes narrowing slightly. "We must find ways to limit our interactions with humans without completely isolating ourselves. Perhaps we could establish designated liaisons between our worlds, ensuring the safety and secrecy of both."

Sakhr snorted, his powerful frame radiating disdain. "Designated liaisons? You would have us answer to such intermediaries? We have ruled ourselves for centuries without the need for human interference. Your belief in their importance is naïve, little genie."

Amir bristled at the jinni king's words, his temper flaring. "Is it naïve to recognize that the human world is evolving faster than ever before? If we do not adapt, we risk losing control of our own realm!"

The exchange between the two supernatural beings grew heated, their voices rising as they argued over power and authority. Anastasia knew she had to intervene before their tempers spiraled out of control.

"Enough!" she shouted, her voice echoing through the chamber. "We will find no resolution if we continue down this path of anger and recrimination."

Anastasia's heart raced as the weight of her responsibility settled heavily upon her shoulders. Her thoughts turned inward, seeking solace in the knowledge that her abilities could guide them toward a peaceful resolution.

"Both of you have valid concerns," she said, attempting to soothe the turmoil that threatened to consume them all. "But we must find a way to address them without allowing our emotions to cloud our judgment."

"Amir, your understanding of the human world is vital to the survival of our realm," Anastasia continued, her words measured and deliberate. "But you must also respect Sakhr's wisdom and experience in maintaining order."

She then turned to the jinni king, her gaze steady and unyielding. "Sakhr, you must acknowledge that change can be necessary for the continued stability of our world. Amir's perspective on adaptation may hold the key to ensuring that our realms remain hidden from prying human eyes."

The room fell silent as Amir and Sakhr considered her words, their expressions a mixture of frustration and begrudging acceptance. Anastasia knew that finding common ground would not be easy, but she was determined to help them see that their shared goal of protecting the supernatural realm was worth setting aside their differences and working together.

Anastasia surveyed the room, the atmosphere thick with tension and unspoken words. The flickering candlelight cast eerie shadows on the ancient walls, and the scent of burning incense filled her nostrils as she steeled herself to intervene in the heated debate before her.

"Enough!" she exclaimed, her voice echoing through the chamber. Both Amir and Sakhr turned to face her, their expressions a mix of surprise and irritation at being interrupted. Anastasia felt her heart pounding in her chest, but she refused to let fear dictate her actions.

"Your bickering will only lead us further from our goal," she declared, her gaze shifting between the two powerful beings. "This is not about who has more authority or control, but about safeguarding our world and the human realm. Do you not see that your constant struggle for power threatens to expose us all?"

Amir's impish eyes widened momentarily, betraying his concern, while Sakhr's dark eyes narrowed as he considered her words. Anastasia allowed herself a small, inward sigh of relief, grateful that her intervention had, at least temporarily, halted the escalating conflict.

"Perhaps," she continued, her tone measured and diplomatic, "we can find a way for both of you to maintain your influence without endangering the delicate balance of our realm. I propose a system of checks and balances that would allow each of you to exercise your powers in a manner that serves our collective interests."

The room fell silent once more, but this time it was charged with anticipation rather than hostility. Anastasia watched intently as Amir and Sakhr processed her proposal, acutely aware of the precarious nature of the situation.

"Checks and balances?" Amir mused, his mischievous grin returning as he mulled over the idea. "An intriguing notion, but how would such a system work?"

"Each of you would have a specific sphere of influence," Anastasia explained, her mind racing to articulate the concept she had only just conceived. "You could work together on matters that affect both the human and supernatural realms, but neither of you would be able to dominate the other completely."

Sakhr's regal bearing seemed to soften for a moment as he contemplated her suggestion. "And what if one of us were to overstep our bounds?" he inquired, his voice low and measured.

"Then the other would have the authority to intervene and restore the balance," Anastasia replied, her confidence growing with each word. "This way, both of you can maintain your power while ensuring that no single entity becomes too dominant."

As the silence stretched on, Anastasia held her breath, hoping against hope that her compromise might just be enough to bring these two formidable beings to a tentative understanding. For the sake of their world, and for the humans who remained blissfully unaware of the danger lurking in the shadows, she prayed that this meeting would mark the beginning of a new era of cooperation between the jinn and genie races.

Amir's impish grin faltered, his mischievous eyes narrowing as he scrutinized Anastasia's proposal. He drummed his fingers on the table, the sound echoing in the vast chamber. Sakhr's dark eyes remained unreadable as they flicked between Amir and Anastasia, his regal bearing a silent monument to his centuries of rule.

"Your proposition is not without merit," Amir conceded, his voice low and thoughtful. "But I must admit, I am hesitant to relinquish any of my influence to another being, even one as powerful as King Sakhr."

"Your concern is understandable," Anastasia replied, her heart pounding with anticipation. "But consider this: if you both maintain your influence and work together for the greater good, not only will the supernatural realm benefit, but so too will the human world that we all share."

As the weight of her words settled over the room, Amir's playful demeanor seemed to recede, replaced by an expression of quiet contemplation. Sakhr, too, appeared deep in thought, his gaze distant as he considered the implications of Anastasia's suggestion.

"Very well," Sakhr rumbled after what felt like an eternity. "I shall entertain your compromise, Anastasia, but know this—I will not hesitate to reclaim my full power should I deem it necessary."

"Nor would I expect you to," Anastasia assured him, her relief palpable. "I trust that both of you will act in the best interests of our world."

"Then we have an accord," Amir declared, extending his hand towards Sakhr in a gesture of goodwill. The jinni king eyed Amir's outstretched hand warily, then sighed and clasped it firmly, sealing their agreement.

Anastasia exhaled, her chest lightening with the knowledge that she had succeeded in brokering peace between these two formidable beings. She knew that the road ahead would not be easy, that tensions between jinn and genies were likely to persist, but for now, she allowed herself a moment of quiet triumph.

"Thank you," she whispered, her voice barely audible as she looked at Amir and Sakhr in turn. "I truly believe that this is the best course for our world."

"Only time will tell if your optimism is warranted," Sakhr replied, his voice somber but not unkind. "But for now, I shall abide by our agreement."

"Indeed," Amir chimed in, his grin returning as he regarded Anastasia with newfound respect. "And perhaps, together, we can find a way to navigate the challenges that lie ahead."

Anastasia smiled, the weight of her responsibility momentarily lifted from her shoulders. For the first time in what felt like ages, she dared to hope that their world might endure, that the delicate balance between human and supernatural realms might yet be preserved. And it was all thanks to one daring compromise, forged in the heart of the storm.

The Were Uprising

The Enchanted Eclipse was a realm of shadow and seduction, nestled deep within the underbelly of Detroit's vibrant nightlife. A pulsating beat echoed through the dimly lit rooms, weaving an irresistible web that drew supernatural beings from every corner of the city. Murmurs of muttered incantations blended seamlessly with the rhythmic music, as vampires, werewolves, and witches alike mingled in an intoxicating blend of power and desire.

At the heart of this swirling vortex of darkness and allure stood Bilquis, the enigmatic queen who ruled over the club and all its shadowy inhabitants. She was a striking woman of African descent, her dark skin gleaming like obsidian beneath the flickering lights. Her eyes, black as midnight and equally as captivating, seemed to hold the secrets of the universe within their depths, drawing everyone who ventured too close into her irresistible orbit.

As she moved through the club, her every step was imbued with a sense of purpose and command that left no doubt of her position within this supernatural hierarchy. The air around her crackled with barely contained energy, a testament to the raw power that flowed through her veins. Yet for all her preternatural strength, there was a quiet elegance to her presence, an ethereal grace that made her seem almost otherworldly.

Bilquis paused by the bar, her keen gaze sweeping across the sea of faces before her. Each one held a story, a tale of magic and intrigue that had led them to this place, this nexus of enchantment and danger. And though they might come from different realms and bear allegiance to different powers, for tonight, they were united under her rule, a single entity bound together by the need for connection and the insatiable hunger for the unknown.

"Bring me a Blood Moon," she murmured to the bartender, her voice sultry and commanding. The man nodded his head in deference, quickly preparing a glass filled with an iridescent crimson liquid that seemed to shimmer and dance beneath the club's dim lighting.

"Of course, Miss Bilquis," he replied, his voice barely audible over the thrumming music as he handed her the drink. She took it, her slender fingers wrapping around the cold glass as she raised it to her lips. The subtle flash of power in her eyes was enough to remind everyone who bore witness that Bilquis was not a woman to be trifled with.

With a subtle gesture from Bilquis, the women surrounding her stepped forward. They were an eclectic mix of beauty and power, each radiating an energy that was as unique as it was spellbinding. These were the members of her coven, the African witches who accompanied her through the labyrinthine world of the supernatural.

One by one, they approached Anastasia, their eyes never leaving hers. There was Makena, with skin as dark as midnight, adorned with intricate white paint that seemed to dance across her body like a living tapestry. Adept at wielding elemental magic, she was a force to be reckoned with. Then there was Iman, with her flowing locks of silver hair that framed a face of ageless wisdom. Her ability to peer into the threads of time made her an invaluable ally in their quest for balance.

"Please, sit," Bilquis gestured to Anastasia, indicating a plush velvet booth nestled in a corner of the club. The pulsating beat of the music faded into a low hum as they settled into the intimate space. The air around them seemed to thicken, charged with anticipation and the promise of secrets yet to be revealed.

"Thank you for coming, Anastasia," Bilquis began, her voice smooth and velvety, her gaze steady and unyielding. "I have brought you here tonight because we face a great threat, one that has the potential to wreak havoc on both our worlds."

Anastasia raised an eyebrow, her curiosity piqued. "What kind of threat?" she asked, her voice betraying no hint of fear or uncertainty.

"His name is Azazil," Bilquis replied, her expression darkening like a storm cloud rolling in. "He was once one of us, but his insatiable lust for power has driven him to unspeakable acts. He seeks to tear apart the fabric that holds our worlds together, to dismantle the delicate balance of power that keeps us all in check."

"Sounds like a guy with too much time on his hands," Anastasia muttered under her breath. She could feel the weight of her dual responsibilities as an FBI agent and a protector of the supernatural world bearing down on her.

"Indeed," Bilquis agreed, her eyes narrowing in determination. "But his actions have grave consequences for both our realms. If he succeeds, chaos will reign, and the line between human and supernatural will blur beyond repair."

"Okay," Anastasia said slowly, processing the information. "And you want me to what, exactly?"

"Help us stop him," Bilquis implored, her captivating eyes boring into Anastasia's soul. "You are uniquely suited to this task, Anastasia. Your connection to both worlds, your strength and courage… We need you."

Anastasia hesitated, torn between her sworn duty as an agent of law and order and her growing allegiance to the supernatural community she had come to know and respect. But as she looked around at the faces of the witches before her, she felt a sense of unity and purpose that couldn't be denied. They were in this together, bound by a common goal and a shared destiny.

"Alright," she finally said with a resolute nod. "I'll help you. But we do this my way."

A slow smile spread across Bilquis's face, a predatory glint in her eyes. "Deal," she agreed, extending her hand to seal their pact. And as they shook on it, the very foundations of their worlds trembled, waiting to see what would come next.

Anastasia's gaze swept across the room, taking in the diverse array of supernatural beings that filled The Enchanted Eclipse. It was a delicate dance of power and alliances, each individual keeping their secrets close to their hearts while attempting to maintain the fragile balance their world depended on. She could feel the tension in the air, like an electric charge crackling just beneath the surface.

"His meddling has stirred up unrest among our kind," Bilquis whispered, her voice barely audible over the pulsating music. "He's turning us against one another, creating chaos that threatens to spill into the human world."

Anastasia glanced at the coven surrounding them, their eyes locked in a silent exchange. They seemed to share a bond that went beyond mere camaraderie—a connection forged through years of loyalty and shared purpose. But even within their circle, she sensed unease, the weight of past betrayals and rivalries still haunting them.

"Can't you see?" Bilquis continued, her eyes searching Anastasia's face for understanding. "We need unity now more than ever. Azazil is a master manipulator, and if we allow him to continue sowing discord, it will be our undoing."

"Unity is easier said than done," Anastasia replied thoughtfully. "You've all got your own agendas, your own loyalties. How can you expect everyone to put aside their differences and work together?"

"Because the alternative is far worse," interjected one of the witches, her dark eyes flashing with determination. "If we don't stand united against Azazil, we risk losing everything."

"Yet some might argue that siding with the humans is a betrayal in itself," countered another witch, her youthful features marred by a scowl. "Why should we trust you, Anastasia? Whose side are you really on?"

"Enough!" Bilquis snapped, silencing the room with a wave of her hand. "We don't have time for petty squabbles and baseless accusations. The fact is, we need each other in order to survive."

Anastasia could see the truth in Bilquis's words. The supernatural realm was a complex web of alliances and enmities, its denizens constantly jostling for power and influence. But if they couldn't learn to work together, their world would be consumed by chaos.

"Tell me more about Azazil's plans," she said finally, her tone resolute. "What does he hope to achieve? And what can I do to help?"

Bilquis hesitated for a moment, clearly weighing her words before speaking. "Azazil seeks to control both our world and the human one, harnessing the combined power of all supernatural beings. If he succeeds, there will be no stopping him."

"Then we must act quickly," Anastasia declared, feeling a newfound sense of determination surging through her veins. "We'll put an end to his schemes and restore the balance between our realms."

"Indeed," Bilquis agreed, her eyes gleaming with a fierce resolve. "Together, we will face this enemy and overcome whatever obstacles stand in our way."

As the coven nodded in agreement, Anastasia knew that the battle ahead would be fraught with challenges and difficult choices. But with the fate of two worlds hanging in the balance, failure was not an option.

Anastasia hesitated, her heart pounding in her chest. She was an FBI agent, sworn to protect the innocent and uphold the law. Now, she stood at a crossroads, grappling with the reality of her supernatural lineage and the responsibility that came with it.

"Can I really do this? Can I truly become a guardian for both worlds?" she questioned inwardly, feeling the weight of her dual roles bearing down on her.

"Your hesitation is understandable," Bilquis said softly, her voice somehow soothing Anastasia's nerves. "But remember, you have a unique perspective, one that can serve as a bridge between our realms. You are more than capable of facing what lies ahead."

Anastasia took a deep breath, trying to find the courage within herself to accept her destiny. As she did so, Bilquis gestured for her coven members to step forward and introduce themselves.

"Meet my sisters," Bilquis said proudly, her gaze sweeping across the group of powerful witches that had gathered around her. "Each with their own unique abilities and strengths."

The first witch to step forward was Nkiru, adorned with intricate tribal markings on her face and arms. Her eyes were a captivating shade of gold, and her presence seemed to emanate strength. "I am skilled in the art of defensive magic," she explained, her voice firm yet gentle. "I will shield us from harm."

"Nice to meet you, Nkiru," Anastasia said, offering a hesitant smile.

"Likewise," Nkiru replied, nodding respectfully.

Next came Ebele, a tall and slender woman with ebony skin that seemed to shimmer like the night sky. She carried an air of mystery about her, and her silver eyes seemed to hold secrets untold. "My talents lie in divination and scrying," she murmured, her voice barely audible. "I will help us navigate the tides of fate."

"Thank you, Ebele," Anastasia replied, intrigued by her enigmatic demeanor.

"Your appreciation is received," Ebele whispered, inclining her head.

The final witch, Kehinde, was a petite woman with a fiery spirit. Her rich, copper-toned skin glowed in the dimly lit room, and her deep brown eyes sparkled with mischief. "My specialty is offensive magic," she declared confidently, a wicked grin on her face. "I'll make sure our enemies regret crossing paths with us."

"Good to know we have some firepower on our side," Anastasia remarked, chuckling slightly at Kehinde's enthusiasm.

"Indeed," Kehinde agreed, grinning broadly. "We'll show them who's boss!"

As Anastasia stood among these formidable witches, she couldn't help but feel a sense of awe mixed with apprehension. They were strong, united in their loyalty to Bilquis and their cause. But could she truly become one of them? Could she find it within herself to embrace her destiny and fight alongside these powerful beings?

"Your journey won't be an easy one," Bilquis said, her voice gentle yet firm. "But trust in yourself and your abilities, Anastasia. We believe in you, and together, we can overcome whatever challenges lie ahead."

Anastasia nodded, taking another deep breath as she steeled herself for the battle to come. She knew that she would face difficult decisions and tests of loyalty, but she also recognized the importance of standing firm against the darkness that threatened both worlds.

"Alright," she said, determination coursing through her veins. "I'm in."

Anastasia followed Bilquis through the pulsating heart of The Enchanted Eclipse, her senses overwhelmed by the cacophony of sights and sounds that surrounded her. She felt a shiver run down her spine as she realized the magnitude of the situation. The supernatural world was far more complex and dangerous than she had ever imagined.

"Tell me more about Azazil's plans," Anastasia said, her voice barely audible above the thumping music as she leaned closer to Bilquis. "What exactly is he trying to achieve?"

Bilquis's eyes narrowed, her gaze intense as she spoke. "He seeks to harness an ancient power, one that could tip the scales in his favor and grant him dominion over both the supernatural and human worlds. If he succeeds, chaos will reign."

"Can't we just stop him?" Anastasia asked, the urgency of the situation gnawing at her. "I mean, you have a whole coven of powerful witches on your side."

"Stopping him won't be easy," Bilquis replied, her face somber. "Azazil has been amassing allies, and his own powers have grown considerably. This is why we need your help, Anastasia. We cannot face this threat alone."

Anastasia took a deep breath, her mind racing as she weighed the risks involved. As an FBI agent, she was sworn to uphold the law and protect the innocent. But now, as a protector of the supernatural realm, she faced a far greater responsibility. The fate of two worlds rested on her shoulders.

"Alright," Anastasia said, determination etching her features. "We'll find a way to stop Azazil, no matter what it takes."

The coven members exchanged glances, their expressions a mix of relief and resolve. They understood the gravity of the situation and were willing to do whatever it took to restore balance.

"Time is of the essence," Bilquis said, her voice laced with urgency. "We must act quickly and decisively before Azazil's plans come to fruition."

Anastasia nodded, well aware of the stakes at hand. Her heart raced as she considered the challenges that lay ahead. The supernatural realm was a complex web of alliances and rivalries, and she knew that navigating it would be no easy task.

"Take heart, Anastasia," said Tari, one of the coven members, placing a reassuring hand on her shoulder. "Remember that you are not alone in this fight. We stand with you, and together we shall triumph over the darkness."

Anastasia met Tari's gaze, finding solace in her words. She couldn't help but feel a sense of camaraderie with these powerful witches, despite their differences. They were united in their pursuit of justice and the protection of both worlds, and Anastasia knew that she had found allies in them.

"Thank you," Anastasia whispered, her resolve strengthened by their support. "Together, we will stop Azazil, and we will restore balance to the world."

She sensed the determination in the air, felt the energy crackle around her as the coven prepared for the battle ahead. In that moment, Anastasia understood that they were more than just a group of supernatural beings – they were a force to be reckoned with, and together, they would face whatever darkness lay ahead.

As Anastasia looked around at the determined faces of the coven members, she felt a sense of unity and trust beginning to form between them. She turned to Bilquis and said, "Tell me more about the individual strengths of your coven members. In order to fight effectively alongside you, I need to understand their abilities."

"Of course," Bilquis replied, her eyes gleaming with pride as she gestured toward each witch in turn. "Tari here is a master of illusion, able to create and manipulate powerful mirages that can disorient and confuse our enemies. Zara possesses the gift of foresight, her visions offering glimpses into possible futures that help guide our decisions. Naya is an empath, able to sense and influence the emotions of those around her, while Amina is skilled in the art of healing, restoring strength and vitality to our wounded."

Anastasia listened intently, already plotting how best to coordinate their efforts against Azazil's forces. She could feel the potential within this group, the power they held when they combined their unique talents.

"Thank you for sharing that with me," Anastasia said, her voice filled with determination. "Together, we will be formidable adversaries."

"Indeed," Bilquis agreed, her expression fierce. "And we must be, for time is running short. We cannot afford to let Azazil continue on his destructive path."

Anastasia nodded, sensing the urgency in Bilquis's words. "We should waste no time, then. Let's begin preparing ourselves for the confrontation ahead."

The witches exchanged nods of agreement, their faces set with resolve. As they gathered in a circle, hands joined, Anastasia could feel the energy building around them, a tangible force that seemed to hum with anticipation. The air crackled with power as they channeled their collective strength, readying themselves for the battle to come.

"Wait," Naya suddenly said, her eyes wide with alarm. "Something's wrong."

Anastasia felt it too – a sudden shift in the atmosphere, a dark, oppressive presence that seemed to loom over them like a storm cloud. The air grew colder, the shadows deepening as an overwhelming sense of dread settled upon the room.

"Show yourself!" Bilquis demanded, her voice ringing out with authority as she stood tall, her coven rallying behind her.

For a moment, there was only silence, the tension in the room reaching unbearable heights. And then, with a sinister laugh that sent shivers down Anastasia's spine, a figure stepped from the darkness.

"Your defiance is amusing, but futile," the figure sneered, his voice cold and menacing. It was clear that Azazil had come for them sooner than they had anticipated, and Anastasia felt her heart race as she stared into the face of their greatest enemy.

"Stand together," Bilquis whispered urgently, her eyes locked on the approaching threat. "We won't let him tear us apart."

As the witches prepared to face Azazil, their powers at the ready, Anastasia knew that this confrontation would change the course of both the supernatural and human worlds forever. The stakes had never been higher, and as the battle lines were drawn, Anastasia could only hope that their newfound alliance would be enough to stop the darkness from consuming all that they held dear.

Anastasia glanced around The Enchanted Eclipse, her eyes taking in the scene before her. Supernatural beings of all shapes and sizes mingled together, their unusual features creating a kaleidoscope of colors and textures. A group of water nymphs danced gracefully near the bar, their shimmering gowns flowing like rivers as they moved. In another corner, a table of djinns debated animatedly in hushed tones, their fiery eyes occasionally flaring with passion.

"Quite a sight, isn't it?" said one of the witches from Bilquis's coven, sidling up to Anastasia. She had dark skin adorned with intricate white markings, her hair woven into countless thin braids that fell past her waist. "I'm Ifeoma, by the way."

"Nice to meet you." Anastasia extended her hand, feeling strangely at ease despite the otherworldly surroundings.

"Your powers are still new to you," Ifeoma observed, cocking her head as she studied Anastasia. "You'll grow into them, don't worry."

"Thank you," Anastasia replied, touched by the witch's gentle reassurance. "I can only hope I'll be able to control them when the time comes."

"Listen," Ifeoma murmured, leaning closer so that her words were barely audible over the pulsating music. "I know it's overwhelming, but we've all been where you are now. You're not alone in this fight."

"Club" was too simple a word for The Enchanted Eclipse; it was an entire world unto itself. Anastasia could feel the hum of energy in the air, the room crackling with magic. It was intoxicating, and terrifying.

"Tell me more about Azazil," she asked Ifeoma, seeking to understand the gravity of the situation. "Why is he such a threat to our world?"

"His plans go beyond mere power or dominance," Ifeoma explained, her expression darkening. "He seeks to unravel the very fabric of reality itself, tearing apart the delicate balance between our worlds."

"Is that even possible?" Anastasia questioned, her mind racing with the potential consequences.

"Unfortunately, yes," Ifeoma said solemnly. "He's already begun his work, causing rifts in the multiverse. But we can stop him, together."

Anastasia hesitated, torn between her duty as an FBI agent and her newfound supernatural responsibilities. She knew she couldn't ignore the danger Azazil posed, but was she ready to embrace the full extent of her powers?

"Your heart is your greatest strength," Ifeoma told her, sensing her internal conflict. "It will guide you on the right path."

"Thank you, Ifeoma," Anastasia whispered, feeling a renewed sense of determination. As she watched the supernatural beings around her – some dancing, others strategizing, all united by their shared existence – she realized that they were all fighting for something greater than themselves.

"Let's do this," she said firmly, meeting Ifeoma's gaze. The witch nodded, her eyes filled with resolve.

Together, they rejoined Bilquis and the rest of the coven, preparing to face whatever challenges lay ahead. They would stand against Azazil and protect the fragile balance between worlds, no matter the cost. And as Anastasia looked around at her newfound allies, she felt a flicker of hope ignite within her – a fire that would not be easily extinguished.

Anastasia's gaze swept across the dimly lit room of The Enchanted Eclipse, lingering on the many supernatural beings that mingled together in harmony. A pair of pixies fluttered above a booth where a group of werewolves shared drinks and laughter. In another corner, vampires discussed matters with fae representatives, their voices low yet animated. It was here, amongst these creatures, that she found herself drawn into a battle for the balance between worlds.

"Are you ready to face this?" Bilquis asked, her voice cutting through Anastasia's thoughts. Her captivating eyes bore into Anastasia, as if searching for any hint of doubt.

"I am," Anastasia responded, her voice steady and filled with determination. She knew what was at stake, and understood the gravity of the situation. "I can't turn my back on either world. I have to protect them both."

"Good," Bilquis said, a hint of pride in her voice. Turning to her coven, she addressed them all. "We must work together with our new ally if we are to defeat Azazil and restore balance."

The witches nodded, their unique features and personalities shining in the dim light. There was Ifeoma, the wise and nurturing one; Kemi, who wielded powerful elemental magic; Mariatu, the healer; and Amara, the fierce warrior. Each had pledged their loyalty to Bilquis and the cause, and now they extended that trust to Anastasia.

"Your abilities will be invaluable to our efforts," Amara told Anastasia, her dark eyes appraising her. "But remember, it is your heart and determination that make you truly powerful."

Anastasia felt a surge of gratitude towards the warrior witch, as well as an understanding of her role in this fight. She was no longer just an FBI agent or even a protector of the supernatural; she was a bridge between two worlds that desperately needed her.

"Thank you, Amara," she said, her voice resolute. "I won't let you down."

"See that you don't," Kemi added with a teasing grin, trying to lighten the mood.

Anastasia's lips curved into a smile, and she felt an unexpected sense of camaraderie with the coven. Together, they formed a united front against the looming threat of Azazil.

"Let us begin our planning," Bilquis declared, motioning for everyone to gather around her. As Anastasia stood shoulder-to-shoulder with her newfound allies, she found herself embracing her new role. She would do everything in her power to protect both the human and supernatural worlds, even if it meant putting her own life on the line.

"Remember," Bilquis said, looking at each member of the coven and finally resting her eyes on Anastasia, "we are stronger together. United, we can face any challenge."

And as they began to discuss their strategy, Anastasia knew that she belonged there – within this circle of powerful beings, bound by a shared purpose. She was ready for whatever lay ahead, and prepared to fight for the delicate balance between worlds.

Duplicity Unveiled

Anastasia sat in her dimly lit apartment, the glow of the city filtering through her sheer curtains. Her legs were tucked beneath her as she stared blankly at the cold tea that had long lost its steam. The weight of her recent encounters with supernatural beings pressed on her chest, making it difficult to breathe. She couldn't shake the feeling that her life was shifting on its axis, and there was no turning back.

Her thoughts swam with visions of the asasiyyin, her newfound lineage, and the potential consequences of embracing this unknown world. A deep sense of loneliness crept into her heart as she considered how isolated she would become if she chose this path. It felt like standing on the edge of a precipice, staring down into darkness and uncertainty.

The air in the room shimmered, and Anastasia looked up to see Zuhra materializing before her. Zuhra's celestial form shimmered with pale light as if the stars were reflected in water,Her soft, cloudlike form was as light as a feather, yet warm like a soft blanket when you're alone on a cold winter's night. Zuhra's eyes, pools of ancient wisdom, met Anastasia's gaze with a gentle reassurance that eased some of the turmoil within her.

"Zuhra," Anastasia murmured, her voice filled with both awe and relief. "I didn't expect to see you tonight."

"Your emotional turmoil called out to me, dear child," Zuhra replied, Her voice was soft like the gentle rustle of leaves through the forest. "I am here to help guide you through these troubled times."

Anastasia hesitated for a moment, then her curiosity pushed her to ask, "How did you become what you are now? What was your journey like?"

Zuhra's lips curved into a gentle smile, her eyes momentarily reflecting a distant memory. "It has been a long and winding journey, one that began many millennia ago. I too was once uncertain and afraid, not knowing what my true purpose was in a world that seemed to be filled with endless chaos."

"Can you share your story?" Anastasia asked, her voice barely above a whisper.

"Of course," Zuhra replied, "but first, let us make ourselves comfortable."

With a wave of her hand, the room was transformed. The cold tea on the table was replaced by two steaming cups of fragrant chai, and plush cushions appeared on the floor for them to sit on. As they settled down, Zuhra began to recount her tale.

"Long ago, I lived a simple life in a small village, unaware of the celestial forces that would one day call upon me. But as fate would have it, I stumbled upon an extraordinary event that altered my destiny forever."

Anastasia listened intently to Zuhra's words, captivated by the story of a woman who had walked a path similar to the one she now found herself on. The details of Zuhra's transformation into a celestial being filled her with hope, but also with trepidation. She knew that such power came with great responsibility, and it was a choice she would have to make carefully.

The weight of Zuhra's celestial form seemed to fill the room, casting a warm glow on the walls as she continued her tale. "In ancient Mesopotamia, I was a young woman, bound by the expectations of my time and place. I had dreams of adventure and discovery, but they seemed distant and unattainable."

"Until one day," she continued, her voice taking on a dreamy quality, "while I was wandering along the banks of the Euphrates River, I stumbled upon a hidden cave. And within it, I found the Celestial Orb."

Anastasia's eyes widened at the mention of the artifact, but she remained silent, allowing Zuhra to continue.

"From the moment I touched the Orb, my life was irrevocably changed. The power that surged through me was unlike anything I had ever experienced. It was overwhelming, terrifying, and exhilarating all at once."

Zuhra paused, her gaze distant, as if reliving the memories of her transformation. Anastasia could only imagine what it must have been like, standing at the precipice of such immense power and potential.

"Those days are long past," Zuhra said, bringing herself back to the present. "But the choices I made and the path I walked have led me here, to you."

"Me?" Anastasia asked, incredulous. "I'm not sure I understand. My life has been normal until recently – just an FBI agent trying to make a difference in Detroit."

"Your lineage is unique, Anastasia," Zuhra explained gently. "You are descended from a line of powerful asasiyyin who have safeguarded the world for centuries. Your recent encounters with supernatural beings were not mere coincidences; they were a call to embrace your true nature."

Anastasia hesitated, grappling with the enormity of the revelation. "I'm not sure I'm ready for that kind of responsibility," she admitted, her voice tinged with uncertainty. "What if I make the wrong choices? What if I lose myself in the process?"

"Those are valid concerns," Zuhra acknowledged, placing a comforting hand on Anastasia's shoulder. "But remember, you are not alone. I am here to guide and support you, as others have done for me."

Anastasia took a deep breath, attempting to process the flood of emotions that threatened to overwhelm her. A part of her longed to embrace her newfound heritage and wield the powers that came with it. But another part of her feared what such a decision would mean for her relationships, her career, and her sense of self.

"Zuhra… how did you find the strength to face your destiny?" Anastasia asked, her eyes searching the celestial being for some semblance of understanding.

"By accepting the power within me and trusting in my ability to make decisions guided by compassion and wisdom," Zuhra replied, her gaze unwavering and full of conviction. "You too must trust yourself, Anastasia. Remember that your path is your own to forge, but you are never truly alone."

Anastasia nodded, taking in the depth of Zuhra's words. The path ahead was uncertain and filled with challenges, but perhaps she could find the courage to navigate it with grace and determination, just as Zuhra had so many centuries before.

Anastasia's gaze lingered on the faint shimmer of Zuhra's celestial form, her mind a swirling vortex of questions and uncertainty. The air in her apartment seemed to vibrate with an otherworldly energy, casting a soft glow over the familiar surroundings.

"Tell me more about the Celestial Orb," Anastasia implored, hoping to find clarity in understanding its power. "What is its true purpose?"

"Ah, the Celestial Orb," Zuhra began, her voice a melodic whisper that seemed to resonate within Anastasia's very soul. "It is a powerful artifact, imbued with the essence of the cosmos itself. Throughout history, it has been sought by those who yearn for the celestial powers it can bestow upon its possessor."

"Like the powers you have?" Anastasia asked, her curiosity piqued.

"Indeed," Zuhra replied, her eyes gleaming with memories of aeons past. "My transformation was a direct result of my encounter with the Orb. Its divine energy altered my very being, allowing me to transcend the limitations of my mortal existence."

Anastasia couldn't help but marvel at the thought of such a powerful object existing in the world around her, hidden from the prying eyes of humanity. But as she considered the implications of the Celestial Orb's existence, a shiver of unease ran down her spine.

"Zuhra, I can't help but feel anxious about the idea of wielding the powers the Orb offers," Anastasia confessed, her fingers tracing the edge of her coffee table absentmindedly. "What if I lose myself in the process? What if I inadvertently hurt someone or cause irreparable damage?"

"Your fears are not without merit, Anastasia," Zuhra acknowledged, her radiant visage taking on a solemn expression. "The path of celestial power is not without its risks, and those who wield it must do so with great care and responsibility. But remember, you are not alone in this journey."

Anastasia's heart ached at the weight of this newfound knowledge, her mind racing to comprehend the monumental decision that lay before her. Was she truly prepared to accept the responsibilities that came with embracing her supernatural lineage?

"Trust in yourself, Anastasia," Zuhra encouraged, her voice a soothing balm for the young woman's troubled thoughts. "You have the strength and wisdom within you to navigate the challenges that lie ahead. And I will be here to guide you, every step of the way."

The soft hum of Zuhra's celestial aura filled the dimly lit room, casting a warm, soothing glow over Anastasia's anxious features. The air around her seemed to vibrate with a quiet power, yet it was the steady reassurance in Zuhra's eyes that anchored Anastasia amidst the storm of her thoughts.

"Being an asasiyyin is not without its challenges," Zuhra admitted, her voice imbued with a gentle understanding that transcended the ages. "But ultimately, the choice to embrace your lineage and the responsibilities that come with it is one that only you can make."

Anastasia turned away, her gaze drifting to the rain-splattered window, where the lights of Detroit danced like distant stars against a canvas of darkness. The world outside seemed so oblivious to the supernatural forces that now sought to pull her from its grasp, and she couldn't help but wonder if things would ever be the same again.

"Zuhra," she began hesitantly, her fingers tapping a nervous rhythm on the windowsill. "What will this mean for my life? My relationships, my career… even my own sense of self?"

"Change is inevitable, dear Anastasia" Zuhra replied, her celestial form shifting, shadows playing across her ethereal visage. "But it is how you choose to navigate these changes that will define you. Do not fear losing yourself; instead, trust in your ability to adapt and grow."

Silence settled between them, broken only by the patter of rain against the glass. Anastasia's thoughts raced, each possible outcome sending ripples through her mind's eye. She imagined herself wielding unimaginable powers – but at what cost?

Would the pursuit of justice be tainted by the temptation to abuse such abilities? Could her relationships withstand the strain that her newfound identity would surely place upon them? And as an FBI agent, would she be forced to make a choice between the mortal law she'd sworn to uphold and the supernatural realm that now beckoned her?

"Remember, Anastasia," Zuhra spoke softly, as if reading her thoughts. "You are not bound by destiny, but by the choices you make. Embrace your heritage with wisdom and care, and you will find your path."

Anastasia exhaled a heavy sigh, feeling the weight of Zuhra's words settle upon her shoulders like a cloak. Steadying her resolve, she turned back to face the celestial being, her eyes shining with a newfound determination.

"Thank you, Zuhra," she said, her voice firm and resolute. "I may not know what lies ahead, but I trust in my ability to navigate this path. And I'm grateful for your guidance."

"Always, Anastasia" Zuhra replied, her warm smile chasing away the last remnants of doubt that still lingered at the edges of Anastasia's consciousness. "Zuhra, call me Nana. My close friends and family call me Nana" " As you wish Nana. Together, we will forge a new future – one where both the mortal and supernatural realms can coexist in harmony."

The lamplight flickered in the dimly lit room, casting shadows across the walls of Anastasia's apartment. In this quiet space, Zuhra's celestial form seemed to grow even brighter, her luminescence filling the air with a gentle warmth.

"Before I became what I am now," Zuhra began, her voice a melodious whisper that seemed to float on the air like a feather, "I was but a simple woman, living in ancient Mesopotamia. My transformation into a celestial being came at a great cost."

Anastasia watched Zuhra carefully, noting the subtle shifts of emotion that played across her radiant face – sorrow, pain, and finally, acceptance. She leaned forward, eager to understand the sacrifices that had shaped the celestial being before her.

"Many loved ones were lost along the way," Zuhra continued, a note of sorrow lingering in her voice. "But it was through those losses that I learned the importance of balance and trust. The supernatural world can be treacherous, and every step must be taken with care."

The words resonated deeply within Anastasia, stirring up memories of her own recent encounters with supernatural beings. She thought of the strange creatures she'd faced, and the secrets that had been revealed about her lineage – her connection to the asasiyyin.

"Zuhra," Anastasia said softly, her voice filled with gratitude. "You have guided me through the darkness, showing me the path that lies before me. I cannot express how much your support has meant to me."

A tender smile graced Zuhra's luminous features, and for a moment, the room seemed to glow even brighter. "Anastasia, we are all connected in ways we cannot fully comprehend," she replied gently. "It has been my honor to walk beside you on this journey."

Within Anastasia, a quiet resolve blossomed. She knew the decision that awaited her would not be easy, but with Zuhra's wisdom and guidance, she felt a sense of hope. Hope that she could embrace her supernatural heritage without losing herself to its seductive power.

"Thank you," Anastasia whispered, her eyes brimming with unshed tears. "I don't know what challenges lie ahead, but I trust in your guidance, and I trust myself."

"Trust is the cornerstone of our existence, Anastasia," Zuhra said, her voice imbued with the wisdom of the ages. "Hold onto it tightly, and let it guide you through the uncertain days to come."

The room seemed to vibrate with Zuhra's celestial presence, the very air shimmering like a mirage. Anastasia couldn't help but be captivated by the ethereal beauty of her otherworldly mentor. It was as if the weight of centuries hung in the air between them, a testament to the wisdom and experience Zuhra carried within her.

"Before I leave you to your own thoughts, Anastasia, remember this," Zuhra said, her voice like the whisper of wind through leaves. "Every decision you make will have consequences – some will be immediate, others may take years to manifest. But trust in yourself, and in your own abilities." She paused, her eyes locked onto Anastasia's with an intensity that seemed to bore into her soul. "You are stronger than you know."

Anastasia nodded, her heart pounding in her chest as she absorbed Zuhra's final words of wisdom. A sense of purpose began to burn within her, fueled by the knowledge that she held the power to shape her own destiny, even in a world filled with supernatural beings and ancient secrets.

"Zuhra, you've given me so much," Anastasia replied, her voice steady and resolute. "I won't let you down. I will face whatever challenges lie ahead, and I will do so with my head held high."

"Your determination is admirable, Anastasia," Zuhra said, her smile warm and encouraging. "I have no doubt that you are capable of great things."

Anastasia felt a surge of gratitude wash over her, and she impulsively reached out to embrace the celestial being before her. To her surprise, Zuhra returned the gesture without hesitation, her arms enveloping Anastasia in a gentle, comforting hold.

"Thank you, Zuhra," Anastasia murmured, her voice muffled by the radiance of Zuhra's celestial form. "I couldn't have come this far without you."

"Remember, Anastasia," Zuhra whispered before releasing her from the embrace, her voice tinged with a note of melancholy. "In this life, there are no certainties – only choices. Trust in your decisions and stay true to yourself, for that will be your greatest strength."

Anastasia drew in a deep breath, the air heavy with a mix of determination and newfound purpose. She realized now that the path she would follow was not set in stone; rather, it was a road she must forge for herself. And as she prepared to face the unknown with courage and conviction, she knew that Zuhra's wisdom and guidance would forever remain a guiding light in the darkness.

"Thank you," she whispered once more, the words barely audible, yet laden with the weight of her gratitude. "I will make you proud."

With a final, reassuring smile, Zuhra's celestial form began to dissolve before Anastasia's eyes. The radiant light that had filled the room slowly faded, leaving only the soft glow of streetlights filtering through the curtains. As she disappeared completely, Anastasia suddenly found herself alone in the familiar confines of her apartment.

"Goodbye, Zuhra," she whispered into the silence, the air still humming with residual energy from their conversation.

The weight of Zuhra's words and revelations settled heavily upon her shoulders, her mind buzzing with thoughts and questions about her future and the Celestial Orb. Despite the clarity and wisdom imparted by Zuhra, the path forward was far from certain.

Anastasia closed her eyes, allowing herself a moment to center and ground herself in the present. She focused on her breathing, inhaling deeply and exhaling slowly, feeling the steady rise and fall of her chest. The soft rustle of leaves outside her window, the distant hum of traffic, and the comforting scent of her favorite jasmine-scented candle served as anchors, pulling her back into the here and now.

"Everything has consequences... Trust yourself..." Anastasia repeated Zuhra's words in her mind, finding solace in their simplicity. It was true; life was an intricate web of choices and outcomes. The decision to embrace her supernatural lineage would undoubtedly change her life forever, but she could not remain paralyzed by fear. She needed to make a choice, to trust in her abilities and the power within her.

Slowly opening her eyes, Anastasia took in the familiar surroundings of her apartment – the well-worn sofa that had seen countless late-night conversations, the small bookcase crammed with an eclectic mix of literature and case files, the framed photograph of herself and her colleagues at the FBI graduation ceremony.

This world, these relationships, were irrevocably intertwined with her destiny. And as difficult as the journey may be, she knew that she could not turn away from the responsibilities that came with her newfound knowledge.

"Zuhra, I hope you're watching over me," Anastasia murmured, feeling a strange mixture of fear and determination settle within her chest. "I'm going to need all the help I can get."

With that, she stood up from the sofa, her hands clenched into fists at her sides. She was prepared to face whatever challenges lay ahead, no matter how great or terrifying they might be. And in that moment of resolution, she felt an unshakable certainty that Zuhra's guidance would continue to light the way forward.

For now, it was time to take the first step on this new path, armed with the wisdom of her celestial mentor and the strength that had always been inside her.

The city lights twinkled in the distance, casting their glow upon the glassy waters of the Detroit River. Anastasia stood by her apartment window, gazing out at the merging of two worlds – the mortal realm she knew and the supernatural one she was just beginning to comprehend. The weight of her decision pressed heavily on her shoulders, but there was also a sense of purpose that coursed through her veins.

"Alright," she whispered to herself, her breath fogging up the windowpane. "This is my path. I must embrace it for the sake of both realms."

As if in response to her declaration, a gust of wind blew through the room, ruffling the pages of a nearby book. Anastasia turned her attention to the tome, a compilation of ancient texts that detailed the history of celestial beings. She traced her fingers along the spines of the pages, feeling a connection with those who had come before her.

"Your lineage is your strength," Zuhra's words echoed within her mind. "Use it wisely, and never forget that you are part of something greater than yourself."

"I won't let you down, Zuhra," Anastasia murmured, the resolve in her voice transforming into steely determination. "I will protect the balance between these worlds, even if it means sacrificing my own peace."

Closing the book, Anastasia strode across the room and retrieved her FBI badge from its resting place on her desk. She held it up to the light, examining the familiar emblem, a symbol of justice and order in the human world. It now seemed to hold an even greater significance, as she would be responsible not only for the safety of mortals but also for maintaining the delicate equilibrium between the realms.

"Amir," she called out, her voice steady and resolute. "I need your help."

The mischievous genie appeared with a flourish, his impish grin seeming to hold a thousand secrets. "Yes, Anastasia Asma'u?" he asked, his eyes gleaming with curiosity.

"From this moment on, I will embrace my supernatural lineage and use it to protect both the mortal and supernatural worlds," she declared, her words ringing with the authority of one who had made a life-altering choice. "I know there will be challenges and danger ahead, but I am ready."

"Ah, a noble decision indeed!" Amir exclaimed, clapping his hands together. "And what would you have me do?"

"Help me find the Celestial Orb," Anastasia replied, her gaze unwavering. "I must understand its power and learn how to wield it responsibly. Only then can I truly fulfill my destiny."

Amir bowed theatrically before her, his grin widening. "As you wish, Anastasia Asma'u," he said, his voice tinged with admiration. "Together, we shall unravel the mysteries of the orb and bring balance to both realms."

Anastasia nodded, her heart swelling with a blend of fear and anticipation. The road ahead would be fraught with peril, but she knew that she was not alone in her quest.

"Thank you, Amir," she murmured, her eyes once again drawn to the cityscape beyond her window. "Let's begin our journey."

And with that, the two allies embarked upon a new chapter in their lives, each step bringing them closer to understanding the true nature of the world they inhabited – a realm where the boundaries between the supernatural and the mundane were beginning to blur, and where a single woman held the key to maintaining the delicate balance between them.

Moonlit Waters

The air hung heavy with tension, electricity crackling in the atmosphere like an invisible storm brewing just beneath the surface. Anastasia Asma'u could feel it in her bones – something was coming, and it threatened to shatter the fragile balance between the human and supernatural worlds. Her hands trembled as she gripped her FBI badge, feeling the weight of her responsibility pressing down on her shoulders.

"Something's not right," she muttered under her breath, scanning the dimly lit street for any signs of trouble. The city of Detroit seemed to hold its breath, waiting for the eruption that would change everything.

As if in answer to her thoughts, a low growl echoed through the night, sending shivers down her spine. A group of imposing figures emerged from the shadows, their eyes glowing like molten gold in the darkness. These were not humans, but were-creatures, beings that walked the line between man and beast. Their presence struck fear into the hearts of those who crossed their path, whether human or supernatural.

"Stay back," Anastasia warned in a hushed tone, her heart pounding in her chest as the were-lion, leader of the pack, fixed his predatory gaze upon her. His massive frame radiated power and danger, exuding an aura of authority that demanded submission. She knew that engaging these creatures meant diving headfirst into the chaos, but there was no turning back now. She had to protect both worlds, human and supernatural alike, from the calamity that loomed on the horizon.

"Human," the were-lion rumbled, his voice a blend of disdain and curiosity. "You reek of magic and fear. What brings you here?"

Anastasia locked eyes with the creature, refusing to let him see her wavering. "I'm here to stop the destruction that's about to befall this city," she replied, her voice steady despite the fear clawing at her insides. The supernatural world was becoming more and more unstable, and she had to act fast before it spilled over into the human realm.

"Bold words," the were-lion snarled, baring his sharp teeth in a menacing grin. "But you're out of your depth, little girl."

"Am I?" Anastasia challenged, her pulse racing as she searched for any sign of weakness in her adversaries. These creatures would not be easily swayed, but she had no choice but to try. "You don't want this chaos any more than we do. Help me stop it, and we can find a way to coexist peacefully."

"Interesting proposition," the were-lion mused, his golden eyes never leaving hers. "But what makes you think you can trust us?"

Anastasia hesitated, her mind racing with thoughts of Artiya'il's guidance and Amir's mischievous grin. She knew that the path ahead was fraught with danger, and that alliances could be both a blessing and a curse. But with so much at stake, she couldn't afford to turn away potential allies.

"Because if we don't work together," she said, swallowing hard, "we'll all be swallowed by the chaos that's coming."

The were-lion's laughter echoed through the abandoned warehouse as he slammed a massive paw onto an old wooden table, splintering it in two. "You humans," he growled, eyes gleaming with amusement, "you've let your cities sprawl and fester, but now that we've come to claim our share, you suddenly want peace?"

Anastasia held her ground, fists clenched at her sides. Her heart hammered wildly, but she refused to let fear dictate her actions. The were-creatures had already caused too much chaos, terrorizing Detroit's communities and claiming territories without regard for the humans who lived there. It was her duty to find a way to restore balance.

"Your demands have consequences," she said, her voice steady as she met the were-lion's gaze. "People are suffering because of your actions."

"Isn't that what humans do?" a were-wolf sneered from the shadows, stepping forward into the dim light. His fur bristled, and his yellow eyes bored into Anastasia. "Suffer each other? Destroy each other?"

"Enough!" The sharp command cut through the air like a gunshot, silencing the bickering around them. All eyes turned to the source of the interruption: a figure emerging from the darkness, their movements fluid, graceful, and powerful all at once. Mami Wata had risen.

Her beauty was overwhelming, drawing every eye to her face. Like water given human form, her ebony skin shimmered with an iridescent sheen. Her smile was captivating, revealing rows of perfect white teeth that glinted with wicked promise. And her eyes, oh, her hypnotic eyes—they seemed to hold depths of ancient wisdom and unfathomable cruelty, swirling like whirlpools threatening to drag anyone who dared look too long into oblivion.

"Are we not all creatures of this world?" Mami Wata murmured, her voice like a siren song that washed over the room. "Why must we fight amongst ourselves when there is so much to be shared?"

"Shared?" The were-lion's lips curled into a snarl. "You would have us share our territory with humans?"

"Share, dominate, coexist," Mami Wata replied, stepping closer to Anastasia. "The choice is yours. But remember, dear ones, that I am the ruler of these waters. Displease me, and you may find your precious territories flooded."

Anastasia shuddered at the thought, feeling the weight of responsibility settle heavily on her shoulders. She couldn't allow this chaos to continue. She needed to find a way to bring peace between the supernatural beings and the human world, and she knew that meant making difficult choices.

"Fine," she whispered, her resolve hardening as she faced the were-creatures. "If it's territory you want, let's talk about what you truly need. But know this: no more innocent lives will be lost. No more chaos."

Anastasia stared into the eyes of the were-creatures, her heart pounding furiously in her chest. The room seemed to close in around her as the supernatural factions faced off, tension thick in the air.

"Enough!" Mami Wata's voice rang out, her hypnotic eyes narrowing dangerously. She stepped between the werewolf and the were-lion, her movements a fluid dance that seemed to defy gravity itself. "We are not here to fight amongst ourselves."

"Then what are we here for?" the werewolf growled, his voice barely contained fury. "The humans encroach on our territory daily."

"Perhaps the time has come to make them pay," the were-lion rumbled, baring his fangs menacingly. As he spoke, storm clouds began to gather outside, darkening the skies above Detroit. Rain pelted against the windows, intensifying with every passing moment.

"Is this your doing?" Anastasia asked Mami Wata, her thoughts racing as she tried to process the sudden change in weather.

"Does it matter?" Mami Wata replied cryptically, her captivating smile never faltering. "What matters is what you're going to do about it."

"Fine," Anastasia said, gritting her teeth. "But first, we need to find some common ground. We can't keep attacking each other like this. It's tearing our world apart."

"Would you have us bow to the humans?" the werewolf snapped, his eyes blazing with anger. "They've pushed us to the brink. They need to see our power."

"Power comes in many forms," Mami Wata interjected, drawing the attention of the room once more. "You don't need to slaughter innocents to prove your strength. Instead, use their fear to your advantage."

"Are you suggesting we manipulate them?" the were-lion asked, his body tense with barely suppressed rage.

"Isn't that what they've been doing to us for centuries?" Mami Wata countered, her voice like a siren's call. "It's time we took back control."

As the supernatural factions debated heatedly, news began to spread throughout Detroit of mysterious disappearances and unexplained phenomena. The city was plunged into chaos as people tried to make sense of what was happening, while Anastasia and the supernatural beings struggled to find a solution in their own world.

"Enough!" Anastasia shouted finally, her voice cutting through the cacophony of voices. "We're getting nowhere like this. We need to find a way to coexist, or we'll destroy each other."

"Your words are wise," Mami Wata said, her hypnotic eyes boring into Anastasia. "But will they listen?"

"Let's hope so," Anastasia replied, swallowing hard as she surveyed the room. The supernatural beings stared back at her, their expressions a mix of defiance and uncertainty. She knew the road ahead would be difficult but, if they could find a way to work together, maybe they could prevent further destruction.

Anastasia's heart raced as she and her allies raced through the streets of Detroit, the cityscape now a battleground for warring supernatural factions. The once-familiar sights were now marred by chaos and destruction. A cold wind whipped through the air, foreboding and unnatural, carrying with it the scent of fear.

"Over here!" Detective Ayo shouted, his voice barely audible over the cacophony of clashing powers and roars of were-creatures. They skidded to a halt in front of an abandoned warehouse where Sakhr, the mighty jinni king, was locked in battle with a group of vicious werewolves.

"Stand back!" Artiya'il warned as he raised his hands, channeling a golden light that struck the werewolves, momentarily halting their advance.

"Are you alright, Sakhr?" Anastasia asked, concern etched on her face.

"I've been better," Sakhr replied through gritted teeth, his eyes still focused on his opponents. "These beasts are relentless."

"Let us help you," offered Amir, the impish grin never leaving his face even amidst the chaos. With a nod from Sakhr, Amir darted forward, unleashing a torrent of fire on the snarling werewolves.

"By Allah, what have we gotten ourselves into?" Anastasia murmured, her gaze flitting between the battles playing out across the city. She could see Zuhra, radiant and fierce, fending off a group of water spirits summoned by Mami Wata herself, while Bilquis led her coven against the shape-shifting Irshi and their myriad forms.

"Focus, Anastasia," Artiya'il urged gently, placing a hand on her shoulder. "We must restore order, one battle at a time."

"Right," Anastasia agreed, determination steeling her resolve. She turned to Detective Ayo, who had been watching the battles with a mix of awe and trepidation. "Ayo, can you help Artiya'il and Amir? They could use your strength."

"Of course," he replied, nodding firmly as he moved to join the fray.

As Anastasia prepared to face the next supernatural threat, she couldn't help but feel the weight of her dual identity bearing down on her. How could she protect both the human world and the supernatural realm when they seemed so intent on tearing each other apart?

"Over there!" Bilquis shouted from across the battlefield, her voice desperate. "Anastasia, we need your help!"

Without hesitation, Anastasia sprinted toward the embattled witch, her heart heavy with the knowledge that she may never find the balance between her two worlds. But for now, she would fight with every fiber of her being to save both realms from descending into chaos and destruction.

Anastasia's eyes widened as the skies above the Great Lakes churned, driven into a frenzy by Mami Wata's escalating powers. The once calm waters thrashed and raged, spilling over onto the shores and flooding Detroit's streets. Boats were tossed about like toys in a whirlpool of destruction, their terrified occupants screaming for help.

"By the heavens," Artiya'il breathed, his voice barely audible over the cacophony of chaos. "Mami Wata has claimed the Great Lakes."

"Whoever dares to challenge me shall face the wrath of my waters!" Mami Wata's voice boomed, her hypnotic eyes gleaming with fury as her laughter echoed around them, cold and merciless.

"Enough!" Anastasia shouted, her fists clenched at her sides. "We cannot allow this to continue. We must put an end to this madness before more innocent lives are lost!"

"Agreed," Detective Ayo said grimly, his eyes scanning the chaotic scene before them. "But how do we stop a force of nature?"

"Perhaps there is a way," Bilquis mused, her brow furrowed in thought. "A powerful binding spell may be able to contain her, but it would require all of our combined strength, and even then, it might not be enough."

"Then we have no choice," Anastasia declared, her heart heavy but resolute.

"We must try. Lives hang in the balance, both human and supernatural. It is our duty to protect them."

"Very well," Bilquis agreed, nodding solemnly. "Gather the others – we'll need everyone for this."

As Anastasia and her allies convened, pooling their resources and knowledge to devise a plan, she couldn't shake the gnawing dread in the pit of her stomach. The stakes had never been higher, and yet, what if their best efforts still weren't enough? What if Mami Wata's power proved too great?

"Focus, Anastasia," she whispered to herself, steadying her breathing. "We can do this. We must do this."

"Ready?" Bilquis asked, her gaze meeting each of theirs in turn.

"Ready," they replied as one, determination burning in their eyes.

"Then let us begin," Anastasia said, raising her hands towards the tumultuous skies above.

As they chanted in unison, a shimmering sphere of energy began to form around Mami Wata, the very air crackling with power. The water spirit snarled in defiance, her beautiful features twisted in rage as she fought against the binds that sought to contain her.

"Your pitiful attempts to hinder me shall fail!" she spat, her voice seething with malice. "You cannot hold me – I am the embodiment of water itself!"

"Perhaps so," Anastasia said through gritted teeth, sweat beading on her brow as she struggled to maintain the spell. "But even the mightiest river can be tamed with time and persistence."

"Then you shall find your persistence rewarded with only death!" Mami Wata roared, her anger causing waves to surge threateningly toward them.

"Stand firm!" Artiya'il cried, his wings flaring out protectively as the waters crashed against them like hammers. "Do not waver, for the fate of both our worlds hangs in the balance!"

With a final surge of effort, Anastasia and her allies tightened the magical bonds around Mami Wata, their voices rising in a crescendo of power and determination. The water spirit screamed in fury, her eyes blazing with hatred, but her struggles began to weaken.

"Let this be a lesson," Anastasia called out, her voice ringing with authority.

"No force, no matter how powerful, can stand against the united strength of those who fight to protect their worlds."

And as Mami Wata's furious cries faded into nothingness, Anastasia knew that they had succeeded – for now. But the battle was far from over, and she would need every ounce of her courage and resolve to face whatever lay ahead.

Anastasia stood at the edge of a crumbling rooftop overlooking the once-familiar streets of Detroit, now a battleground for supernatural forces. She gripped her weapon tightly, feeling the weight of responsibility growing heavier with each passing moment. The city she loved was tearing itself apart, and it was up to her and her allies to restore order.

"Are you ready for this?" Detective Ayo asked, his deep voice betraying a hint of concern.

"I have to be," Anastasia replied, her dark eyes narrowing as she surveyed the chaos below.

"Remember what Artiya'il taught you," Sakhr, the jinni king, added, his regal bearing a contrast to the destruction around them. "You have the power within you to stand against these forces."

Anastasia took a deep breath, reminding herself of the celestial messenger's words – and her own newfound strength. She had come a long way since discovering her supernatural lineage, but now she faced her greatest challenge yet.

"Let's go," she said with determination, leaping from the rooftop and landing gracefully on the street below, her allies following close behind.

"Over there!" Bilquis shouted, pointing to a group of were-creatures who had surrounded a terrified family. Their golden eyes gleamed menacingly in the dim light, their snarls sending chills down Anastasia's spine.

"Leave them be!" Anastasia called out boldly, drawing her weapon and charging towards the fearsome creatures.

"Who dares to challenge us?" The were-lion roared, his powerful form looming over the others.

"Someone who will put an end to your reign of terror," Anastasia retorted, lunging forward and engaging the were-creatures in a fierce battle. Her movements were swift and precise, showcasing the skills she had honed through countless hours of training.

"Your courage is admirable," the were-lion growled as he parried Anastasia's attack, "but it will not save you."

"Courage is only part of it," Anastasia replied, her eyes locked on her opponent. "I fight for something greater than myself."

"Your conviction means nothing in the face of raw power!" The were-lion roared, launching a devastating attack that sent her flying back.

"Ugh!" Anastasia hit the ground hard, her body aching from the impact. She struggled to rise, her vision blurred and her breath coming in ragged gasps. *I cannot fail,* she thought desperately, pushing through the pain.

"Leave her alone!" Amir cried, unleashing a torrent of magical energy that forced the were-lion to retreat momentarily. Anastasia seized the opportunity, mustering all her strength and resolve for one final strike.

"Your reign ends here!" she shouted, her weapon glowing with ethereal light as she lunged at the were-lion.

"NO!" he roared, his golden eyes widening in surprise as Anastasia's weapon found its mark. With a final, agonized cry, the mighty were-lion fell, defeated by a mortal who had embraced her supernatural destiny.

Anastasia stood victorious, breathing heavily, her allies rushing to her side. Relief washed over her, but it was short-lived as a chilling laughter echoed through the night air.

"Bravo, little protector," a voice whispered, full of malice and darkness. "But your true test has only just begun."

"Who's there?" Anastasia demanded, her senses on high alert.

"Show yourself, coward!" Detective Ayo added, his skepticism replaced by fierce loyalty to Anastasia.

"Patience, my dear adversaries," the voice taunted, sending shivers down their spines. "Soon enough, you shall know the full extent of my power. And when that day comes, you will wish for death."

The laughter faded away, leaving Anastasia and her allies shaken but more determined than ever to protect their city and its people – both human and supernatural.

"Let them come," Anastasia whispered, her eyes flashing with newfound resolve. "I will be ready."

As the first light of dawn broke over the shattered skyline, a new chapter in Detroit's history began – and with it, the rise of a protector who would stop at nothing to defend her world.

Weaponry of the Heavens

The air was ripe with defeat, the lingering scent of burning ozone and blood a stark reminder of the battle that had just torn through the city streets. Anastasia raced through the wreckage, her heart pounding in her chest as panic clawed at her throat. She skid to a halt as she finally spotted what she was looking for.

"Harut!" she cried out, her voice strained with desperation.

Her allies had already gathered around him, their faces etched with concern and disbelief. The enigmatic fallen angel lay motionless on the ground, his once-powerful wings crumpled like discarded paper. Harut's dark eyes, which always seemed to hold secrets, were glazed over and unfocused. His breathing was shallow, each breath a laborious struggle. Even with her limited knowledge of supernatural beings, Anastasia knew that he was on the brink of death.

"Is he...?" stammered one of her allies, unable to finish the question.

"Quiet," snapped another, his voice heavy with fear and frustration. "We need to focus."

Anastasia knelt beside Harut, her hands hovering over his broken form. There were deep gashes across his body, blackened edges indicating that some sort of dark energy had accompanied the attack. Blood seeped from his wounds, pooling beneath him, a testament to the severity of his injuries.

"Stay with us, Harut," Anastasia whispered urgently, trying to keep the tremor from her voice.

Gritting her teeth, Anastasia began to chant an incantation she had learned from Zuhra, a close supernatural ally. She could feel the energy coursing through her veins, filling her with a sense of power and determination. Her hands glowed faintly as she placed them on Harut's battered body, attempting to heal his most severe wounds.

"Come on," she muttered under her breath, willing the magic to work. "Stay with us."

Her allies watched in tense silence, their expressions a mix of hope and resignation. They knew this was far beyond Anastasia's capabilities, but they couldn't help but hold onto the sliver of hope she offered.

As seconds turned into minutes, it became clear that Anastasia's attempts were futile. The glow from her hands began to flicker, growing weaker by the moment. Harut's breathing did not improve, and his eyes remained vacant, staring into the void.

"Damn it!" Anastasia slammed her fist onto the ground, frustration boiling over. The pain in her hand was nothing compared to the emotional turmoil raging inside her.

"None of this should have happened," she whispered fiercely, tears stinging at the corners of her eyes. "I should have been able to prevent it."

She thought back to the events leading up to their devastating defeat – the negotiations that had crumbled before her eyes, the fragile alliances shattered, and the enemy that had struck with terrifying swiftness. As an FBI agent tasked with dealing with supernatural cases, she felt responsible for the chaos that had unfolded. If only she had been more skilled, more knowledgeable…

"Hey," said one of her allies gently, placing a hand on her shoulder. "This isn't your fault, Anastasia. You've done everything you can."

"Everything I can?" she replied bitterly, looking down at Harut. "It doesn't seem like enough."

"None of us could have predicted this," another ally chimed in. "We're all hurting, Anastasia. But blaming yourself isn't going to help Harut or stop the chaos that's been unleashed."

Anastasia clenched her jaw, knowing they were right but unable to shake the heavy weight of guilt pressing down on her. She looked at each of her allies – supernatural beings who had put their trust in her, who believed she could bring peace and stability to their world. The pressure was immense, and the fear of failing them gnawed at her soul.

"Then what do we do now?" she asked, her voice cracking with emotion.

"First, we need to get Harut someplace safe," said one of her allies, determination sparking in their eyes. "We'll regroup and figure out our next move. We can still turn this around, Anastasia. We just need to stay strong and keep fighting."

Anastasia nodded, tears streaming down her face as she took a deep breath. They were right; she couldn't afford to wallow in self-pity. Lives were at stake, both human and supernatural, and it was up to her to restore balance. She knew she couldn't do it alone, but with her allies by her side, maybe, just maybe, they could find a way to rise from this devastating defeat.

"Alright," she whispered, wiping away her tears. "Let's save Harut. And then… we'll find a way to save everyone else."

A chilling wind blew through the ruined streets, as if the city itself mourned their crushing defeat. Anastasia stood amidst the wreckage, her allies gathered around Harut's crumpled form. With each labored breath he took, resentment and bitterness festered within the group, threatening to tear them apart.

"Shouldn't you have known this was going to happen?" a werewolf growled, baring his teeth at Anastasia. "You're supposed to be our leader."

"Enough, Jarek," Zuhra interjected, her celestial aura soothing the tension in the air. "Now is not the time for blame."

Anastasia clenched her fist, the weight of her failure bearing down on her shoulders. She couldn't let it destroy everything they'd worked so hard to build. Her eyes met Zuhra's, and she found a flicker of hope amidst the despair.

"Zuhra, you've guided me through so much," Anastasia said, her voice trembling slightly. "What do we do now? How do we save Harut and protect our world?"

Zuhra placed a gentle hand on Anastasia's arm, her touch as warm as sunlight. "I cannot give you all the answers, dear one. But remember that you have more than just my guidance – you have the strength and wisdom of all your allies."

"Then let's put our heads together," Anastasia declared, determination fueling her resolve. "We'll find a solution, no matter how hopeless things seem."

"Very well," an ancient vampire murmured, stepping forward. "Perhaps there are old spells or rituals that could help us heal Harut."

"Or maybe we can seek out other supernatural beings who share our goal," a fae suggested, her lilting voice hesitant but hopeful.

"Right," Anastasia agreed, her mind racing with possibilities. "We need to pool our resources and knowledge. We can't afford any more mistakes."

As they began to strategize, the strain between Anastasia and her allies slowly dissipated, replaced by a shared determination to right their wrongs and protect their world. Though doubt still gnawed at the edges of Anastasia's mind, she refused to let it consume her; instead, she focused on the task at hand, drawing strength from her allies and the wisdom of Zuhra.

"Failure is not an option," she whispered to herself, gritting her teeth. "We will find a way – we must."

Though the path before them was uncertain and fraught with danger, Anastasia knew that only by standing together could they hope to overcome the darkness threatening to engulf their world. And as long as she had Zuhra's guidance and the support of her allies, she would fight until her last breath, striving to save not only Harut but all those who depended on her.

The sky overhead churned with unnatural fury, the clouds a dark and foreboding omen that seemed to reflect the chaos brewing within the supernatural world. Anastasia stood beneath their shadow, feeling the weight of her responsibility settling heavily on her shoulders. Time was running out – she knew it, and so did her allies.

"Have you learned anything new from Zuhra?" Sakhr asked, his voice strained with anxiety. The jinni king's eyes were narrowed, as if he were trying to peer through the veil of darkness that had descended upon them.

"Nothing that can help us immediately," Anastasia admitted, frustration tightening her chest. "She speaks in riddles and half-truths, leaving me grasping at straws."

"Maybe we're missing something," Irshi suggested, their form flickering like a candle flame caught in a draft. "We need more insight, more information."

Anastasia clenched her fists, her nails biting into her palms. She felt the pressure mounting, threatening to crush her under its unbearable weight. It wasn't just Harut who was in danger now – it was everyone. If she couldn't find a way to broker peace between the warring factions, the supernatural world would be plunged into chaos. And it would be on her head.

"Perhaps there's someone else who can help," Bilquis said quietly, her captivating eyes filled with concern. "Another source of wisdom, another ally we haven't yet considered."

"Like who?" Detective Ayo demanded, his skepticism evident in every line of his body. "We've already tried reaching out to every being we know, and look where it's gotten us."

"Enough," Anastasia snapped, her anger flaring. "Arguing among ourselves won't help us find a solution."

"Then what will?" Ayo shot back, his dark eyes challenging hers. "We can't just keep spinning our wheels here, Anastasia. We need to act."

Anastasia turned away from the group, feeling their eyes on her as she stared out at the darkened cityscape. She knew they were right – that every moment they wasted only brought them closer to disaster – but she couldn't shake the gnawing doubt that had taken root in her mind.

"Am I truly capable of fulfilling my role as a protector?" she wondered, pressing a hand to her heart. "Or am I leading us all to ruin?"

"Trust yourself, Anastasia," Artiya'il murmured, his celestial presence a comforting balm amidst the turmoil. "You have the wisdom and strength within you to overcome this darkness."

"Then why do I feel so lost?" she whispered, her voice barely audible above the howl of the wind.

"Because the path before you is shrouded in shadows," he replied gently. "But even in the darkest night, there is always a glimmer of light to guide your way."

"Where do I find that light, Artiya'il?" Anastasia asked, her desperation clear.

"Look within, Anastasia," he said, his ethereal gaze steady and reassuring. "And trust in the connections you've forged with those who stand beside you."

She nodded, drawing strength from his words. Though she was scared – terrified, even – she refused to let fear paralyze her. She owed it to Harut, to her allies, and to herself to keep fighting, to keep searching for a way to bring peace to the supernatural world. And if the solution wasn't yet clear, then she would simply have to work harder, dig deeper, and refuse to give up until the path forward revealed itself.

"Alright," she said, turning back to face her friends and allies, her expression resolute. "Let's find that light and drive back the darkness. Together."

Anastasia stood at the precipice of two worlds, the mundane and the supernatural, feeling the weight of responsibility bearing down on her shoulders. She stared out at the city skyline from her apartment window, the golden glow of streetlights casting a halo around each building. Her FBI badge lay on the table beside her, a symbol of her duty to protect and serve the people of Detroit.

"Agent Anastasia," Detective Ayo said as he approached, his voice heavy with concern. "You've always been committed to your work, but you can't be both an FBI agent and a protector of the supernatural world. You need to make a choice."

She turned to face him, her dark eyes meeting his steady gaze. "I know how this looks, Ayo," she admitted quietly, "but I believe there must be a way to reconcile my two worlds. I just need time to figure it out."

"Time is something we don't have," Ayo replied, frustration lacing his words. "The city is on the brink of chaos, and we need you focused on the task at hand."

Anastasia's hands clenched into fists at her sides. "I am focused," she insisted, her tone resolute. "I won't fail either of my responsibilities. We just need new strategies, alternative paths to restore balance."

"Then what do you propose, Anastasia?" Bilquis asked, her captivating eyes fixed on her, expecting results.

"First, we need to understand our enemies better," Anastasia said, her mind racing as she tried to piece together a plan. "We must find out their motives, their weaknesses. If we know what they want, we might be able to use that information against them."

"Sounds risky," Amir chimed in, his impish grin betraying his curiosity. "But I like it. Who doesn't love a good spy mission?"

"Secondly," Anastasia continued, "we need to strengthen our alliances. We can't defeat our enemies alone. We must unite the supernatural world and present a united front against the forces that threaten us."

"Unifying the supernatural world won't be easy," Sakhr cautioned, his regal bearing commanding attention. "But it's a worthy goal. Perhaps we can begin by forming a council of representatives from each faction."

Anastasia nodded, encouraged by their support. "Lastly, we need to prepare for battle. Our enemies won't wait for us to come up with a perfect plan. We must be ready to fight at a moment's notice."

"Agreed," Mami Wata said, her voice like a siren's call. "We will train our people in the ways of war and magic, honing our skills until we are an unstoppable force."

"Then let's get to work," Anastasia concluded, feeling a newfound determination coursing through her veins. "Together, we can forge a path to peace and restore balance to both of my worlds."

Though the road ahead was filled with uncertainty and danger, Anastasia refused to let fear control her. She would find a way to protect the city she loved, no matter the cost. And as she stared out once more at the skyline, a symbol of human resilience and progress, she knew deep down that she could not let her city - or her allies - down.

With the weight of her dual responsibilities pressing down on her, Anastasia locked herself away in her makeshift war room. Maps of Detroit's supernatural hotspots lined the walls, and she poured over every detail, searching desperately for a solution to the seemingly insurmountable challenge before her.

"Any luck?" Amir asked, materializing beside her with a concerned look on his impish face.

"Nothing yet," she admitted, frustration lacing her words. "I just don't know how we're going to find a way to unite everyone and stand against our enemies."

"Keep trying," Artiya'il urged gently, resting a comforting hand on her shoulder. His ethereal presence brought a momentary sense of calm to her frazzled nerves. "You have a strong spirit, Anastasia. You will find a way."

"Perhaps there is an answer hidden within your own heritage," Zuhra suggested, her celestial wisdom radiating from her like the morning sun. "Your ancestors were powerful protectors, after all."

Anastasia's eyes widened as she remembered a tale her grandmother had once told her about a sacred relic that held immense power. It was said to be capable of uniting different factions and could only be wielded by a true protector. The mere thought of it sent a shiver down her spine.

"Could it be possible…?" Anastasia wondered aloud, her mind racing with possibilities.

"Only one way to find out," Detective Ayo chimed in, his skepticism tempered by curiosity. "We'll have to follow the clues and see where they lead us."

"An ancient relic, you say?" Sakhr mused, stroking his chin thoughtfully. "Such a thing could indeed turn the tide in our favor."

"Then let us search for it," Bilquis declared, her eyes flashing with determination. "Together, we shall uncover its secrets and bring hope to our people."

As Anastasia and her allies set off on their quest, a flicker of hope ignited within her. Though the path they walked was fraught with danger and uncertainty, she knew that she must persevere in order to save both the city she loved and the supernatural world that had become her responsibility.

"Let's do this," Anastasia whispered to herself, steeling her resolve. "For Harut, for Detroit, and for all those who depend on us."

The chapter closed with a sense of anticipation and trepidation as Anastasia and her eclectic group of allies embarked on a journey that would either unite them or tear them apart. With the fate of the city hanging in the balance, only time would tell if they could rise above their devastating defeat and find a way to save them all.

Heart of Detroit

Anastasia sat on the edge of her worn, beige sofa, her fingers idly tracing the frayed threads as she stared into the dark recesses of her apartment. The moonlight seeping through the blinds cast eerie shadows on the walls, amplifying her feeling of isolation. Her life had taken a sudden, strange turn, and now she found herself grappling with the duality of her identity - FBI special agent by day, supernatural warrior by night.

"Can I really handle this?" she whispered to the silence around her, her voice laden with uncertainty. "Am I strong enough to carry both these burdens?"

The weight of her doubts bore down on her like an oppressive fog, wrapping its tendrils around her thoughts until they were obscured, leaving only a heavy darkness in their wake. She clenched her fists, nails biting into her palms, as her frustration bubbled under the surface.

"God, please give me strength," she prayed. "I don't want to fail those who depend on me."

Images of her recent encounters flickered through her mind - Artiya'il, the celestial messenger, revealing her destiny; Amir, the mischievous genie, assisting her in her pursuits; Sakhr, the powerful jinni king, his gaze filled with centuries of secrets; Ayo, the skeptical detective, drawn into her world despite his disbelief. Each of them represented a piece of the puzzle that was her life, a life divided between two worlds that seemed increasingly incompatible.

"Is it even possible to find balance in this chaos?" she wondered, her heart aching with the desire for answers.

In that moment, Anastasia felt the crushing weight of responsibility press upon her shoulders, threatening to break her resolve. She longed for guidance, for someone who could help her navigate the complexities of her existence. But as the darkness of doubt threatened to consume her, Anastasia knew that the only way forward was to confront her fears and find the strength within herself to continue her journey.

Anastasia's pacing intensified, her footsteps echoing through the empty apartment like a heartbeat. Each thud of her soles against the cold wooden floor seemed to punctuate her worries, amplifying them in her mind. The walls that had once provided solace now felt like a prison, trapping her in a constant loop of doubt and frustration.

"Can I truly manage both worlds? Am I capable enough?" she muttered under her breath, her words barely audible. Anastasia's eyes darted around the room, searching for some sort of escape from her racing thoughts, but finding none. She clenched her fists at her sides, knuckles turning white as she struggled to maintain control.

Suddenly, a gentle warmth filled the room, easing the tension that had coiled within Anastasia like a taut spring. The air grew thick with an otherworldly energy, and a shimmering light began to dance before her eyes. It swirled and twisted, weaving itself into a familiar figure that radiated wisdom and reassurance.

"Zuhra," Anastasia whispered, her voice trembling with a mix of relief and awe.

"Peace, child," Zuhra said softly, her ethereal presence casting a calming glow across the room. Her eyes held the wisdom of the ages, their deep blue depths reflecting the countless souls she had guided throughout time. "You are not alone on this journey. Remember, you are stronger than you realize."

"Is it possible to find balance in this chaos?" Anastasia asked, her voice cracking with emotion. "I feel like I'm being torn apart, trying to exist in two worlds that seem increasingly incompatible."

"Balance is never easy, dear one," Zuhra replied gently, her celestial gaze unwavering and kind. "But it is achievable if you learn to trust yourself and the path that has been laid before you. Your dual roles are not a punishment, but an opportunity to grow and evolve. Embrace them, and you will find the harmony you seek."

Anastasia's chest heaved with each breath, her eyes glistening with unshed tears as she drank in Zuhra's words. She could feel the weight of her doubts beginning to lift, replaced by a quiet determination that resonated within her very core.

"Thank you, Zuhra," Anastasia murmured, her voice stronger and steadier than before. "Your guidance means more to me than I can express."

"Trust yourself, Anastasia," Zuhra repeated softly, her form beginning to dissolve back into the shimmering light from which it had emerged. "You have the strength and wisdom to navigate this journey. Remember that, above all else."

Anastasia stared at the ethereal figure before her, feeling a mix of relief and desperation well up inside her. The shimmering light that surrounded Zuhra seemed to pierce through the darkness of her doubts, offering a glimmer of hope in her tumultuous existence.

"Zuhra, I need your guidance," Anastasia implored, her voice thick with emotion. "I'm struggling to find my place in this world, torn between my responsibilities as a protector and my desires as a human being. How can I possibly fulfill both roles without losing myself?"

Zuhra regarded Anastasia with infinite patience, her celestial eyes reflecting the wisdom she had gathered throughout the ages. "You must learn to trust yourself, dear one," she said softly, her voice like a soothing balm to Anastasia's frazzled nerves. "Trust in your ability to navigate these challenges, for you have been chosen to walk this path for a reason."

Anastasia clenched her fists, frustration simmering beneath her skin. "But how can I trust myself when I feel so lost?" she demanded, her voice cracking under the weight of her uncertainty.

"By recognizing that you are not alone in your struggle," Zuhra replied gently, her radiant figure casting a warm glow across the otherwise dim room. "There are those who share your burden, who will help guide and support you through the trials that lie ahead. Together, you will find the balance that you seek."

Anastasia took a deep, steadying breath, trying to absorb Zuhra's words into her very being. She looked down at her hands, still trembling with pent-up emotions, and then back up at the celestial being before her. "How do I find them, Zuhra? How do I connect with those who can help me on this journey?"

Zuhra smiled warmly, her shimmering form flickering like a candle in the wind. "By opening your heart and allowing yourself to trust in others, as well as yourself. The connections you seek will reveal themselves in time, and when they do, you must be prepared to embrace them with open arms."

"Thank you," Anastasia whispered, her eyes brimming with determination as she clung to Zuhra's words like a lifeline. "Your wisdom gives me strength, even in my darkest moments."

"Remember, dear one," Zuhra said softly as her form began to fade back into the shadows, "trust is crucial to maintaining balance. Trust in yourself, trust in those who share your journey, and trust in the path that has been laid out before you."

Anastasia looked into Zuhra's wise and knowing eyes, feeling the weight of her mentor's words settling upon her shoulders. "I understand the importance of trust, but how do I know when to trust myself? How can I be sure that my decisions are the right ones?"

"Ah, Anastasia," Zuhra began, her voice a soothing balm to Anastasia's frayed nerves. "The truth is, there is no certainty in life. You must learn to trust not only in your choices but also in your ability to adapt and grow from the consequences of those choices."

Anastasia clenched her hands into fists at her side, frustration bubbling up within her. "But what if I make the wrong choice, Zuhra? What if my actions lead to more harm than good?"

"Every choice carries with it the potential for both light and darkness," Zuhra replied gently. "The key is to accept that you cannot control everything, and to have faith in your ability to rise above any challenges that may come your way."

Anastasia's brow furrowed as she grappled with Zuhra's words. She felt the tendrils of doubt slowly loosening their grip on her heart, replaced by a flicker of hope. "So, it's not about making perfect decisions, but rather trusting in my resilience and ability to learn from my experiences?"

"Exactly," Zuhra affirmed, a smile spreading across her luminescent features. "You possess an inner strength, Anastasia, one that has carried you through countless trials and tribulations. Trust in that strength, and know that you are never alone on this journey."

With each word spoken by Zuhra, Anastasia could feel the cloud of uncertainty surrounding her begin to dissipate like morning mist under the warmth of the sun. A sense of renewed determination began to take root within her, a fierce and unyielding resolve that seemed to surge through her very veins.

"Thank you, Zuhra," Anastasia said, her voice firm and resolute. "Your guidance has helped me find my way amidst the storm of doubt that threatened to consume me."

"Remember, Anastasia," Zuhra replied as her shimmering form began to fade once more, "you are never alone in this journey. Trust in yourself, trust in those around you, and trust in your path. Embrace who you are and all that you are capable of, and I have no doubt that you will succeed."

With that final piece of wisdom, Zuhra disappeared, leaving Anastasia standing tall and filled with newfound purpose. She knew that the road ahead would not be easy, but she was no longer afraid to face it. For the first time in what felt like an eternity, Anastasia felt ready to step back into the world and continue her journey, buoyed by the knowledge that she was not alone in her trials and that she carried within her the strength to overcome any obstacle.

As Anastasia stood there, a profound shift seemed to take place within her. The tense lines of worry that had etched themselves across her face began to ease, and her furrowed brow smoothed out. Her shoulders, which had been hunched defensively, now rolled back and down, as if releasing the weight of the world that had been resting upon them.

"Thank you, Zuhra," she said once again, her voice now steadier, almost melodic in its newfound confidence. She looked into Zuhra's eyes, filled with gratitude for the celestial being who had guided her through this storm of self-doubt.

Zuhra smiled warmly at Anastasia, her own form radiant with pride at the transformation taking place before her. "It is my honor to guide you, dear one. Remember that your strength has always been within you; I am merely here to help you recognize it."

Anastasia nodded, feeling a sense of clarity wash over her like a cool, refreshing wave. It was as if the fog that had clouded her thoughts had suddenly lifted, leaving behind an unobstructed view of her path forward. The air around her seemed to vibrate with purpose, and even the room itself appeared brighter, more vibrant than it had moments ago.

"Embrace your dual roles, Anastasia," Zuhra continued, her words resonating within Anastasia's very soul. "You were chosen for this journey not in spite of your humanity, but because of it. Your unique blend of gifts, experiences, and emotions is what will set you apart and enable you to succeed where others have faltered."

With each word that Zuhra spoke, Anastasia felt another layer of doubt peel away from her heart, revealing the solid core of determination that lay beneath. Her hands, which had been clenched tightly at her sides, slowly unfurled, and she took a deep, grounding breath.

"I understand now," Anastasia said, her voice ringing with conviction. "I cannot let my fears hold me back. I must learn to balance my dual roles and trust in myself, my allies, and the path that lies before me."

"Exactly," Zuhra agreed, her smile broadening as she watched the spark of determination ignite within Anastasia's eyes. "You are more than capable of navigating this journey, dear one. Trust in your own strength and resilience, and you will find yourself able to face any challenge that comes your way."

As Anastasia absorbed Zuhra's words, she felt an overwhelming sense of purpose settle around her like a protective cloak. With each breath she took, her resolve grew stronger, until it seemed to radiate from her very being, filling the room with its potent energy.

Anastasia's shoulders, once hunched with the burden of self-doubt, straightened as if an invisible force had lifted them. She rolled her shoulders back, feeling the tension dissipate and be replaced by a newfound resolve. Her hands, which had been clenched into fists, now hung loosely at her sides, relaxed yet ready to spring into action.

"Thank you, Zuhra," she whispered, her voice brimming with gratitude and newfound confidence.

The celestial being nodded, her eyes shimmering with pride. "You have come so far, Anastasia. I have no doubt that you will continue to grow and find the balance you seek."

Anastasia drew herself up to her full height, her dark and expressive eyes alight with determination. The room seemed to hum with the energy that radiated from her, as if it too were preparing for the challenges ahead.

"Very well," she declared, her tone resolute. "I am ready to face whatever lies before me."

Zuhra offered one last, warm smile, a beacon of reassurance in the dimly lit room. With a slight nod, she began to fade away, her radiant form dissolving into a shimmering light that gradually vanished.

Left alone in the quiet apartment, Anastasia took a deep, steadying breath, letting the air fill her lungs and then releasing it slowly. She closed her eyes for a moment, allowing herself to feel the strength of her conviction surging through her like a powerful current.

"Alright," she murmured to herself, opening her eyes and fixing her gaze on the door that led back into the world beyond her sanctuary. "Let's do this."

With renewed purpose, Anastasia strode confidently towards the door, knowing that, no matter what challenges awaited her on the other side, she was ready to meet them head-on. She reached for the doorknob, her hand steady and sure, and as she stepped out into the world, she felt the weight of her doubts and fears fall away, leaving only resolve and determination in their place.

Ties That Bind

The wind howled through the narrow alleyways of Detroit, carrying with it an air of tension and unease. Anastasia stood in a secluded corner of the city, her back pressed against the cold brick wall of an abandoned building. The dim glow of a flickering streetlight cast eerie shadows on the ground, mirroring the turmoil that stirred within her.

Anastasia's heart raced as she unfolded the crumpled piece of paper she had found hidden within the pages of her grimoire. Her hands trembled as she read the hastily scrawled words, each line revealing more about Bilquis's manipulation than the last. As much as she wanted to deny it, there was no escaping the truth; she had been betrayed by someone whom she had considered an ally.

"Can this be true?" Anastasia whispered to herself, her voice barely audible above the distant sirens and the relentless wind. She read the note once more, desperately searching for any indication that it might be a ruse or a mistake. But the evidence was undeniable, and with each passing moment, the gravity of the situation weighed heavier upon her.

"Damn it, Bilquis," she muttered under her breath, her anger boiling to the surface like hot magma threatening to erupt. How could she have been so blind? And yet, there was something about Bilquis that had always seemed… off. A sense of danger lurking just beneath the surface, hidden behind her captivating eyes and enigmatic smile.

Anastasia clenched her fists, nails biting into her palms as she fought to regain control of her emotions. Panic threatened to overtake her, but she knew that now was not the time for fear. What mattered most was finding a way to counter the treachery that had been set in motion.

"What have you done, Bilquis?" she breathed, feeling a chill run down her spine as the implications of her discovery began to sink in. She knew that she could no longer trust anyone, not even those closest to her.

"Think, Anastasia," she urged herself, forcing her mind to focus on a plan of action. No matter how overwhelming the situation seemed, she knew that she couldn't afford to let her guard down – not when the entire city was at stake.

As the wind continued to whip around her, Anastasia took a deep breath and prepared herself for what lay ahead. She knew that confronting Bilquis would be no easy task, but it was a challenge she had no choice but to face. And as the flickering streetlight above her cast long, distorted shadows on the ground, Anastasia knew that she would need every ounce of strength and cunning she possessed if she hoped to protect Detroit from the chaos that threatened to consume it.

As Anastasia stood in the dimly lit alley, she desperately attempted to process her thoughts. Who could she trust now? The sense of betrayal gnawed at the edges of her heart, spreading like a stain through her veins. Her mind raced, trying to make connections and find patterns in the chaos that had been thrust upon her.

"Everything I thought I knew was a lie," she whispered to herself, feeling a mixture of anger and despair taking root in her chest. She clenched her fists, nails digging into her palms, as if physical pain could somehow dull her emotional turmoil.

"Focus," she reminded herself. Losing her composure would only serve Bilquis's scheme. Anastasia couldn't allow that – too much rested on her shoulders.

She breathed deeply, forcing her thoughts to turn towards the Shadow Amulet. It pulsed with a dark energy that seemed to consume the air around it, as though it fed on the very atmosphere. The amulet's power radiated through its obsidian core, tendrils of shadow snaking their way outwards like tendrils seeking prey. Its aura weighed heavily on her senses, as if bearing the burden of all the darkness in this world and beyond.

"Such an artifact shouldn't exist," she muttered under her breath, her fingers instinctively reaching for the protective talisman hanging around her neck. The Shadow Amulet held the potential to unleash unimaginable havoc, not just within the supernatural community, but also the human world. If left unchecked, it could blur the boundaries between the realms, turning Detroit into a living nightmare.

"Is that what you want, Bilquis?" Anastasia seethed, her eyes narrowing as she tried to decipher the motives of the enigmatic witch. "To control both worlds? Or is there something even darker driving you?"

The wind picked up, whipping her hair across her face. In that moment, Anastasia made a decision. She couldn't confront Bilquis on her own – not without risking everything they had worked so hard to protect. But she could find allies, those who would stand by her side in the face of such treachery.

"Trust," she breathed, realizing that while betrayal had shattered her confidence in others, it was trust that would ultimately save them. Trust in her allies, in their shared goal of maintaining the balance between worlds, and in her own strength to see this through.

"Be prepared, Bilquis," Anastasia vowed, determination igniting within her like a phoenix rising from the ashes. "I will not let you succeed. The Shadow Amulet's power will not be your weapon."

With renewed focus, she set off into the darkness, her steps light but purposeful. Time was running out, and every second counted. Anastasia knew that the battle ahead would test her limits, but she refused to back down. For the sake of both worlds, she would do whatever it took to stop Bilquis and secure the Shadow Amulet.

And as she disappeared into the shadows, the city seemed to hold its breath, waiting for the storm that was about to erupt.

Anastasia's mind raced as she hurried through the darkened streets, her thoughts a whirlwind of possible strategies and potential outcomes. The city's shadows seemed to whisper around her, urging her on like a tidal wave of darkness. How could she bring down Bilquis without causing further harm? She needed a plan – something that would strike at the heart of the issue while minimizing collateral damage.

"Think, Anastasia," she muttered under her breath, her footsteps echoing on the pavement like a metronome ticking away the seconds. "You've faced worse than this before."

She stopped suddenly, her breath catching in her throat as an idea struck her like lightning. It was risky, but it just might work. They needed to exploit Bilquis's weaknesses, use her own desires against her. If they could convince her that the Shadow Amulet was more trouble than it was worth…

"Focus on her ambition," Anastasia whispered to herself, a slow grin spreading across her face. "That's the key."

Without wasting another moment, she dashed towards the hidden sanctuary where her most trusted allies were waiting. Bursting through the door, she found them huddled together over a makeshift map of Detroit's supernatural districts.

"Guys," she panted, feeling the weight of responsibility press down on her shoulders. "I think I have a plan."

"Finally!" Malik exclaimed, his eyes narrowing with determination. "What do you propose?"

"First, we need to gather intel on Bilquis's coven," Anastasia began. "We need to know their strengths, weaknesses, and how far they're willing to go for their leader. Then, we'll use that information to sow discord among their ranks."

"Interesting," Priya mused, one hand resting on her chin. "But how exactly are we going to accomplish that?"

"By creating doubt within the coven," Anastasia replied, her voice steady despite the fear gnawing at her insides. "We'll make them question if Bilquis's pursuit of the Shadow Amulet is what's best for them."

"Ah, divide and conquer," Jamal said with a nod. "Classic strategy."

"Exactly," Anastasia agreed. "But we must be careful not to alert Bilquis to our interference. The more subtle our actions, the more effective they will be."

"Count me in," Malik declared. "I've got connections in the supernatural underworld who can help us gather intel on the coven."

"Same here," Priya added, her eyes gleaming with determination. "My research on ancient artifacts might reveal some information about the Shadow Amulet that could be useful in undermining Bilquis's plans."

"Good," Anastasia said, feeling a surge of hope as her allies rallied around her. "But remember, time is of the essence. We need to act quickly before Bilquis consolidates her power."

"Agreed," Jamal replied, rolling up the map and tucking it under his arm. "Let's get to work."

As they dispersed to begin their tasks, Anastasia couldn't help but feel a flicker of uncertainty. She knew the stakes were high, and the risks even higher. But for the sake of both worlds, she had to believe that their plan would succeed.

Anastasia stood at the edge of a rooftop, overlooking Detroit's skyline, the wind whipping her hair and the city's vibrant energy flowing through her veins. The sense of urgency was palpable, and she knew that every moment they spent planning brought Bilquis closer to harnessing the dark power of the Shadow Amulet.

"Alright," Anastasia spoke into her phone, her voice firm and resolute. "We don't have much time. I've got a plan in motion, but we need to act fast."

"Are you sure about this, Anastasia?" Jamal's voice sounded concerned on the other end. "Confronting Bilquis is risky."

"Riskier than letting her control the Shadow Amulet?" Anastasia countered, her eyes narrowing as she scanned the city below. "I can't just stand by knowing what she's capable of. We must protect both worlds."

"Understood," Jamal replied, his tone shifting to one of determination. "What do you need us to do?"

"Malik, you and Priya focus on gathering intel on the coven members and their loyalties. I'll confront Bilquis directly," Anastasia instructed, her heart pounding with equal parts fear and resolve. "The sooner we sow doubt among her followers, the better our chances of stopping her."

"Be careful, Anastasia," Malik warned. "Bilquis is cunning and ruthless.

She won't hesitate to strike if she senses you're a threat."

"I know," she answered, her grip tightening on her phone. "But we can't afford to wait any longer. The balance between our worlds is hanging by a thread."

"Stay connected with us," Priya advised, her voice calm and steady. "If anything goes wrong, we'll be there for backup."

"Thank you," Anastasia said, grateful for their unwavering support. With a deep breath, she ended the call and leaped from the rooftop, her supernatural agility carrying her safely to the ground below.

As she made her way through the bustling streets, dodging pedestrians and weaving between cars, Anastasia's mind raced with the possible outcomes of her upcoming confrontation with Bilquis. She knew that the Shadow Amulet's power could wreak havoc on both the human and supernatural worlds, and the thought of that dark energy in Bilquis's hands sent shivers down her spine.

"Focus," she whispered to herself, steeling her resolve as she approached the entrance to Bilquis's club. "You can do this."

With every step she took towards the club, Anastasia felt the weight of responsibility bearing down on her. The fate of Detroit—of both worlds—rested on her shoulders. And as she pushed open the heavy doors and stepped into the dimly lit space, her determination never faltered.

"Time to face the music, Bilquis," Anastasia murmured under her breath, her pulse quickening at the thought of what lay ahead. "Your reign ends tonight."

Anastasia stood outside the entrance of a small, dusty bookstore tucked away in a forgotten corner of Detroit. The shop's windows were obscured by grime and layers of old newspapers, but she could feel the potent energy emanating from within. She knew that this was where she would find the resources she needed to face the formidable Bilquis.

"Time is running out," she muttered under her breath, her eyes darting across the street as she slipped inside the dimly lit shop.

The air inside was heavy with the scent of old parchment and ink. Anastasia's eyes adjusted to the darkness, and she saw shelves upon shelves of ancient texts stacked precariously high. Her heart raced at the thought of the potential knowledge contained within these pages.

"Find what you need, and quickly," she told herself, scanning the titles before her.

"Can I help you?" a raspy voice called from behind an enormous stack of books. A tiny, wizened figure emerged, squinting up at Anastasia through thick, round glasses.

"Actually, yes," she replied, addressing the elderly shopkeeper with quiet urgency. "I'm looking for information on the Shadow Amulet and how to counter its power."

"Ah, the Shadow Amulet," the shopkeeper murmured, stroking his beard thoughtfully. "That's a dangerous subject to delve into. Follow me."

Anastasia trailed the shopkeeper through the labyrinthine passages of the store, her mind racing with thoughts of her plan.

"Amir, Sakhr, Detective Ayo—I need you all to gather intel on Bilquis's coven and any potential weaknesses we can exploit," Anastasia whispered into her earpiece as they navigated the narrow aisleways. "Artiya'il, Zuhra, keep watch over the city. We need to know if the amulet's influence starts spreading." She paused for a moment before adding, "And please, all of you, be careful."

"Understood," Amir's voice crackled through the earpiece. The others chimed in with affirmations, their determination echoing Anastasia's own.

The shopkeeper stopped before a hidden alcove, pulling back a tattered curtain to reveal a small collection of books bound in dark leather. "These should help," he said solemnly, handing her a thick volume titled 'Forbidden Artifacts and Their Power.'

"Thank you," Anastasia replied, flipping through the pages with trembling hands. She knew that time was working against them, and she needed to find a way to neutralize the Shadow Amulet before Bilquis could unleash its full potential.

"Good luck," the shopkeeper whispered as Anastasia hurried out of the store, clutching the ancient tome to her chest.

"Alright, team," she whispered into her earpiece, her heart pounding in her ears. "I've got what we need. Let's move."

Anastasia's allies responded with a chorus of assent, each one committed to their part in the upcoming confrontation. They would face Bilquis together, united by their shared purpose of protecting Detroit and maintaining the fragile balance between the worlds.

"Stay focused," Anastasia reminded herself, opening the book to a page marked with an illustration of the amulet, its dark aura seeming to seep from the page. "We can do this."

Anastasia stood at the edge of a dimly lit alley, hidden in the shadows. The cold air bit at her skin as she stared at the entrance to Bilquis's underground club, her breath forming small clouds that dissipated into the night. Her team was in position, poised for action, and yet she couldn't shake the gnawing feeling in her gut.

"Is everyone ready?" she whispered into the earpiece, her voice tense and wavering slightly.

"Ready," came the hushed replies from Amir, Ayo, and Sakhr, each stationed strategically around the perimeter.

"Remember, we need to retrieve the Shadow Amulet before it causes irreversible damage," Anastasia reminded them, her eyes fixed on the door, watching as the bouncer allowed another patron inside. "But be cautious. We don't know what other forces Bilquis has enlisted."

"Understood," Ayo murmured, his voice steady and reassuring. Anastasia took a deep breath, drawing strength from her allies' resolve.

"May Allah guide us," she muttered under her breath, her fingers absently tracing the crescent moon pendant around her neck. As much as she wished she could simply march into the club and confront Bilquis head-on, she knew that they needed a more strategic approach. One false move could jeopardize their entire mission, and possibly their lives.

"Alright," she said, steeling herself. "Let's move."

A flicker of doubt danced through her mind as she stepped out of the shadows, her nerves buzzing with anticipation. She hesitated, her hand hovering above the amulet tucked safely within her pocket. What if her plan failed? What if they were unable to neutralize the amulet's dark power?

"Are you okay, Anastasia?" Artiya'il's soothing voice echoed through her earpiece, his celestial presence a comforting balm to her frayed nerves.

"Y-yes," she stuttered, swallowing hard. "I'm just… concerned about the outcome."

"Trust your instincts," Artiya'il advised gently. "You were chosen for this task for a reason. Have faith in yourself and in your allies."

"Thank you, Artiya'il," Anastasia whispered, drawing a shaky breath. She knew that hesitation could be their downfall, but the weight of their decisions weighed heavily on her shoulders. The lives of countless innocents rested in her hands, and the thought of failure was almost too much to bear.

"Let's do this," she said quietly, her voice wavering but determined. "For Detroit. For the balance between worlds."

"Agreed," her allies murmured, their voices resolute.

Anastasia took a final deep breath, preparing to step into the club and confront Bilquis. But just as she lifted her foot, a chilling scream pierced the night air, followed by the sound of shattering glass. Her heart leaped into her throat, and terror gripped her chest.

"Something's happening," Ayo's alarmed voice crackled through the earpiece. "We need to move, now."

"Stay focused, everyone," Anastasia commanded, her voice steadier than she felt. "Stick to the plan, but be prepared for anything."

As they rushed toward the entrance of the club, Anastasia's mind raced with possibilities. Had Bilquis already set something in motion? Was it too late to stop her?

"Wait!" Sakhr suddenly shouted, his voice urgent and uncharacteristically panicked. "There's a barrier – we can't enter!"

The team skidded to a halt just outside the doors, staring at the invisible force field blocking their path. They could see chaos unfolding inside the club, bodies writhing in pain as dark tendrils of energy snaked through the air.

"Find a way to break the barrier," Anastasia ordered, her heart pounding in her chest. "We have to get inside and neutralize that amulet before it's too late."

"Leave it to me," Irshi said, their form shifting rapidly as they searched for the right configuration to pass through the barrier.

"Be careful," Mami Wata warned as she watched them work, her hypnotic eyes filled with concern.

Anastasia clenched her fists, watching helplessly as her plan teetered on the brink of collapse. But she couldn't afford to doubt herself now – not when so much was at stake. She had to believe in her abilities, in her team, and in their shared determination to save Detroit from the darkness threatening to consume it.

"Got it," Irshi finally announced, having found the right shape to slip past the barrier. "Let's go!"

As the team crossed the threshold into the club, bracing themselves for the battle ahead, a sinister laugh echoed through the building, chilling Anastasia to her very core.

"Welcome, Anastasia Asma'u," Bilquis purred, her voice dripping with malice. "I've been expecting you."

The chapter ended, leaving the reader on the edge of their seat, eager to see how Anastasia and her team would face this new challenge and the darkness that awaited them within.

Bilquis's sinister laughter still echoed in Anastasia's ears as she and her team stood within the dark, pulsating heart of the supernatural club. The air was thick with an oppressive energy that seemed to seep into their very bones. Around them, distorted reflections of their faces stared back from the mirrored walls, each twisted visage a haunting reminder of the duality they all carried within themselves.

"Keep your guard up," Anastasia commanded, her voice steady despite the tremor of fear coursing through her veins. "We don't know what she has planned for us."

"Whatever it is, we'll face it together," Detective Ayo vowed, his eyes scanning their surroundings with a steely determination that belied the uncertainty churning inside him.

"Indeed," Sakhr intoned solemnly. "United, we are strong."

"Speak for yourself," Amir muttered under his breath, fidgeting nervously as he hovered nearby. "I'd rather be anywhere but here right now."

"Focus," Artiya'il admonished gently. "Now is not the time for distractions."

As they crept deeper into the club, every step weighed down by the heavy atmosphere, Anastasia couldn't help but feel an icy dread tightening around her heart. The darkness seemed to whisper terrible secrets into her ear, secrets that threatened to drown her in despair.

But she couldn't afford to give in to her fear. Not when so much was at stake – not just for her, but for everyone who called Detroit home. She had to stay strong, for all of them.

"Over there," Mami Wata hissed suddenly, pointing toward a shadowy corner where the flickering lights didn't quite reach. "Something's not right."

"Be ready for anything," Anastasia instructed, her fingers gripping her weapon tightly as adrenaline surged through her.

As they approached the area, the darkness seemed to shift and coalesce, forming a terrifying figure with sharp, gleaming eyes that bore into Anastasia's very soul. Her heart hammered against her ribs, but she refused to back down.

"Show yourself!" she demanded, her voice ringing out with all the authority she could muster.

"Very well," the figure replied, stepping from the shadows with a predatory grace. It was Harut, his dark eyes gleaming with a dangerous amusement as he sized up the group before him. "I must say, I didn't expect you to make it this far."

"Save your taunts for someone who cares," Anastasia spat, her anger momentarily overpowering her fear. "Where's Bilquis? What have you done with the Shadow Amulet?"

"Ah, dear Anastasia," Harut drawled, his lips curling into a wicked smile. "So eager to jump to conclusions. But if it's answers you want... I suppose I can oblige."

"Enough of this," Zuhra snapped, her celestial radiance casting eerie shadows on the walls around them. "Tell us what we need to know, or face the consequences."

"Fine," Harut sighed, feigning disappointment. "Bilquis awaits you in her inner sanctum, where she has already begun harnessing the power of the Shadow Amulet. The longer she remains unopposed, the more destruction she will unleash upon this city."

"Then we have no time to waste," Anastasia declared, her resolve hardening like steel. "Let's go."

"Wait," Irshi cautioned, their ever-changing form shifting uneasily. "There may be traps or enchantments designed to thwart us. We should proceed with caution."

"Agreed," Artiya'il nodded solemnly. "The stakes are too high to risk making a misstep now."

"Right," Anastasia agreed, her gaze never leaving Harut's smirking visage. "But remember – every second we delay, the danger grows greater. We must act swiftly and decisively if we hope to save Detroit from the darkness that threatens to engulf it."

"Lead the way, Anastasia Asma'u," Sakhr intoned, his voice filled with a quiet reverence. "We will follow you into battle, no matter what awaits us on the other side."

As Anastasia and her team braced themselves for the confrontation ahead, they knew that their greatest challenge still lay before them. But together, united by their shared determination to protect the city they loved, there was nothing they couldn't overcome.

"Let's do this," Anastasia whispered, her heart pounding in her chest as they stepped forward into the unknown.

Anastasia's pulse raced as she led her trusted allies through the labyrinthine streets of Detroit, the city's familiar hum providing a stark contrast to the turmoil brewing in her mind. The revelation of Bilquis's manipulation weighed heavily on her heart, and every step closer to the witch's lair seemed to intensify her discomfort.

"Remember, we have to act quickly," Anastasia whispered under her breath, her hands trembling slightly. "The Shadow Amulet is already in Bilquis's possession, and who knows what chaos it'll cause if we don't stop her."

Irshi, their form shifting hues like ink on water, nodded their agreement. "We understand, Anastasia. But the danger lies not only in the amulet itself but also in the trust we've lost. If Bilquis has deceived us, who else might be hiding something?"

"Focus," Artiya'il said, his wings folded tightly against his back. "Bilquis is our priority now. We can deal with the other uncertainties later."

As they neared their destination, the oppressive aura of the Shadow Amulet grew stronger, tendrils of darkness seeming to seep from every corner. It was clear that the artifact's power had begun to infuse itself into the very fabric of the city, blurring the line between the supernatural and human worlds.

"Any ideas on how to counteract the amulet's power?" Anastasia asked her companions, her tone dripping with worry.

"Perhaps we could seek the counsel of Harut and Marut," Sakhr suggested hesitantly. "They may know of a way to neutralize the amulet or at least contain its effects."

"Even if they do, can we really trust them?" Anastasia questioned, her eyes narrowing. "We need to be certain that they're truly on our side before involving them further."

"Let's try to retrieve the amulet first," Artiya'il interjected. "Then we can decide how best to handle it and who to involve. Time is of the essence."

"Agreed," Anastasia said, taking a deep breath to steady herself. "Let's go."

As they approached Bilquis's lair, hidden beneath the shimmering neon lights of her underground club, Anastasia felt a renewed sense of determination. She would do whatever it took to ensure Detroit's safety, even if it meant confronting someone she once considered a friend.

"Stay on your guard," Anastasia warned her allies as they slipped inside, the pulsating music barely muffling their cautious footsteps. "We don't know what awaits us in here."

"Lead the way, Anastasia," Irshi urged, their ethereal voice barely audible over the clamor. "We trust you."

With her companions' unwavering support at her back, Anastasia forged ahead into the dimly lit depths of the club. The weight of their responsibility bore down on her, but the fire of her resolve burned brighter than any fear or doubt that threatened to consume her.

"Let's end this," she murmured, steeling herself for the confrontation to come.

147

"Let's end this," she murmured, steeling herself for the confrontation to come.

Battle of Two Worlds

Anastasia sat on the floor of her dimly lit apartment, her legs folded beneath her and her hands resting on her knees. Her gaze lingered on the delicate patterns of the prayer rug before her, the intricate designs a testament to her faith. She could feel the weight of her responsibilities pressing down on her shoulders like an invisible burden, threatening to consume her spirit.

The shadows in the room seemed to whisper doubts into her mind, taunting her with her insecurities. Am I truly capable? Can I protect both worlds? Her thoughts swirled around her, darkening the already somber atmosphere.

"Enough," she murmured to herself, shaking off the tendrils of fear that sought to ensnare her heart. Taking a deep breath, she straightened her back and closed her eyes, focusing her thoughts on the divine.

Anastasia began the Dhikr, reciting the names of Allah in a soft, rhythmic cadence. "Ya Hayy, Ya Qayyum, Ya Rahman, Ya Rahim…" The words flowed through her, each syllable weaving a protective cocoon around her soul.

Her breaths slowed, synchronizing with the sacred verses, and she felt the tension in her body gradually dissipate. The whispers of doubt were silenced, replaced by the soothing hum of devotion that reverberated within her.

"Ya Alim, Ya Hakim, Ya Latif, Ya Wadud…" As she continued the Dhikr, Anastasia found solace and strength in the ritual. The presence of Allah enveloped her, a shelter from the storm of her conflicted emotions.

With each name, Anastasia felt her connection to the supernatural world grow stronger, as if the Dhikr was not only bridging the gap between her and the divine but also solidifying her bond to the hidden realm that she was destined to protect. Her faith served as an anchor, grounding her amidst the chaos that threatened to engulf her.

"Ya Fattah, Ya Ghafoor, Ya Tawwab, Ya Ra'oof..." The doubts and insecurities that had plagued her seemed to recede, pushed back by the simple act of remembering and invoking the divine presence. Anastasia felt a renewed sense of purpose and determination fill her being, empowering her to face whatever challenges lay ahead.

And in this moment of quiet devotion, she found not only solace but also the strength to embrace her newfound abilities and the responsibilities that came with them. She would forge her own path, guided by her faith and resolve, and she would protect both worlds with all the might and wisdom Allah had granted her.

Anastasia's fingers traced the beads of her tesbih, each one a reminder of the divine presence she sought to invoke. Her breath steadied as she whispered the names, her voice barely audible but resonant with power. "Ya Alim, Ya Hakim, Ya Latif..." She felt the warmth of each word suffuse her being, a balm for her troubled thoughts.

"Ya Wadud... Ya Fattah... Ya Ghafoor..." The repetition of these sacred names soothed her anxious heart, their syllables weaving an ethereal tapestry that enveloped her in tranquility. Her mind, previously a whirlwind of doubts and fears, began to settle like sand carried by the wind, finally finding reprieve.

The gentle click of the door resounded through the room, pulling Anastasia out of her meditative state. Detective Ayo stood in the doorway, his imposing figure momentarily filling the frame, tension etched across his features. The concern in his deep-set eyes was evident even before he spoke. "Anastasia, are you alright?"

She nodded, her hands still clutching the tesbih. "I am now, thanks to Dhikr," she said, offering him a tentative smile. He crossed the room to stand beside her, his presence a steadying force amidst the turmoil within her.

"Your distress reached me from afar," Ayo admitted, his gaze never leaving her face. "Our bond is growing stronger, it seems." The sincerity in his voice was unmistakable, and Anastasia couldn't help but feel grateful for the connection they shared.

"Thank you for coming," she murmured, grateful for the solace his mere presence offered. She could sense his unwavering support, even as his own connection to the supernatural world continued to surprise him.

"Of course," Ayo replied, his voice a soothing balm. "You do not have to face this alone, Anastasia."

As they stood together, their shared determination and faith in Islam a beacon of hope in the darkness, Anastasia's heart swelled with gratitude for her newfound ally. With Ayo by her side, she knew that whatever challenges lay ahead, they would confront them as one, united by their trust in the divine and their duty to protect both the human and supernatural worlds.

The flickering light from the candles cast dancing shadows on the walls of Anastasia's apartment, their warmth a stark contrast to the chill that had settled in her bones. Anastasia hesitated, feeling an unfamiliar vulnerability gnawing at her insides. Detective Ayo stood beside her, his mere presence a solid anchor in the stormy sea of her emotions.

"Detective Ayo," she began, her voice barely above a whisper, "I need to tell you something." She paused, wondering if he would dismiss her fears as the ramblings of a novice, but his steady gaze encouraged her to continue.

"Ever since I learned about my asasiyyin lineage and my abilities, I've felt like I'm drowning in expectations. I feel like I have this immense power within me, but at the same time, I can't help but wonder if I'm truly capable of wielding it."

Ayo listened intently, the empathy in his eyes telling her that he understood her struggle. He offered her a reassuring smile, his deep voice wrapping around her like a warm blanket. "Anastasia, it's normal to be afraid. Just because you possess power, doesn't mean you're expected to control it flawlessly from the start."

"Still," she continued, her doubts spilling forth like water breaking a dam,

"I fear that I'll fail to protect those I care about, both human and supernatural. It's a crushing responsibility, and I don't know if I'm strong enough to carry it."

"Strength isn't just about physical power or even magical abilities, Anastasia," Ayo said gently, his words underscored by the wisdom of his own experiences. "True strength is found in our ability to adapt, to learn, and most importantly, to rely on the support of those around us."

"Trust is not easily given, especially in a world where the supernatural and human realms collide," Anastasia admitted, her eyes moist with unshed tears. "But I trust you, Detective Ayo, more than I ever thought possible."

"Your trust means more to me than you know," Ayo said, his voice thick with emotion. "And I promise to do everything in my power to support you in this journey. Together, we'll face whatever challenges come our way."

Anastasia breathed in deeply, feeling as though an immense weight had been lifted from her shoulders. She glanced at the tesbih beads still clutched in her hand, their smooth surface a tangible reminder of the strength she drew from her faith.

"Thank you, Ayo," she whispered, daring to hope that perhaps, with his support, she could find the courage to embrace the responsibilities that lay ahead. "For being here, for believing in me, and for accepting the reality of the supernatural world that now entwines us both."

"Of course," he replied softly, his eyes filled with sincerity, "I believe in the power of faith, and I have faith in you, Anastasia."

In the dim glow of the candles, they stood together, united by their shared beliefs and their resolve to protect both the human and supernatural worlds. The burdens that had once seemed insurmountable now appeared lighter, as if borne by two sets of shoulders instead of one. In that quiet moment, Anastasia knew that no matter what lay ahead, they would face it together, their bond forged by trust and a shared conviction in something greater than themselves.

Anastasia's fingers slid smoothly over the tesbih beads, her voice lilting in a soothing chant as she recited the ninety-nine divine names of Allah. Her breaths deepened and slowed with each repetition, creating a rhythmic cadence that resonated within her very being. The doubts and insecurities that had plagued her only moments before began to recede, replaced by an inner calm that radiated outwards like ripples on a still pond.

"Ya Salaam… Ya Mumin… Ya Hayy…"

The words flowed together, taking on a life of their own as they merged with Anastasia's steadily beating heart. She felt her connection to the supernatural world around her grow stronger, pulse by pulse, as if the very essence of her asasiyyin lineage was awakening within her.

"Ya Qayyum… Ya Quddus… Ya Azeez…"

A sudden surge of energy coursed through her body, igniting her senses and sharpening her mind. It was as if she could feel the air around her, each individual molecule vibrating with unseen power. Her fingertips tingled where they touched the beads, and she sensed the energies swirling within them, a testament to the countless prayers and devotions they had borne witness to.

"Ya Jabbar… Ya Mutakabbir… Ya Khaliq…"

Her surroundings came into razor-sharp focus, the colors and textures of her apartment appearing more vivid than ever before. She could hear the faint hum of electricity from the streetlights outside, the distant murmur of conversation from her neighbors, even the flutter of a moth's wings as it danced around a flame.

"Ya Bari… Ya Musawwir… Ya Ghaffar…"

Anastasia's heart swelled with gratitude for this newfound clarity, understanding that her faith and devotion had unlocked something within her—something that had always been there, waiting to be discovered. She realized that by embracing her asasiyyin heritage and placing her trust in Allah, she could tap into a wellspring of power beyond anything she had ever imagined. And with this power came an even deeper sense of responsibility and purpose.

"Ya Ghafur… Ya Rahim… Ya Malik…"

As the final name left her lips, Anastasia opened her eyes, their dark depths now shimmering with newfound strength and resolve. She turned to Detective Ayo, who had been watching her transformation with a mixture of awe and wonderment.

"Did you feel it, Ayo?" she asked breathlessly, excitement shining in her eyes. "The energy, the connection—this is what I've been searching for."

Ayo nodded solemnly, his deep-set eyes reflecting the magnitude of her discovery. "I felt it too, Anastasia. Your faith and dedication have unlocked something truly powerful within you, something that will change not only your life but the lives of those around you."

Anastasia's chest swelled with pride and determination, knowing that her journey had only just begun. The path ahead would undoubtedly be fraught with danger and uncertainty, but she was no longer alone in her quest to protect both the human and supernatural worlds. With her unwavering faith and the support of her allies, she was ready to embrace her destiny as an asasiyyin, a guardian of the balance between realms.

"Alhamdulillah," she whispered, her voice filled with gratitude and conviction, "I am ready to face whatever lies ahead."

Anastasia and Detective Ayo stood side by side, their silhouettes framed against the setting sun that cast a warm golden hue throughout the room. The air was charged with determination, a shared resolve that seemed to speak volumes between them without the need for words.

"Thank you, Ayo," Anastasia said softly, her voice thick with gratitude. "I couldn't have come this far without your unwavering support."

Ayo's deep-set eyes met hers, and he gave her a reassuring smile. "We're in this together, Anastasia. No matter what challenges we face, I'll be by your side."

The room seemed to vibrate with their combined energy and conviction, as if the very fabric of reality was acknowledging their pledge. Their unspoken understanding was palpable; they were bound not only by their faith but also by their devotion to protecting both the human and supernatural worlds.

Taking a step closer, Anastasia reached out and placed her hand upon Ayo's forearm, feeling the steady rhythm of his pulse beneath her fingertips. His muscular build and imposing height provided reassurance and comfort, a steadfast pillar in the whirlwind of uncertainty that had become her life.

"Your belief in me, despite your initial skepticism, means more than I can express," she confessed, her dark eyes locked onto his. "Together, we'll navigate the dangers ahead and ensure the balance between realms remains intact."

Detective Ayo nodded, his expression solemn yet brimming with trust. "You've shown me that there is more to this world than I ever imagined, and I'm ready to embrace it as long as we stand side by side."

Anastasia smiled at him, her heart swelling with appreciation and new-found confidence in her abilities. She could feel the power coursing through her veins, an ever-present reminder of the legacy she was now a part of. With Ayo by her side and her faith as her guide, she knew they were ready to face whatever challenges lay ahead.

"Alhamdulillah," Anastasia whispered, her voice filled with conviction. "Together, we will protect both worlds."

A silence enveloped the room as Anastasia and Detective Ayo stood side by side, their gazes fixed on the distant horizon beyond the apartment window. The setting sun painted the sky in hues of orange and pink, casting a warm glow upon their faces. In this quiet moment, shared reflections created an unspoken bond between them, forged in faith and trust.

"Sometimes, I still find it hard to believe all that has happened," Ayo admitted softly, his deep voice barely above a whisper. "But seeing you embrace your powers, witnessing your unwavering determination… It fills me with hope."

Anastasia turned her gaze towards him, her eyes shimmering with gratitude and understanding. She reached for his hand, their fingers intertwining as they stood together, united by both their physical connection and their spiritual ties. "Your support has given me the strength to face my fears, Ayo. I can't imagine walking this path without you."

In response, Ayo gave her hand a gentle squeeze, his eyes conveying his commitment to their cause. They stood there, hands clasped, as the final rays of sunlight dipped below the horizon. It felt as though the world was holding its breath, waiting for them to take up arms against the darkness that threatened to consume both realms.

"Tomorrow, we begin," Anastasia murmured, her voice filled with resolute determination. "We'll face whatever comes our way, knowing that Allah is guiding our steps and that we have each other's back."

"Indeed," Ayo agreed, his voice steady and unwavering. "Together, we are stronger than any force we may encounter."

As the first stars began to flicker in the twilight sky, Anastasia allowed herself to fully embrace the responsibilities that came with her newfound powers. She sensed a shift within herself, a deepening connection to the supernatural world and the ability to draw strength from the spiritual realm.

"Let's make a promise," Anastasia proposed, her voice filled with conviction. "No matter what lies ahead, we will never lose sight of who we are and what we stand for. Our faith will remain our beacon, guiding us through the darkest of nights."

"Agreed," Ayo nodded solemnly, his grip on her hand tightening with determination.

As they stood together, bathed in the last fading light of day, their bond grew stronger, fortified by shared purpose and unwavering trust. Though the challenges that awaited them were vast and uncertain, Anastasia knew that, with Ayo by her side, she was ready to face whatever lay ahead. With renewed hope and determination burning in their hearts, Anastasia and Detective Ayo prepared to step into the unknown, ready to protect and defend both realms as guardians of the balance between worlds.

A City's Soul

Anastasia stood in the center of the abandoned warehouse, her breath visible in the cold air. The wind howled outside, seeping through the cracks in the walls and making her shiver. Her eyes were darting around the dimly lit room, trying to sense the presence of her allies.

"Detective Ayo!" she called out, her voice echoing through the empty space. "Harut! Irshi!"

One by one, they emerged from the shadows. Detective Ayo's muscular frame was hunched, his deep-set eyes scanning their surroundings with an uneasy skepticism. Harut, the enigmatic fallen angel, glided into view, his unreadable dark eyes seeming to hold secrets beyond comprehension. And there was Irshi, a shape-shifting being whose appearance was constantly changing, their mercurial temperament making them as unpredictable as the wind.

"Everyone is here," Anastasia said, her voice firm but filled with tension. "We must prepare for the upcoming confrontation. The fate of Detroit hangs in the balance."

"Are you certain about this?" asked Ayo, his voice betraying his lingering disbelief in the supernatural world he had been thrust into.

"More certain than I've ever been," Anastasia replied. "In order to protect the city we love, we have to defeat those who threaten it."

Ayo nodded tersely, looking to Harut and Irshi for support. They exchanged knowing glances before turning their attention back to Anastasia.

"Then let us begin our preparations," Harut said, his voice calm yet foreboding.

Anastasia took a deep breath and turned towards the makeshift basin of water, feeling the weight of responsibility on her shoulders. She knew that in order to face what lay ahead, she would need strength and guidance from a higher power. With a determined resolve, she began the process of making Wudu.

She washed her hands three times, cupping the cold water in her palms and feeling it cleanse her skin. As she rinsed her face, she whispered a prayer for guidance, her words barely audible above the howling wind. She continued with her arms, head, and feet, each time reciting another verse of her prayer, seeking solace in the familiar ritual.

As she finished, she raised her hands to the heavens and closed her eyes. In that moment, the chaos of the world around her seemed to quiet, replaced by a sense of connection to a power greater than herself. In her heart, she knew that she had been chosen for this battle, and that she would not be alone in facing the darkness.

"Please guide us through this fight," she murmured, her voice filled with emotion. "Help us restore balance and protect the city we love."

Her allies watched her in silence, their expressions a mix of awe and respect. They understood the magnitude of the task ahead, and the importance of Anastasia's connection to her faith.

"Let's get ready," Anastasia said finally, opening her eyes and meeting the gaze of her comrades. "Together, we will defeat Azazil, Bilquis, and Mami Wata. For Detroit!"

Their voices rang out together, a chorus of determination and hope as they faced the dark uncertainty of the battle to come.

From the shadows, a figure emerged, taking form before Anastasia and her allies. It was Artiya'il, the celestial messenger, his ethereal presence radiating wisdom and kindness. His eyes gleamed with a divine light as he spoke, his voice soothing yet authoritative.

"Children of Earth, you face great peril, but know that you are not alone," he began. "Anastasia, daughter of faith, your devotion has granted you a protective force shield from the Almighty. With this shield, no harm shall come to you, so long as your heart remains pure and your purpose true."

Anastasia's eyes widened, feeling a warmth around her body, invisible yet tangible. She understood the weight of this gift and the responsibility it entailed.

"Thank you, Artiya'il," she whispered, her voice full of gratitude and determination.

"The battle is upon us," Detective Ayo said, his deep-set eyes scanning the dark horizon. "We must stand united against these forces threatening our world."

"Agreed," Harut added, his enigmatic gaze never leaving Anastasia. "Together, we will prevail."

As they prepared to face their enemies, Anastasia felt a surge of power within her. She took a deep breath, knowing that the time had come to confront Azazil, Bilquis, and Mami Wata.

The sky darkened, and thunder rumbled overhead as the supernatural forces descended upon them. They fought back, their unique abilities shining through in the chaos of battle.

"Stay close!" Anastasia shouted, her blade slicing through the air as she fended off demonic creatures. Her shield shimmered around her, deflecting attacks, guided by her unwavering faith and pure heart.

"Got your back, Anastasia!" Detective Ayo called out, his fists connecting with fierce precision, sending were-creatures reeling. His skepticism had long vanished, replaced by an unshakable resolve to protect his city.

"Watch out!" Harut warned, slashing through a group of malevolent spirits with his celestial sword. His fallen angel status was evident in his ferocity and cunning, yet there was a hint of redemption in his eyes as he fought alongside Anastasia.

The Irshi shape-shifted rapidly, their forms adapting to counter various threats. One moment they were a fierce lion, the next a swift falcon, always unpredictable and lethal.

Anastasia's heart raced, her mind focused on the mission at hand. They were outnumbered and facing great danger, but she knew that they could not afford to fail. The balance between the human and supernatural worlds hung in the balance, and she was determined to restore it.

"Stay strong!" she called out to her allies, her voice rising above the din of battle. "We can do this!"

Her blade flashed, her shield glowed, and her faith remained steadfast as she fought for the city she loved and the people she sought to protect. With every strike, every parry, Anastasia felt the power of her connection to a higher purpose, guiding her through the perilous confrontation.

In the midst of the chaotic battle, Anastasia found a brief moment of respite. The protective force shield surrounding her shimmered like an ethereal veil, deflecting curses and attacks with ease. For a fleeting instant, she felt invincible.

"Alhamdulillah," she whispered, her heart swelling with gratitude for the aid bestowed upon her.

Her gaze swept across the battlefield, taking in the struggles of her allies. Ayo's steadfast determination wavered under the relentless assault of Azazil's hellfire; Harut's celestial sword clashed against Bilquis's dark sorcery, sparks of divine and arcane energies illuminating their desperate dance; and the Irshi, though fierce and adaptable, were visibly tiring as they tried to evade Mami Wata's watery tendrils.

"Enough!" Anastasia roared, her voice carrying across the battlefield. "We must stand united!"

"Fall back!" she ordered, slicing through an attacking creature with a swift, decisive stroke. "Form the crescent moon and star formation!"

Her allies heard her command and swiftly regrouped. Ayo took his position at one end of the crescent, while Harut marked the other. The Irshi formed the curve between them, their shapes shifting rapidly, poised for any attack. In the center, Anastasia stood as the guiding star, her blade raised and shield held firm.

"Follow my lead!" she instructed, her mind racing with strategy. "Together, we can defeat them!"

As if sensing their renewed vigor, Azazil, Bilquis, and Mami Wata redoubled their efforts, unleashing a maelstrom of dark power. Yet, the crescent moon and star formation held strong, each ally covering the others' weaknesses, their combined might repelling the fearsome trio's onslaught.

"Channel your faith into your strikes!" Anastasia called out, her voice unwavering as she cut down a vengeful spirit. "Believe in our victory!"

"Your faith is contagious, Anastasia!" Ayo shouted back, his fists glowing with renewed energy, striking down a demonic assailant. "We won't let you down!"

Harut and the Irshi echoed their agreement, their resolve solidifying under Anastasia's leadership. They fought as one, each movement in harmony with the others, an unstoppable force united by their shared purpose.

The tide of battle began to turn, the once-overwhelming odds now more manageable. Anastasia could feel the momentum shifting in their favor, and though she knew there was still much to be done, hope bloomed within her heart like a desert flower after a rare rain.

In the midst of their fierce battle, Anastasia scanned the battlefield, taking in the crescent moon formation her allies had adopted at her command. Despite their unwavering faith and determination, she could see the weariness in their movements as they fought off Azazil, Bilquis, and Mami Wata's minions. With a sudden flash of inspiration, she called out to her comrades.

"Listen closely, everyone!" Anastasia shouted above the chaos. "We must make use of the force shield granted to us by our faith! Each of you take turns stepping into the center of the formation—the star—and perform Wudu!"

"Are you certain this will work?" Harut asked skeptically, his sword slicing through an enemy with a burst of light.

"Trust me," Anastasia responded firmly, her eyes flashing with conviction. "The power of our faith will protect us!"

One by one, Anastasia's allies stepped into the star's center and made Wudu, their faces a mixture of concentration and reverence as they cleansed themselves with water summoned from Amir, the genie. As each completed the ritual, a shimmering barrier enveloped them, much like the one that had protected Anastasia earlier.

"By the grace of the Almighty, it works!" Detective Ayo exclaimed as he finished his own Wudu, his fists now glowing even brighter as they smashed through the darkness that threatened to engulf them.

Anastasia watched in awe as her allies became increasingly more powerful and untouchable, their movements fluid and precise. The once formidable foes that had overwhelmed them now struggled to land a single blow, their attacks thwarted by the divine shield.

"Amazing, Anastasia!" Irshi cried out, their form shifting rapidly between animal and human as they tore through an onslaught of demonic creatures. "Your faith has given us the strength we need to prevail!"

"Let this be a lesson to us all," Anastasia thought, her heart swelling with pride and gratitude. "Our faith can be our greatest weapon when we truly believe in its power."

With renewed vigor, the group pressed on, their crescent moon and star formation cutting through the horde like a divine blade. Azazil, Bilquis, and Mami Wata could only look on in horror as their forces crumbled beneath the unyielding might of Anastasia and her allies, united and empowered by the strength of their shared faith.

Anastasia's gaze narrowed, her focus shifting from the carnage around them to the three imposing figures that had orchestrated this chaos: Azazil, Bilquis, and Mami Wata. Clenching her fists, she felt a surge of determination course through her veins, fueled by her unwavering faith.

"Enough!" Anastasia shouted, her voice carrying above the din of battle. "This ends now! We will restore balance to our world, and it begins with your defeat!"

Her words seemed to echo through the air, catching the attention of the formidable trio. They exchanged dark glances before turning their full attention toward her, the energy in the air palpable as they prepared for the inevitable confrontation.

"Come on, then," Bilquis taunted, her melodious voice dripping with malice. "Show us what you've got, little girl."

"Let us see if your faith can save you now," Mami Wata hissed, her hypnotic eyes gleaming with malicious intent.

"Be careful what you wish for," Anastasia retorted, steeling herself for the battle ahead.

With a roar, she launched herself at her adversaries, her movements swift and precise. Her hands were ablaze with divine light, each strike aimed to cripple and disarm. Azazil, Bilquis, and Mami Wata responded in kind, their collective power creating a maelstrom of supernatural energy that threatened to consume everything in its path.

"Your hubris will be your downfall!" Azazil sneered, his sinister form weaving through the onslaught of Anastasia's attacks.

"Angels have fallen," Anastasia thought, "and so shall demons."

"Is that all you have?" Bilquis taunted, as she deflected a blow from Anastasia's glowing fist. "You'll need more than faith to best me."

"Faith is the foundation," Anastasia replied, dodging a vicious swipe from Mami Wata's razor-sharp claws. "But it's not all I have."

As if on cue, Harut appeared at her side, his celestial form radiating divine power. Together, they launched a barrage of attacks at their foes, forcing them back with every blow.

"Your cause is lost!" Anastasia cried out to her enemies, her voice filled with conviction. "The balance will be restored!"

"Never underestimate the strength of humanity," Harut added, his own words carrying an air of authority that seemed to bolster Anastasia's resolve even further.

Azazil, Bilquis, and Mami Wata faltered, their once-confident expressions now marred by doubt and fear. They exchanged uneasy glances, realizing that the tide had turned against them.

"Your time has come," Anastasia declared, her eyes blazing with divine light. "Surrender, or face the consequences."

"Know this," she thought, as she prepared for one final push. "It was not my faith alone that brought you low. It was our combined strength—our unwavering belief in each other, and in the power of righteousness—that has sealed your fate. Our world shall be free of your darkness, and balance will be restored."

With a battle cry that echoed through the heavens, Anastasia led her allies in a final charge, their hearts filled with hope and determination as they fought to vanquish the darkness that threatened their world.

Anastasia, her determination unwavering, led her allies through the chaotic battleground. As they engaged in fierce combat against the forces of darkness, she couldn't help but notice a subtle shift in the tide of the battle. Detective Ayo, Harut, and the Irshi, now protected by the force shield and empowered by Wudu, began to regain their strength.

"Stand firm, my friends!" Anastasia called out as she dodged a vicious strike from Azazil. "We are stronger together. Allow the divine protection to guide you!"

The Irshi, their eyes glowing with renewed vigor, unleashed torrents of elemental magic upon their enemies. Fire and lightning danced alongside gusts of wind, while the very earth trembled beneath the onslaught. In response, Harut brandished his celestial sword, its gleaming blade slicing through the air as he launched devastating attacks at Bilquis and Mami Wata.

"Your reign of terror ends today," Detective Ayo shouted, his voice filled with conviction as he expertly fired enchanted bullets, each one striking true against the dark forces.

"Unleash your full potential! Show them the power of unity and faith!" Anastasia commanded, her heart swelling with pride as she witnessed her allies' relentless assault.

"Righteousness shall prevail!" Harut roared, his booming voice resonating across the battlefield.

"Let's end this, once and for all," Anastasia thought, her mind racing with strategy and anticipation. The time had come for a coordinated attack, one that would demonstrate the full extent of their combined abilities.

"Harut, engage Azazil!" she ordered, her voice carrying over the din of battle. "Ayo, focus on Mami Wata! Irshi, keep Bilquis occupied!"

"Understood!" they replied in unison, their voices resolute and determined.

As they moved into position, Anastasia channeled her newfound power, focusing her divine energy into a brilliant beam of light that pierced the sky. Azazil hissed in pain as Harut's celestial blade found its mark, while Mami Wata recoiled from Detective Ayo's relentless barrage of enchanted bullets.

"Feel the wrath of our combined might!" Anastasia thought, a fierce smile playing on her lips as she unleashed a torrent of divine energy upon Bilquis. The witch stumbled back, weakened by the onslaught of magic from both Anastasia and the Irshi.

"Your defeat is at hand," Anastasia whispered, her voice a promise of retribution.

"Your cause is doomed," Harut added, driving Azazil back with another powerful swing of his sword.

"Your darkness will be cleansed from this world," Detective Ayo vowed, his eyes locked on Mami Wata, who writhed under the weight of his unrelenting assault.

As Anastasia watched her allies press their advantage, she knew that victory was within their grasp. Together, they would restore balance to the human and supernatural worlds, vanquishing the forces of evil that sought to plunge them into chaos.

In the heat of battle, Anastasia could sense the tide turning. Her allies' renewed strength coursed through her like a surge of electricity, invigorating her with renewed determination. Azazil, Bilquis, and Mami Wata were formidable, but they had underestimated the power of unity and faith.

"Harut, now!" Anastasia shouted, her voice thundering above the cacophony of combat. The angel's celestial blade sliced through the air, its divine light searing into Azazil. The demon shrieked in agony as his dark essence began to dissipate.

"Your reign of torment ends here," Harut declared, his voice resonating with divine authority. Azazil's form flickered and waned until he vanished, consumed by the light of Harut's blade.

"Detective Ayo, aim for Mami Wata's heart!" Anastasia ordered, her gaze fixed on the water spirit thrashing under the relentless assault of enchanted bullets.

"Got it!" Ayo replied, his voice steady despite the intensity of the moment. He took careful aim and fired, the bullet imbued with his unwavering resolve. The shot pierced Mami Wata's chest, and her hypnotic eyes widened in shock as her watery form shattered into a thousand droplets, evaporating into the air.

"Your treachery has been washed away," Ayo murmured, his eyes reflecting the weight of his actions.

"Irshi, together we'll finish Bilquis!" Anastasia called to the enigmatic Irshi, who nodded in silent agreement. They moved in unison, their combined magical force converging on the weakened witch.

"Your ambition has brought you ruin," Anastasia whispered, her words laced with finality. With a final surge of energy, she and the Irshi struck Bilquis down, her body crumbling to ash that was swept away by the wind.

As the last remnants of their enemies faded, an eerie silence fell over the battlefield. The adrenaline that had fueled Anastasia and her allies began to dissipate, replaced by a heavy exhaustion. They gathered together, leaning on each other for support as they surveyed the devastation around them.

"Is everyone alright?" Anastasia asked, her eyes scanning her friends for injuries as she fought to catch her breath.

"We're alive, thanks to you," Ayo replied, wincing as he touched a bruise on his face. "Your plan worked perfectly, Anastasia."

"Indeed," Harut agreed, his celestial form flickering slightly, weakened from the intense battle. "You have proven yourself to be a true leader and protector of both worlds."

"Thank you," Anastasia murmured, her heart swelling with gratitude and relief. "But we couldn't have done it without each other."

As the group tended to their wounds, the sun broke through the clouds, casting golden rays upon their weary faces. In that moment, Anastasia knew that they were more than just a collection of individuals; they were a united force, bound by their commitment to protect the world from darkness.

"Let's go home," Anastasia said softly, her voice tinged with both weariness and hope. Together, they turned their backs on the ravaged battlefield, their steps resolute as they prepared to heal the scars left by the conflict and build a brighter future for Detroit.

Anastasia stared out at the city skyline, the setting sun casting long shadows across the broken streets. The once-thriving heart of Detroit was now a battleground littered with the remnants of their struggle against Azazil,

Bilquis, and Mami Wata. The city's buildings stood tall and proud, but bore wounds from the conflict that needed healing.

"Look at what we've accomplished," Ayo said softly, joining Anastasia as she gazed out at the city. "We saved countless lives today."

Anastasia nodded, her dark eyes filled with determination. "But there is still much to be done. We need to help rebuild this city and ensure that its people are safe from any future threats."

"Agreed," Harut chimed in, his celestial form still flickering but regaining strength. "Now that we have vanquished our enemies, it is time for us to restore balance and peace to both worlds."

Anastasia turned to face her allies, her heart swelling with pride and gratitude. She could see the exhaustion etched on their faces, but also the resolve that burned within them. They had come together as strangers, brought by fate and circumstance, but now they were united as one formidable force.

"Everyone, listen up," Anastasia called out, her voice steady and strong. "Our victory today has shown me that we are capable of great things when we stand together. But our work is far from over."

"Indeed," Amir agreed, his impish grin returning to his face as he floated by her side. "It is not enough just to defeat our enemies. We must also heal the wounds they have inflicted upon this world."

"Let us start by helping those who have been affected by this battle," Zuhra suggested, her radiant presence filling the group with warmth and hope. "There are many who have been displaced or injured, and they will need our assistance in the days to come."

"Then let's get to work," Anastasia declared, her eyes brimming with determination. "Together, we can bring peace and hope back to this city."

Her allies nodded in agreement, their hearts filled with renewed purpose. They knew that the road ahead would be long and challenging, but they had faced darkness before and emerged victorious. With Anastasia's leadership and their combined strength, they were ready to face whatever challenges lay ahead.

As the sun dipped below the horizon, casting the city in a warm, golden glow, Anastasia and her allies set out on their mission to restore Detroit. Hand in hand, they walked through the shattered streets, their spirits buoyed by the knowledge that together, they could heal the wounds of the past and forge a brighter future for all.

Claiming The Heritage

The sky above the battlefield was an angry swirl of black and indigo, lit only by the jagged streaks of lightning that tore through the heavens. Thunder roared as if heralding the end of days, echoing across the ravaged landscape like a war drum. Amidst the chaos stood Anastasia, her dark eyes gleaming with resolve, her hands ablaze with divine power. The air around her crackled with energy, a counterpoint to the storm raging overhead.

Facing her were the forces of Azazil and Mami Wata, their grotesque forms leering out of the swirling mist that clung to the ground. Their unearthly cries pierced the night, drowning out the wails of the wounded and dying. At the head of this unholy legion stood Mami Wata herself, her hypnotic eyes locked on Anastasia, her captivating smile belying the deadly intent in her fluid movements.

"Your struggle is futile, child!" Mami Wata called out, her melodic voice barely audible above the din of the battle. "You cannot hope to stand against us!"

Anastasia's lips curved into a defiant smile as she raised her hands high, unleashing a torrent of searing light towards her enemies. "Watch me," she whispered fiercely.

The divine power surged forth, enveloping the monstrous horde in its purifying embrace. Screams of agony tore from their throats as they were consumed by the heavenly blaze, their twisted bodies falling to ash upon the charred earth. Through the haze of smoke and fire, Anastasia could see Mami Wata falter, her enchanting visage replaced by one of frustration and fury.

"Enough!" the water spirit hissed, lashing out with tendrils of liquid darkness that snaked through the carnage towards Anastasia.

"Return from whence you came!" Anastasia cried, her voice echoing with the weight of divine authority. With a sweeping gesture, she banished the sinister tendrils back towards their master, watching as Mami Wata was forced to retreat before her onslaught.

The remaining minions of Azazil and Mami Wata found themselves scattered and disoriented, their combined strength no match for the righteous fury of the young warrior. Some were captured by Anastasia's allies, bound and held for judgment, while others were driven back into the shadows from which they had emerged. The battlefield grew quiet, save for the ragged breaths of the weary combatants and the distant rumble of retreating thunder.

Anastasia surveyed the scene, her heart swelling with pride at the sight of her vanquished foes. She knew that the road ahead would be long and fraught with danger, but this victory filled her with hope – a hope that balance could be restored and peace brought back to both the human and supernatural worlds. Her divine powers still humming in her veins, Anastasia stood tall and resolute, ready to face whatever challenges lay ahead.

Amidst the settling dust and debris, Anastasia's eyes darted across the battlefield, searching urgently for a familiar face. The cries of the retreating forces of Azazil and Mami Wata provided a chaotic backdrop to her frantic search. A sudden flash of movement caught her attention - a figure emerging from the smoke, barely visible against the backdrop of destruction.

"Is that…?" Anastasia's heart hammered in her chest as she recognized the enigmatic presence of Bilquis. Her relief was tempered with concern, and she sprinted towards her friend, her divine powers momentarily forgotten. Anastasia had fought alongside many allies during the battle, but it was Bilquis who had been by her side throughout it all, aiding her in her quest to restore balance.

"Watch out!" an ally shouted behind her, but Anastasia didn't hesitate. She reached Bilquis, who looked battered and weary but still possessed that commanding aura. The chaos around them seemed to fade into the background as Anastasia threw her arms around the woman, enveloping her in a desperate embrace.

"Are you alright?" she whispered urgently, her voice trembling with emotion. "Did any of my actions harm you?"

Bilquis leaned into the embrace, her breathing labored. "I'm fine, Anastasia," she assured her, though the strain in her voice betrayed her exhaustion. "Your powers protected us both."

Anastasia pulled back slightly, her gaze locked on Bilquis' captivating eyes. A million unspoken thoughts swirled between them, their connection deeper than words could express. In that moment, the weight of the battle seemed to lift from their shoulders, replaced by a shared sense of triumph and relief.

"Thank God," Anastasia breathed, allowing herself a small smile. She knew full well that the victory they had achieved today would have ripple effects throughout the supernatural community. The respect and understanding that had been forged on this battlefield would be crucial in maintaining peace between the human and supernatural worlds.

But for now, she allowed herself to revel in the simple joy of having Bilquis by her side – a trusted friend and ally who had risked everything for the cause they both believed in. Together, they turned their attention back to the battlefield as the last remnants of their enemies retreated or were captured, ready to face whatever the future held.

A sudden hush fell over the battlefield as Anastasia stepped back from Bilquis, her hands still gripping the other woman's arms protectively. The storm of chaos that had raged only moments before seemed to recede like a tide, leaving behind an eerie silence in its wake.

"Listen to me," Anastasia called out, her voice carrying across the desolate landscape. Every eye turned towards her, drawn by the authority and strength that radiated from her very being. "There is something you all must know about Bilquis."

The assembled warriors leaned in closer, their expressions a mixture of curiosity and suspicion. It was well known that the enigmatic leader of Detroit's underground supernatural club had been playing both sides of the conflict, but none had suspected the true extent of her duplicity.

"Throughout this struggle, Bilquis has been working covertly to undermine Azazil and Mami Wata from within," Anastasia revealed, her voice tinged with admiration for the courage and cunning displayed by her ally. Murmurs of astonishment rippled through the crowd, mingling with the whispers of the wind that danced around them.

"Her actions were guided by my strategy," Anastasia continued, stepping closer to Bilquis, who stood taller at her side, "a strategy informed by the wisdom of the Holy Quran, Surah 9 verse 5: When preparing for war use every stratagem of war.' So I use it, we battle them from the inside and the outside!"

She paused, allowing the words to sink in, her eyes scanning the faces of those gathered before her. "This passage teaches us the importance of striking decisively against our enemies, but also reminds us of the need to maintain peace and balance in our world. By infiltrating the ranks of Azazil and Mami Wata, Bilquis was able to weaken their stronghold on our city and prevent even greater destruction."

Anastasia's chest heaved with the effort of her speech, her heart racing with a mixture of adrenaline and relief. She knew that the revelation of Bilquis' true role carried significant risk, but she also believed in the power of trust – both in the divine guidance of the Quran and in the strength of the bond she shared with her trusted ally.

"Today, we have struck a decisive blow against those who sought to bring chaos and darkness into our world," Anastasia concluded, her voice swelling with pride and conviction. "Together, we will continue to fight for peace, balance, and justice – guided by the wisdom of our faith and the courage of our hearts."

As the echoes of her words faded away, replaced once more by the quiet rustling of the wind, Anastasia turned to Bilquis, her eyes shining with gratitude and respect. The two women exchanged a silent nod, their unspoken understanding transcending the boundaries of language and experience. In that moment, standing amidst the ruins of a war-torn battlefield, they had never been more united – or more determined to forge a brighter future for their city and its people.

The hush that had fallen over the battlefield seemed to hang heavy in the air, as if every creature present held their breath in anticipation. Anastasia's allies slowly turned to one another, their expressions a mix of shock and awe. In the eyes of those who had fought alongside her, there was now something more than just admiration – it was reverence.

"By Allah," whispered Amina, one of Anastasia's closest companions, her voice trembling with emotion. "Her faith and courage know no bounds."

"Indeed," agreed Tariq, a seasoned warrior who had seen his fair share of battles. "To trust Bilquis so completely, even under such dire circumstances… it takes great wisdom and conviction."

As the reality of the revelation settled in, murmurs of agreement rippled through the ranks, each acknowledging the depth of Anastasia's vision and the strength of her leadership. It was clear to all that she had risked much by placing her trust in Bilquis, but her gamble had paid off, and the tide of battle had turned in their favor.

With renewed determination, Anastasia's allies turned their attention back to the scattered remnants of Azazil and Mami Wata's forces. The once-mighty army was now in disarray, their morale shattered by the sudden loss of their key support. Some creatures retreated into the shadows, desperate to escape the wrath of Anastasia and her warriors, while others surrendered or were captured, unable to continue fighting against the overwhelming force of righteousness.

"Push forward!" Anastasia commanded, her voice ringing out like a clarion call across the battlefield. "We must not let them regroup! Show them that they are no match for those who stand united in faith and purpose!"

As she spoke, her words seemed to echo within the minds of her allies, reinforcing their newfound trust in her leadership. They surged forward, cutting down the fleeing enemies and capturing those who surrendered, their movements swift and decisive. It was a sight to behold – a testament to the power of unity, faith, and unwavering conviction.

And as the last remnants of their foes were either driven away or captured, Anastasia could feel the relief radiating from her allies. They had achieved victory against all odds, and the knowledge that they had done so while guided by the wisdom of the Holy Quran only deepened their sense of accomplishment.

"Alhamdulillah," Anastasia murmured to herself, even as she scanned the battlefield for any remaining threats. "Thanks be to Allah for guiding us to this victory."

In her heart, she knew that the battle had been won not only through strength of arms but also through the power of trust and faith. And with each passing moment, the bond between her and her allies only grew stronger, solidifying their resolve to face whatever challenges lay ahead.

Anastasia stood amidst the battlefield, her chest heaving with each heavy breath she took. The adrenaline that had fueled her during the intense battle now receded, leaving in its wake a bone-deep weariness. Her allies, too, seemed to be feeling the impact of the ferocious conflict, their exhaustion evident in the way they slumped against one another or leaned on their weapons for support.

"Everyone, gather around!" Anastasia called out, her voice hoarse but still strong enough to carry across the field. "We must tend to our wounded and assess the situation."

As they congregated, she couldn't help but notice how some of her allies shot wary glances at Bilquis, their expressions a mixture of curiosity and uncertainty. She knew that trust would not come easily, especially after the revelation of Bilquis' double agent status. Yet Anastasia could also see the first signs of respect creeping into the eyes of those who had fought beside them.

"Will you help me?" Anastasia asked Bilquis softly, seeking her assistance in healing those who were injured.

"Of course," Bilquis replied without hesitation, her dark eyes momentarily softening.

Together, they moved among their comrades, using their divine powers to mend torn flesh and soothe aching bodies. With each act of kindness,

Anastasia saw the barriers between them and Bilquis slowly dissolving, as their shared struggle began to foster a sense of camaraderie.

"Never thought I'd see the day when we would fight alongside witches," a shapeshifter named Hassan murmured, his voice tinged with both disbelief and respect, as Bilquis expertly wrapped a bandage around his arm. "But then again, I never thought I'd see someone like Anastasia either."

"None of us did," another ally, a djinn named Fatimah, chimed in, her eyes fixed on Anastasia as she helped a wounded comrade to his feet. "She's shown us that we can rise above our differences and work together for the greater good."

As she listened to their words, Anastasia felt a strange mix of emotions welling up within her: pride in her allies, relief that they had survived the battle, and an immense gratitude towards Bilquis for her invaluable assistance.

"Things are changing," Anastasia thought, as she looked around at the faces of those who had fought beside her. "And we must change with them if we are to protect both the human and supernatural worlds."

"Are you alright?" Bilquis asked, breaking into Anastasia's reverie.

"Yes, I am," Anastasia replied, giving her a small smile. "I am just… grateful. Grateful that you were here with us, and grateful for the seeds of understanding that have been sown today."

"Indeed," Bilquis agreed, her captivating eyes gleaming with a newfound respect for Anastasia. "You have shown all of us that there is a better way, one that does not involve needless conflict and division."

"Let this be the start of something new," Anastasia declared, her voice firm and resolute despite her exhaustion. "Together, we shall forge a future built on trust and unity – one that will make both our worlds stronger and more secure."

And with those words, she knew that the path they had chosen would be fraught with challenges and obstacles. But she also knew that with the support of her allies and the bonds forged in the heat of battle, they would overcome whatever trials lay ahead.

Anastasia stood at the edge of the battlefield, her eyes scanning the scarred landscape. The once pristine park now bore the marks of their fierce struggle, its grass trampled and stained with otherworldly residue. She could still feel the tremors of magic that permeated the air, a lingering reminder of the power unleashed during their confrontation with Azazil and Mami Wata's forces.

"Taking risks is part of our lives," Bilquis' voice startled Anastasia from her thoughts, "and I'm glad you took that risk with me."

Turning to face her ally, Anastasia couldn't help but feel a swell of gratitude toward the enigmatic woman. Her decision to trust Bilquis had been a gamble, one with potentially catastrophic consequences. Yet the outcome had been a victory, not just for them, but for the entire supernatural community.

"Without balance and trust between our worlds," Anastasia responded thoughtfully, "we would have descended into chaos and destruction. Your role as a double agent was crucial in maintaining that delicate equilibrium."

"Still, it was a difficult path we chose," Bilquis remarked, brushing a stray lock of hair from her face. "But, it seems to have paid off."

"Indeed," Anastasia agreed, her gaze returning to the battlefield before them. "The supernatural community has been shaken by the revelation of your true allegiance. It will take time to rebuild what has been broken, but I believe we can do it. Together."

"Your faith is admirable, Anastasia," Bilquis said earnestly. "I hope it will serve us well in the days to come."

"Hope is all we have," Anastasia replied softly, her eyes glistening with determination. "We must cling to it, even when the darkness threatens to consume us."

With that, she turned to survey the gathered allies who were tending to their wounds and consoling one another. Though the battle had left them physically and emotionally drained, she could see the spark of renewed purpose in each of their eyes.

"Let's begin the healing process," Anastasia said, addressing her allies with a strong voice that belied her exhaustion. "For both our worlds."

As the sun dipped below the horizon, casting long shadows across the battlefield, Anastasia and her newfound comrades began the arduous task of repairing the damage wrought by their conflict. And as they worked side by side, the seeds of trust and unity took root, promising a brighter future for all who called the human and supernatural realms home.

Resolution

The battle had ended, but the air still hung heavy with a mixture of smoke, ash, and the faint scent of blood. Anastasia Asma'u surveyed the wreckage around her: shattered windows, scorched walls, and the debris of both supernatural and human origin. The streets of Detroit had transformed into a warzone, a testament to the ferocity of the conflict that had just taken place.

"Are we all accounted for?" Anastasia called out, her voice hoarse from shouting orders during the clash.

"Everyone's here," Detective Ayo confirmed, his deep-set eyes scanning the faces of their ragtag group of survivors. The exhaustion was evident in his posture, his usually broad shoulders slumped as if weighed down by the invisible burden of their fight.

"Good," Anastasia said, nodding her approval. "We need to start healing and rebuilding right away."

"Agreed," Amir chimed in, his impish grin replaced with a somber expression. "There's much work to be done."

Anastasia could see the physical and emotional toll the conflict had taken on her friends and allies. Artiya'il's ethereal presence seemed dimmed, his celestial glow now flickering like a candle nearing its end. Sakhr, the mighty jinni king, leaned heavily against a nearby wall, his regal bearing diminished by fatigue. Even Bilquis, the enigmatic leader of the witches, appeared shaken, her usual captivating eyes clouded with uncertainty.

"Let's split up and tend to the injured," Anastasia suggested, taking command of the situation. "Artiya'il, can you help with the supernatural beings? Amir, you and Bilquis can assist the humans. Ayo, come with me; we'll do what we can for both groups."

"Of course," Artiya'il replied, his soothing voice slightly strained but still filled with kindness. "We'll do our best to ease their suffering."

"Right," Amir said, his voice more determined than before. "Let's get to work."

As they moved through the wreckage, Anastasia could feel the weight of her dual identity as both a devout Muslim and a supernatural being heavy upon her. She had never imagined her life would lead her here, but now that it had, she was committed to restoring balance and harmony to these worlds.

"Are you alright?" Ayo asked, concern etched on his face as he walked beside her.

"Yes," she replied, taking a deep breath and trying to steady herself. "I'm just tired. We all need rest, but there's so much to be done."

"Hey, we'll get through this," Ayo assured her, placing a hand on her shoulder. "Together."

Anastasia looked into his eyes and saw the sincerity in his gaze. Despite everything they had been through, she couldn't help but feel a sense of hope. Together, they would heal the wounds inflicted by the conflict and, in doing so, forge a newfound understanding between the supernatural and human worlds.

Anastasia surveyed the scene around her, the smell of burnt wood and torn earth filling the air. Exhausted bodies, both human and supernatural, lay scattered amidst the debris, their faces etched with pain and fatigue. A sense of urgency burned within her, fueled by a responsibility she could no longer deny.

"Artiya'il," Anastasia called out, her voice strong despite her own weariness. "We need to gather everyone together. We must start the healing process."

"Of course, Anastasia," the celestial messenger replied, his ethereal presence wrapping itself around the wounded like a comforting embrace.

"Amir, Sakhr, Bilquis, Were-lion, Mami Wata, Zuhra, Harut, Irshi," Anastasia addressed each in turn, aware of the weight her words carried. "I understand that we all come from different backgrounds and beliefs, but it's crucial that we put aside our differences and work together. Our strength will come from unity."

"Agreed," Sakhr rumbled, his dark eyes holding centuries of secrets softening slightly. "We have all suffered losses in this conflict. It is time for healing."

"Forgiveness and compassion are key principles in Islam," Anastasia continued. "They are central to finding peace, both within ourselves and with others. This is the path we must now walk."

"An admirable sentiment," Bilquis murmured, her captivating eyes searching Anastasia's face. "But how do you propose we begin?"

"First, we must tend to the injured," Anastasia said, her gaze sweeping over the broken bodies around them. "Artiya'il, your celestial powers can help heal those who are suffering. The rest of us can assist by providing comfort and care."

"Very well," Artiya'il agreed, his voice soothing as he knelt beside a wounded witch, his hands glowing with a soft, healing light.

"Next, we must clear away the debris and rebuild what has been destroyed," Anastasia continued, her tone firm. "We will work as one, humans and supernatural beings alike, to restore our world."

"Your faith and determination are admirable," Zuhra said, her warm presence a balm amidst the chaos. "We shall follow your lead in this endeavor."

"Thank you," Anastasia replied, her heart swelling with gratitude for their support. She turned to Ayo, who had remained by her side, his deep-set eyes filled with concern. "Will you help me, too?"

"Of course," Ayo said without hesitation. "I'm with you every step of the way."

As they began working together, Anastasia could feel the threads of unity weaving through the group, binding them with a shared purpose. Forgiven slights and past animosities faded in the face of their collective efforts, replaced by a sense of camaraderie that transcended their differing origins.

Though the road ahead would be long and difficult, Anastasia knew that through forgiveness, compassion, and unity, they would ultimately triumph - not just over the wounds of the conflict, but over the divisions that had once seemed insurmountable. And in that moment, she felt a renewed sense of hope for the future, both for herself and for the worlds she was now sworn to protect.

The air in Detroit was thick with the scent of burnt wood and charred metal, a poignant reminder of the destruction that had ravaged the city. Anastasia surveyed the scene around her, a mixture of pain and determination etched on her face. She knew now, more than ever, the importance of restoring balance and harmony between the two worlds.

"Amir, can you help heal the injured?" she asked, addressing the impish genie as he darted between the fallen.

"Of course," Amir replied, his grin never fading despite the grim situation. With a snap of his fingers, his small form began to shimmer and multiply, creating duplicates of himself that set about tending to the wounded.

Supernatural beings and humans alike were being tended to by the multiple Amirs, their dedication to healing evident in the gentle touch and soothing words they offered to each patient. Sakhr, the mighty jinni king, knelt beside an injured police officer, carefully applying a poultice to the man's burns. The officer looked up at the regal being with a newfound respect in his eyes, whispering his thanks.

"Your bravery is commendable," Sakhr replied, his deep voice resonating with genuine admiration. "We shall restore this city together."

Anastasia walked through the wreckage, stopping to share words of encouragement with those who labored tirelessly to rebuild what had been destroyed. She paused when she spotted Artiya'il and Mami Wata working together, their ethereal beauty contrasting sharply with the chaos around them. The celestial messenger and the water spirit were using their combined powers to purify the tainted waters that had flooded the streets, cleansing the area of any lingering darkness.

"Is there anything I can do to help?" Anastasia asked, her dark eyes filled with the desire to contribute.

"Spread your message of unity," Artiya'il said, his voice soothing and authoritative. "Remind the people that they are not alone in this endeavor."

"Your faith has brought us together," Mami Wata added, her hypnotic gaze never leaving Anastasia's. "Now, we must work as one to ensure that such devastation does not happen again."

Anastasia nodded, understanding the importance of their words. She turned to address the gathered crowd, human and supernatural alike. "We are united in our purpose," she declared, her voice strong and unwavering. "Together, we shall rebuild our homes and mend the wounds of our world. We stand as one, a testament to the power of forgiveness, compassion, and unity."

The crowd responded with a chorus of determined affirmation, their voices carrying through the ruined streets. Anastasia felt a surge of hope rise within her, fueled by the newfound understanding between the two worlds. They had come together in the face of adversity, and now they would heal and grow stronger because of it.

"Let us begin," she said, her eyes shining with determination. And so, side by side, humans and supernatural beings set about restoring balance and harmony to their shattered city, bound together by a shared purpose and an unbreakable bond.

As the sun dipped below the horizon, casting a warm, golden glow over the city, Anastasia Asma'u stood among the rubble, watching as the people she had united worked tirelessly to heal the wounds their world had suffered. She felt a swell of pride and gratitude at the sight before her, but beneath it all, an undercurrent of exhaustion tugged at her very core. The weight of her responsibilities threatened to crush her, even as she tried to remain strong for those who looked to her for guidance.

"Looks like we've got a long road ahead," Detective Ayo said as he approached her, his deep voice tinged with weariness. He rubbed the back of his neck, wincing slightly at the bruises that marred his skin.

Anastasia turned to face him, noting the dark circles under his eyes and the lines that etched his brow more deeply than before. "Yes, we do," she agreed, her voice soft with empathy. "But we'll walk it together, side by side."

Ayo hesitated for a moment, his gaze flickering between her eyes and the ground at their feet. Then, taking a deep breath, he spoke again, his words laced with vulnerability. "Anastasia, there's something I need to tell you."

She tilted her head, curious and concerned by the sudden shift in his demeanor. "What is it, Ayo?"

"I…" He swallowed hard, steeling himself. "I've been feeling… different since we started working together. And after everything we've been through, I can't keep it to myself any longer."

Anastasia held her breath, her heart pounding in her chest as she waited for him to continue.

"Aasma'u, I've fallen for you. Your strength, your courage, your unwavering faith—I admire it all so much." Ayo's eyes searched hers, filled with a mixture of hope and fear. "I know we come from two different worlds, but I want to be part of yours. I want to stand by your side not just as a partner in this fight, but… as something more."

Anastasia's eyes widened in surprise, her breath catching in her throat as his confession reverberated through her mind. She'd sensed the connection between them, but she'd never imagined he would put such feelings into words. An unfamiliar warmth spread through her chest, but it was quickly tempered by the realization that her faith might not allow for such a relationship.

"Detective Ayo, I…" Her voice wavered as she struggled to find the right words. "I'm honored by your feelings, truly. But I must tell you, my faith is at the center of who I am. As much as I may be drawn to you as well, I can't ignore the principles that guide me."

Ayo nodded solemnly, his expression a blend of understanding and disappointment. "I know, Anastasia. Your commitment to your faith is one of the things I admire most about you. And I wouldn't ask you to change any part of yourself for me."

"Thank you," she whispered, touched by his respect for her beliefs. Still, she couldn't help the sinking feeling in her stomach as she considered the path that lay before them—a path that seemed to hold no easy answers.

"Whatever happens," Ayo said softly, his gaze unwavering, "I'll be here, ready to support you in any way I can. We'll face whatever comes our way, together."

Anastasia smiled at him, her heart aching with both gratitude and uncertainty. "Together," she echoed, taking comfort in the knowledge that, no matter what the future held, she wouldn't have to face it alone.

A soft breeze rustled through the ruined streets, stirring up dust and debris as it whispered past Anastasia Asma'u and Detective Ayo. The air was heavy with the scent of scorched earth and the aftermath of battle—an image that mirrored the turmoil within Anastasia's heart. She looked into Ayo's eyes, seeing the vulnerability he had just laid bare before her. In that moment, she knew that they needed to set boundaries in order to protect both their hearts and their faith.

"We can navigate this new terrain together," Anastasia began, her voice steady despite the storm of emotions swirling inside her. "But we must do so according to the teachings of Islam. There are rules that we need to follow, both for our own well-being and out of respect for our beliefs."

"Of course," Ayo replied, his deep voice filled with understanding. "I know that your faith is important to you, and I would never ask you to compromise it."

Anastasia smiled gratefully at him, warmed by his acceptance. "These rules are not meant to be burdensome, but rather a means of protection and guidance. One such rule is that we maintain appropriate boundaries. We should avoid being alone together in private spaces, and physical contact should be limited until we're certain about our future."

"Understood," Ayo said, nodding in agreement. His gaze remained steady on her face, his eyes filled with sincerity and determination. "I'm willing to take things slow and do what's necessary to honor your faith and our relationship."

Anastasia felt a rush of relief wash over her, knowing that Ayo was willing to walk this cautious path with her. But amidst the relief, there was still a small, nagging fear that clawed at her insides. She glanced around at the desolation left by the supernatural conflict, a stark reminder of the precarious balance between their two worlds.

"Thank you, Ayo," she whispered, her dark eyes shimmering with gratitude. "Your understanding means more to me than you can possibly know."

As they stood there amidst the wreckage, Anastasia felt a renewed sense of hope and determination surge within her. The path before them was fraught with challenges and uncertainty, but together, they would face it with patience and respect for one another's beliefs. And as long as they remained steadfast in their faith and commitment, no obstacle would be insurmountable.

Anastasia couldn't shake the image of her and Ayo standing there, in a moment of emotional vulnerability surrounded by the chaos. As she sat down on a nearby bench, she tried to reconcile the different aspects of her identity: a devout Muslim, an FBI agent, and now, a supernatural being caught in a battle between worlds.

"Hey," Ayo said softly, joining her on the bench. "You look like you're carrying the weight of two worlds on your shoulders."

She smiled wearily. "I suppose I am, in a way."

"Want to talk about it?"

Anastasia looked at him, appreciating his concern, but hesitated. How could she put into words the myriad of emotions swirling within her? Nevertheless, she took a deep breath and tried. "It's just… I've always had this clear vision of who I am and what I stand for. But now, with everything that's happened, it feels like my entire world has been turned upside down."

Ayo nodded, understanding in his eyes. "I can only imagine how difficult that must be for you. But if there's one thing I know about you, Anastasia Asma'u, it's that you have an incredible inner strength. You'll find a way to make sense of it all."

His words brought her both comfort and resolve. She was determined to do what was right—both for herself and the worlds she now straddled. "Thank you, Ayo," she said, her voice filled with conviction. "I will do whatever it takes to protect both worlds and uphold my faith."

"Good," he replied, his hand brushing against hers in a brief gesture of support. "And I'll be by your side every step of the way. We may not have all the answers right now, but we'll figure them out together."

Anastasia's heart swelled with gratitude for Ayo's unwavering support. Despite the lingering doubts and fears that gnawed at her, she knew that with him by her side, anything was possible.

"Promise me one thing, though," she said, locking eyes with him.

"Anything."

"Promise me that we'll always be honest with each other, even when it's difficult. Our relationship can only survive if we trust and respect each other's beliefs and boundaries."

Ayo's gaze never wavered. "I promise, Anastasia. I have no intention of losing you because of a lack of honesty or understanding."

"Thank you," she whispered, her heart lighter than it had been in days.

As they sat on the bench together, a sense of hope and possibility bloomed between them. Their path would not be easy, their worlds fraught with danger and uncertainty. But with patience, respect, and an unshakable bond, Anastasia Asma'u and Detective Ayo were ready to face whatever fate had in store for them. And as they stood up, side by side, they knew they were stronger together than they ever could be apart.

Returning Home

Anastasia strode through the bustling FBI headquarters, her polished boots clicking rhythmically on the marble floor. She nodded to colleagues as they passed, their greetings warm and respectful. A familiar sense of purpose filled her chest as she approached her superior's office.

"Agent Anastasia," greeted Special Agent Daniels, his graying temples and firm jawline adding a distinguished air to his authoritative presence. "I've been meaning to speak with you about your recent performance. Outstanding work."

"Thank you, sir," Anastasia replied, standing at attention before him. Her dark eyes were unflinching, a testament to her unwavering dedication to her job.

"Please, have a seat," Daniels gestured to one of the chairs in front of his desk, and Anastasia obliged. "You've proven yourself to be an invaluable part of our team. Your ability to think outside the box has solved cases that would've otherwise gone cold. Keep up the good work."

"Thank you, sir. I'll do my best," Anastasia said, feeling a spark of pride at the praise. She had worked incredibly hard to earn her place here, and it felt good to know that her efforts were recognized.

As she left Daniels' office, Anastasia couldn't help but reflect on how much her life had changed since discovering her supernatural lineage. The knowledge of her true heritage had given her a greater understanding of herself and her place in the world. It was now her responsibility to protect both the human realm and the supernatural world – a task she took very seriously.

Anastasia paused near a window, gazing out over the Detroit skyline. The sun was setting, casting fiery hues across the horizon. Embers of memories stirred within her, tales of ancient ancestors who held the same powers she now wielded. She felt a profound connection to them, their struggles, and their triumphs.

"Hey, Anastasia," called a friendly voice, drawing her attention back to the present. "How's it going?"

"Hi, Kyle," she responded, offering a genuine smile to one of her colleagues. "I'm doing well. Just taking a moment to appreciate our beautiful city."

"Can't argue with that," Kyle said, joining her in looking out the window. "By the way, I heard you were instrumental in solving that missing persons case last week. You're really making a name for yourself around here."

"Thanks, Kyle," she replied, touched by his kind words. "It was a team effort, but I'm glad I could play my part."

The conversation turned lighthearted as they discussed upcoming cases and office gossip. But beneath the surface, Anastasia felt a deep reverence for the heritage that had granted her the unique abilities and perspective that set her apart. She knew that she was part of something much larger than herself – a legacy that spanned centuries and continents, connecting her to an ancient world filled with magic and power.

Anastasia vowed to honor that legacy, using her newfound knowledge and skills to protect both the human and supernatural realms. It wouldn't be easy, but she knew that she couldn't turn away from the destiny that awaited her. And so, with renewed determination, she dove headfirst into her work, committed to fulfilling her role as a protector and guardian, no matter the challenges that lay ahead.

The sun dipped below the horizon, casting a vibrant mix of oranges and reds across the sky. Anastasia stood on the rooftop of the FBI headquarters, her eyes closed as she murmured an ancient incantation under her breath. She felt the familiar presence of her supernatural allies gather around her, their energies intertwining with her own.

"Thank you for coming," she said softly, opening her eyes to see the ethereal forms of her ancestors and mystical creatures. "I seek your guidance in my mission to protect both worlds."

An elderly ancestor stepped forward, his voice gentle yet powerful. "We are proud of your determination, Anastasia. Remember that our wisdom and experience will always be at your disposal."

"Your dedication to this cause is commendable," added a majestic djinn, floating gracefully within the circle of beings. "Call upon us when you need assistance, and we shall do our best to aid you."

Anastasia nodded gratefully and began discussing recent events and challenges with her supernatural allies. They shared insights and offered advice, helping her navigate the complexities of her dual responsibilities.

"Detective Ayo," she mentioned, hesitating before continuing. "He's been a valuable partner, but he's still skeptical about the supernatural world."

"Trust in your connection with him," the elderly ancestor advised. "In time, he may come to understand the truth of our existence."

"Indeed," agreed a shape-shifting leopard. "You and the detective share a bond that could prove beneficial in the battles to come."

Anastasia thanked her allies and ended the meeting, feeling strengthened by their support. She descended to street level just as Detective Ayo pulled up in his car, his muscular frame unfolding from the driver's seat as he approached her.

"Late night at the office?" he asked, his deep-set eyes twinkling with amusement.

"Something like that," Anastasia replied, unable to suppress a smile. "Ready to grab some dinner?"

"Absolutely," Ayo said, holding the car door open for her.

As they drove through the city streets, their conversation flowed effortlessly between work and personal topics. Anastasia found herself increasingly drawn to Ayo's sharp mind and pragmatic nature, which provided a grounding influence amidst the supernatural chaos she navigated daily.

"Have you always been so skeptical of things beyond logic?" she asked, curious about his perspective.

"Growing up in a world that constantly demands proof makes it difficult to believe in anything without evidence," he admitted. "But I've seen enough strange things working with you to question my own beliefs."

"Perhaps there's more to the universe than meets the eye," Anastasia suggested gently, hoping to nudge him toward greater openness.

"Maybe," Ayo conceded, his gaze lingering on her for a moment before returning to the road. "And if anyone could convince me of that, it's you."

The chemistry between them was palpable, each interaction fueling the growing attraction that neither had yet acknowledged. But as the night wore on, and they continued to delve deeper into each other's thoughts and experiences, it became clear that their connection was more than just professional – it was something powerful and profound, a force that had the potential to redefine their lives and the worlds they sought to protect.

Anastasia stood at the edge of the crime scene, her eyes scanning the area with a mix of professional detachment and heightened awareness. The grisly sight before her – a body twisted into an unnatural position, as if every bone had been shattered – sent a shudder down her spine. Ayo, standing beside her, jotted down notes in his worn notepad, his brow furrowed in concentration.

"Whatever did this wasn't human," Anastasia murmured, crouching down to examine the victim's wounds more closely.

"Agreed," Ayo replied, his skepticism momentarily forgotten in the face of such carnage. "But what do you think it was?"

A flicker of uncertainty crossed Anastasia's face as she considered the question. On one hand, she knew that her supernatural allies might be able to shed light on the situation; on the other, involving them could potentially expose her secret life and jeopardize her career. And yet, the stakes were too high – innocent lives hung in the balance, and the last thing she wanted was to let fear hold her back from doing what was right.

"Let me make some inquiries," she said finally, pushing aside her doubts and focusing on the task at hand. "I'll get back to you with my findings."

"Alright," Ayo agreed, trusting her judgment implicitly. "I'll keep working on the case from my end."

As they parted ways, Anastasia felt the weight of her dual roles settling heavily upon her shoulders. Though she had always known that balancing her two worlds would be a challenge, the reality of the situation was far more complex than she could have anticipated. She was constantly torn between her duty to her fellow agents and her loyalty to her supernatural allies, each side demanding her full attention and commitment.

Walking briskly through the city streets, Anastasia mulled over the consequences of her actions. If she chose to involve her supernatural allies, there would be a risk of exposing their existence to the world – a dangerous prospect for all involved. On the other hand, if she kept them out of it, she might be putting human lives at risk.

"Am I doing the right thing?" she wondered, her thoughts a tangled mess of worry and determination. "Or am I only making things worse?"

It was a question that haunted her every step, but one that she knew she couldn't afford to dwell on for long. With each passing moment, the threat loomed larger, and the need for answers grew more urgent. Steeling herself, Anastasia reached out to her supernatural allies, seeking their wisdom and guidance in the face of an enemy unlike any they had ever encountered before.

As Anastasia and Ayo reconvened, she relayed her findings with caution. "I've learned that we're dealing with a powerful supernatural entity," she informed him, watching his reaction carefully.

"Okay," he said slowly, taking it in stride. "What do we do?"

"Let's work together," Anastasia proposed, her voice firm with conviction. "We'll combine our strengths, knowledge, and resources to bring this creature to justice."

Ayo nodded, understanding the unspoken trust between them. They were in this together, their complementary skills uniting in a formidable partnership against the darkness that threatened both worlds.

"Let's do this," he agreed, and together, they set off to confront the unknown.

Anastasia stood in the dimly lit warehouse, her eyes scanning the scene before her. The air was thick with tension and the smell of damp concrete mixed with something far more sinister – death. A body lay sprawled on the ground, evidence markers surrounding it like a swarm of bees. The victim's lifeless eyes stared blankly at the ceiling, as if searching for answers in the unforgiving darkness above.

"Agent Anastasia," said Special Agent Gibbs, her superior, "what can you tell us about this?"

"Based on the wounds, I'd say we're dealing with something supernatural," she replied, trying to keep her voice steady despite the growing sense of unease that coiled within her. She could feel the energies in the room, dark and twisted, pulsing through her veins as she struggled to maintain control over her own powers.

"Supernatural?" Gibbs raised an eyebrow skeptically. "Are you sure?"

"Positive," she confirmed, meeting his gaze with unwavering determination. "I can sense it."

"Alright," he conceded, giving her a nod of approval. "Show us what you've got."

Drawing upon her inherent connection to the supernatural realm, Anastasia closed her eyes and reached out with her senses, feeling the lingering traces of magic that permeated the crime scene. As she did so, a series of arcane symbols began to manifest themselves in her mind's eye, etched in blood-red ink against the backdrop of her psyche.

"Here," she said suddenly, pointing to a spot on the floor near the body. "There's a sigil hidden here. It's faint, but it's definitely there."

Crouching down, Ayo carefully brushed away the layer of dirt and grime to reveal the intricate symbol beneath. His deep-set eyes widened in surprise as he looked up at Anastasia, newfound respect and curiosity gleaming in their depths.

"Good work," he said, his voice tinged with awe. "I don't know how you did that, but it's impressive."

"Thank you," she replied, feeling a surge of pride at his praise. They had come a long way since their initial meeting, and the trust they had built between them was palpable.

As the crime scene was processed and the evidence collected, Anastasia and Ayo found themselves standing alone in a quiet corner of the warehouse, away from the prying eyes of their colleagues.

"Listen, Anastasia," Ayo began, his tone hesitant and cautious. "I wanted to talk to you about… well, us."

"Us?" she echoed, her heart skipping a beat as she looked up into his dark, searching eyes.

"Yeah," he nodded, his cheeks flushing slightly under her scrutiny. "I mean, we've been working together for a while now, and I can't deny that there's something between us. More than just professional respect, I mean."

Anastasia felt warmth flood her chest, her pulse quickening at the unspoken confession. She knew he was right – their chemistry was undeniable, and the attraction between them had only grown stronger over time.

"However," he continued, his brow furrowing with concern, "I'm worried about the challenges we might face as a couple, given your dual roles as an FBI agent and a protector of the supernatural. I don't want our relationship to jeopardize your mission or put either of us in danger."

Anastasia exhaled slowly, contemplating his words. She understood his fears – the complexities of balancing her responsibilities were overwhelming at times, and the consequences of her actions weighed heavily on her conscience.

"I won't lie," she admitted softly, meeting his gaze with equal parts vulnerability and determination. "It won't be easy. But I believe that we can navigate these challenges together, as a team. Our trust and understanding have already proven strong enough to bridge the gap between our worlds, so why not our hearts?"

"Alright," Ayo said after a moment's pause, his features softening as he reached out to gently squeeze her hand. "I'm willing to give it a try if you are."

"Then let's make this work," she whispered, smiling up at him with a mixture of relief and anticipation. And as they stood there, hand in hand amidst the shadows and secrets that surrounded them, Anastasia knew that their connection would be the key to unlocking a brighter future for both the human and supernatural realms – a future forged in love, trust, and the unbreakable bonds of partnership.

The rain pattered against the windowpanes, casting a melancholic sheen over the Detroit streets as Anastasia sat in her office, sifting through the latest case file. The scent of damp earth and wet asphalt mingled with the faint aroma of her chamomile tea, creating an oddly soothing atmosphere.

"Agent Anastasia," a voice called from the doorway, causing her to look up from the stack of papers on her desk. Detective Ayo stood there, eyes troubled as he held out a small slip of paper. "I just received an anonymous tip about a series of unexplained disappearances."

"Disappearances?" Anastasia asked, accepting the note and scanning the hastily scribbled information. Her heart skipped a beat as she caught sight of the locations listed – all of them were known supernatural hotspots, places where the veil between the human and mystical realms was at its thinnest.

"Something doesn't feel right about this, Anastasia," Detective Ayo admitted, concern evident in his voice, but also a hint of excitement. "If there's a supernatural threat involved, you're the best person to handle it."

"Thank you for trusting me with this, Ayo," she said, grateful for his unwavering support despite the challenges they faced. She knew she couldn't do this alone; it was time to consult her otherworldly allies.

***

"Is it possible that someone is deliberately targeting these vulnerable spots?" Anastasia asked as she sat in the dimly lit room, surrounded by her supernatural confidants – Artiya'il, Sakhr, Amir, and Bilquis. Their collective wisdom and insight would be invaluable in solving this mystery.

"Unlikely," Artiya'il replied, his celestial eyes reflecting the soft glow of the candles that flickered around them. "These locations are well-guarded by powerful forces both seen and unseen. Penetrating their defenses would require immense power and cunning."

"Still, we mustn't underestimate our adversaries," Bilquis interjected, her voice as smooth and commanding as ever. "The balance between our worlds is delicate, and even the slightest disturbance could have catastrophic consequences."

"Then we need a plan to investigate these disappearances without alerting whoever is behind them," Anastasia said, determination burning in her eyes. "We need to find out who's responsible and put an end to this before it's too late."

"Agreed," Sakhr rumbled, his dark gaze betraying the depth of his concern. "But tread carefully, Anastasia. The shadows are growing deeper, and we cannot afford to lose you to their embrace."

"Thank you for your guidance, but I won't let you down," Anastasia assured them, heartened by their support. "And with Ayo by my side, we'll face whatever dangers lie ahead – together."

As they strategized late into the night, Anastasia couldn't help but feel a sense of trepidation mingled with anticipation. This new threat would test her abilities to their limits, but it would also strengthen the bonds she had forged with her supernatural allies and with Detective Ayo – bonds that might just be the key to saving both worlds from the encroaching darkness.

"Let us hope that our efforts will be enough to vanquish this unseen foe," Artiya'il murmured, his ethereal voice heavy with the weight of their shared responsibility. "For the sake of both realms, we must prevail."

Anastasia and Detective Ayo crouched behind a crumbling wall, the moon casting eerie shadows over the abandoned warehouse district. The air was thick with anticipation, both of them poised for action. Anastasia could sense the supernatural energy emanating from one of the dilapidated buildings, an uneasy feeling settling in her gut.

"Are you sure this is the place?" Ayo whispered, his eyes scanning the darkened windows for any signs of movement.

"Positive," Anastasia murmured, her voice barely audible. "It's like a beacon to me." She glanced at Ayo, seeing the trust in his deep-set eyes, despite the skepticism that had once defined him. They had come a long way since their first encounter, and now they were united by a common cause – to protect both worlds from the encroaching darkness.

"Okay," he said, nodding. "You lead the way, and I'll watch your back."

With a silent agreement, they crept towards the building, their senses on high alert. Inside, they found themselves in a vast, dimly lit chamber filled with ominous-looking artifacts and strange symbols etched into the floor. In the center of the room, a swirling vortex seemed to be drawing the very essence of the supernatural world into itself.

"Looks like we found our problem," Ayo muttered, his gaze fixed on the vortex.

Anastasia nodded, her mind racing as she considered their next move. "We need to neutralize this vortex before it consumes the entire supernatural realm," she said, her voice tight with urgency. "But we have to be careful not to trigger any traps or alarms."

"Leave that to me," Ayo assured her, pulling out a small device from his pocket. "I've been studying some of the supernatural tech we've encountered, and this little baby should help us disable any security measures."

Anastasia couldn't help but feel a surge of pride at Ayo's adaptability and ingenuity. They made a formidable team, their complementary skills and growing trust forging them into an unstoppable force.

"Ready?" she asked, her eyes meeting his.

"Always," he replied with a confident grin.

Working in tandem, they approached the vortex cautiously, Ayo using his device to neutralize various traps while Anastasia focused on deciphering the symbols surrounding the vortex. With each passing moment, she felt her connection to the supernatural world strengthening, guiding her towards the right course of action.

"Okay, I think I've got it," Anastasia whispered, her fingers hovering over the final symbol. "On my signal, we'll activate the counter-sequence, which should close the vortex."

"Let's do it," Ayo said, his hand resting on her shoulder, offering both support and reassurance.

Drawing upon her supernatural abilities, Anastasia initiated the counter-sequence, feeling the energy around her shift as the vortex began to waver. Ayo's steady presence at her side bolstered her resolve, and together, they watched as the vortex shrank and finally disappeared, leaving behind a faint echo of its once-threatening presence.

"Is that it?" Ayo asked, his voice tinged with disbelief. "We did it?"

Anastasia nodded, her chest swelling with relief and triumph. "Yes," she breathed. "Together, we closed the vortex and protected both worlds."

In the aftermath of their victory, both human and supernatural realms were safe – for now. But as Anastasia looked at Ayo, her heart brimming with gratitude and warmth, she knew that whatever challenges lay ahead, they would face them together, united by their shared purpose and the bond that had formed between them. And that knowledge filled her with hope, even in the face of the unknown.

As Anastasia and Ayo walked away from the site where the vortex had been, the world around them seemed to take on a new sense of vibrancy. The city skyline shimmered in the twilight, casting a kaleidoscope of indigo and violet hues across their path, while the sounds of traffic and distant laughter filled the air with an almost palpable energy.

"Feels like we've earned ourselves a break, don't you think?" Ayo said, his voice breaking through Anastasia's reverie. She glanced at him, taking note of the slight smile that played at the corners of his lips. His eyes sparkled with a newfound curiosity – a testament to the supernatural world he had recently come to accept.

"Perhaps," Anastasia replied, her thoughts tumbling over one another as she considered the implications of their partnership. "But I have a feeling our work is far from over."

"Of course," Ayo conceded, his gaze lingering on her for a moment before turning back to the cityscape. "But for now, we can enjoy this victory, right?"

Anastasia couldn't help but smile at his optimism, finding it contagious. "Yes, I suppose we can."

The two continued their walk, the weight of their previous challenges momentarily dissipated by the simple pleasure of each other's company. As they passed by a street vendor selling fragrant jasmine tea, Anastasia found herself caught up in memories of her grandmother, who had taught her about her heritage and the supernatural responsibilities tied to it. An unexpected surge of gratitude washed over her – not only for her grandmother, but also for those who had supported her journey, including Ayo.

"Thank you," she murmured, her eyes meeting Ayo's as a soft breeze danced through the air, carrying whispers of jasmine.

"For what?" Ayo asked, genuinely curious.

"Everything," Anastasia replied, her heart swelling with an unfamiliar emotion. "For believing in me, for standing by my side, and for trusting that together, we can make a difference."

Ayo's eyes searched hers, his expression softening. "You don't have to thank me, Anastasia. It's been an honor to work with you. And besides," he added, a playful grin appearing on his face, "how could I resist the allure of the supernatural?"

Anastasia laughed, feeling a warm connection igniting between them. They continued walking, their conversation turning to lighter topics as they enjoyed the crisp evening air. But beneath the surface, she couldn't shake the sense that this was just the beginning – that there were countless unknown challenges waiting for them on the horizon.

Together, she thought, her hand brushing against Ayo's for a brief moment, sending a shiver down her spine. Whatever comes our way, we'll be ready.

Epilogue

Detroit had come alive, the city pulsating with renewed energy and vibrant hope. The streets were filled with laughter and music, a testament to the harmony that now existed between humans and supernatural beings. Colorful murals adorned the walls of once-abandoned buildings, while markets bustled with activity as people and creatures from all walks of life traded goods and stories.

Skyscrapers gleamed in the sunlight, casting long shadows across the cityscape, while the scent of fresh-baked pastries and spiced foods mingled with the fragrance of newly planted flowers. The air buzzed with the hum of conversations, both mundane and magical, as the people of Detroit embraced their new normal.

In the heart of it all, FBI Special Agent Anastasia Asma'u sat at her desk, her dark, expressive eyes scanning through reports and updates on various cases. Her strong, athletic build tensed as she focused on her work, her commitment to maintaining the delicate balance between the human and supernatural worlds evident in every movement.

"Agent Anastasia," called a voice from the doorway. It was her supervisor, Director Johnson, a gruff man with salt-and-pepper hair who had initially doubted her abilities, but had since come to respect her dedication and talent. "I've got something for you."

Anastasia looked up, curious, and saw him holding a small, velvet-lined box. He placed it on her desk, his own eyes displaying a hint of pride. "You've been awarded the Medal of Valor for your role in maintaining the peace and stability of this city," he said, nodding at the gleaming medal nestled within the box. "Congratulations, Anastasia."

"Thank you, sir," she replied, her fingers tracing the intricate design on the medal. A surge of pride swelled in her chest, but she knew she couldn't have achieved any of this without the help of her supernatural allies.

"Your work is making a real difference, Anastasia," Johnson continued. "The crime rates have dropped significantly, and there's a sense of unity that I haven't seen in years. You've built bridges between worlds that many thought were impossible."

Anastasia smiled softly, acknowledging the truth in his words but still feeling humbled by the responsibility that came with her dual identity. In her thoughts, she thanked Artiya'il for revealing her destiny, Amir for his impish yet invaluable assistance, and Sakhr for the support and guidance he had given her as she navigated the world of the jinni.

"Thank you, sir," she said again, her voice filled with gratitude. "I couldn't have done it without the help and trust of our supernatural allies. It's been an incredible journey so far, and I'm honored to be a part of it."

"Keep up the good work, Agent," Johnson said with a smile before leaving her office.

About The Author

Tony Pang, a remarkable African-American author, is a beacon of hope and love in the literary world. Born in Mobile, Alabama, and deeply rooted in his mantra, "Healing Hearts with Hope," Tony's writings reflect his profound commitment to this belief. A Marine and a Martial Artist, his discipline and dedication shine through not just in his professional pursuits but also in his personal passions. Whether it's a day spent fishing, where the joy is found even when the fish aren't biting, or an evening immersed in the soulful tunes of Bobby Blue Bland and BB King, Tony's zest for life is palpable.

With an impressive average rating of 4.38 from 125 ratings and 12 reviews, Tony's literary contributions span genres like Nonfiction, Fiction, and Philosophy. His influences range from the poetic musings of Hafiz and Khalil Gibran to the thrilling narratives of Sidney Sheldon and Anne Rice. Among his notable works are "Anesthesia Technician Survival Guide" and "Healing Status," both of which have garnered significant acclaim.

Beyond his books, Tony's love for Blues music is so profound that he often quips, "you can get me to do just about anything if you play some Bobby Blue Bland or BB King." A man of many talents, Tony's journey from leading the Dali Lama in prayer to showcasing his art in galleries and mingling with diverse groups of people showcases his multifaceted personality.

With a strong online presence, Tony engages with his readers and followers on platforms like Goodreads, where he candidly answers questions and shares insights about his writing process and inspirations. His website and active Twitter handle further bridge the gap between the author and his readers, making him not just a writer but a community figure who resonates with many.

In essence, Tony Pang is not just an author; he's a storyteller, a healer, and a beacon of hope. Dive into his world, and you'll find tales that heal, inspire, and resonate with the heart.

www.ingramcontent.com/pod-product-compliance
Lightning Source LLC
Chambersburg PA
CBHW041054310726

48978CB00011BA/554